Also by Kiera Stewart
Fetching

How to Break a Heart

KIERA STEWART

Disney • Hyperion

LOS ANGELES   NEW YORK

All rights reserved. Published by Disney • Hyperion, an imprint of Disney Book Group.
No part of this book may be reproduced or transmitted in any form or by any means, electronic
or mechanical, including photocopying, recording, or by any information storage and retrieval
system, without written permission from the publisher. For information address
Disney • Hyperion, 125 West End Avenue, New York, New York 10023.

First Edition, December 2015
10 9 8 7 6 5 4 3 2 1
FAC-020093-15288

Printed in the United States of America

Library of Congress Cataloging-in-Publication Data
Stewart, Kiera.
How to break a heart / Kiera Stewart.—First edition.
pages cm
Summary: "Thirteen-year-old Mabry Collins gets advice from her friend Thad about
how to break a heart after a humiliating breakup"—Provided by publisher.
ISBN 978-1-4231-7181-2 (hardback)—ISBN 1-4231-7181-0
[1. Love—Fiction. 2. Dating (Social customs)—Fiction.] I. Title.
PZ7.S84935Ho 2016
[Fic]—dc22   2015006989

Reinforced binding

Visit www.DisneyBooks.com

SUSTAINABLE FORESTRY INITIATIVE   Certified Sourcing
www.sfiprogram.org
SFI-00993

THIS LABEL APPLIES TO TEXT STOCK

For Michele
Princess Leia and the Eskimo forever

The Breaking of the Hearts

Good-bye.

First, the word floats in the air, like a satellite scouting out the most vulnerable areas. Your eyes, your neck, the ticklish spot under your arm. Anywhere open and unguarded, unspoiled—at least as of yet.

Then, the missiles hone in, and once they do, watch out. They launch into your soft spots, blasting through the skin, the bone, anything that lies in the way of the heart. Once they pierce that all-important organ, it will feel like something has been shattered, crushed, bludgeoned, maybe even ripped out. Excoriated. Now there's a word. You may feel that word. You may never know exactly what it means, but oh, you will know how it feels.

And even though your heart is the ultimate victim, every cell in your body and brain will cry out for sympathy. You will feel pain in the roots of your hair, the knuckle of your thumb, your appendix. Various fluids will start to pour from the holes on your face. Tears. Snot. Slobber. You will become a most unattractive version of yourself—red, puffy, swollen, and unkempt. Needy, insecure, clinging.

This, my friends, is love. It should be wrapped in yellow caution tape. Surrounded by orange cones. Labeled with a skull and crossbones. It should be kept out of the hands of minors. If love were an actual drug, the FDA would not approve.

Love. Flip it over and here's what you have: heartbreak. The remainder; the ruins of love.

romper *to break*

yo rompo

tú rompes

ella rompe

nosotros rompemos

ellos rompen

Cristina is sitting on the edge of her bed, holding a rock and crying—a picture of tragic perfection. Her tears are plump little drops that travel down her face with dignity, leaving her perfectly applied makeup respectfully in place. The camera pans to the rock, which is cradled in both palms. The etching reads *C.A.* ♥ *L.A., Para Siempre.* Forever.

"So what happened—he's dead or something?" Sirina asks. She's talking about Cristina's husband, Luis.

"No," I say, wanting her to be quiet. "Missing."

"Missing how?"

"Kidnapped. *Shhh!*"

"Wow," Sirina says, standing up. "Okay, I'm going."

"No!" I say, and pull her back down to the couch. "Stay. *Please.*"

She crosses her arms. "Fine. But only if you're going to pay attention to me and not your stupid telenovela."

"It's almost over," I tell her. On the screen, Mariela, the Queen of Heartbreak, is packing up her suitcases, her *maletas*. She shows no emotion, but Armando, the rich, powerful guy who owns most of Suelo, their town, is turning into a train wreck. He's practically on his knees, professing his love and pleading for her not to go. *"¡Te quiero! ¡No te vayas!"* And then the credits for *La Vida Rica* start to roll.

"That's Mariela?" Sirina asks.

I nod.

"I think I like her best," she says.

"Why?" I ask, feeling a little betrayed. "Cristina's so much better. She's so strong, so loyal, so passionate—"

"So *sad*." She looks at me. "*Blech*. She's always so pathetic."

"*Pathetic?*" I say, offended.

"Well, you know. It seems like she's always crying over something. Mariela's just—I don't know—more powerful."

"Yeah, well, Mariela doesn't really love anyone, that's why!"

"She definitely seems to be doing okay."

"You don't get it." I sigh and slump back on the couch. "You just don't believe in love."

My dog, Hunter, is lying on the couch next to Sirina. He stretches, straightening his four legs. "Who doesn't believe in love, Hunter? I love *you*, don't I? Yes I *doooo*," Sirina says in her gooshy voice. And then she leans over and starts kissing his big chocolaty-Lab head. "You're a sweet boy, aren't you?"

She looks over at me and I smirk back at her. "Not the same," I say.

I can't really blame Sirina. She's never had a boyfriend. She's never been in love. I almost feel sorry for her—she really doesn't know what she's missing. I mean, what's life without passion? Without romance? Without love?

Love—that's something Sirina and I don't have in common, at least not yet. I think she just hasn't met the right guy. I mean, we're thirteen, so there's a little time, but *still*. I can't wait till we have boys in common. Me and Nick, her and some awesome guy with a name like Romario, going out to a fabulous dinner—one with special forks and fancy napkins. Maybe even salsa dancing or something. I will be wearing a short but flouncy skirt and daringly high heels, and my honey-colored hair will shine under the light of the moon. And I'll throw my head back and laugh, and show off my full lips (ruby red) and straight teeth (white, very white), and Nick will gaze at me admiringly and—

My phone hums from between the couch cushions.

"Let me guess. Nick," Sirina says, sounding less than supportive.

I look at my phone. *Nicolás*, the screen reads. My Spanish translation of him. I smile.

"*Hiiii*," I say, song-like, into the phone.

"Mabry?"

My nerves jolt awake like I've been jabbed with a sharp needle. It's a woman's voice! *Oh. My. God.* Nick must have a secret girlfriend. An older woman!

"Who *is* this?" I say to this other woman. I hear my heartbeat in my ear. My skin feels tingly. My armpits itch. I bet her name is Rocío and she has dark, flowing hair that actually *does* shimmer in the moonlight. And possibly cleavage. HOW CAN I POSSIBLY COMPARE!?

"This is Mrs. Wainwright."

Oh. Okay. No need to panic, then. But wait. Why is Nick's mom calling me? Is he in trouble? Is he in the hospital? What if he's in one of those full-body casts like Enrique had after he got in the airplane crash in episode four? What if he's completely wrapped in bandages, mummy-like, and my very first kiss *ever* has to be through his breathing hole?

This is the man I love! My heart races. "I'll be right there!" I say.

"Where? *Here?*" She sounds confused. "Uh, well, no, Mabry, you don't need to come over—Nick's not even home."

Of course he isn't! "Not to the house," I say. "The *hospital!*"

Sirina shoots me a look of concern.

"What? Who's in the hospital?" Mrs. Wainwright asks.

"Uh, well, I mean, I just thought," I stumble. "Um. Where's Nick?"

"Nick's at karate."

"Oh, right," I say. I laugh a little, relieved—although the hospital scene was starting to seem kind of amazing. The room would smell of fresh lilacs, and I would gently cradle his bandaged head so he could drink his dinner through a straw. My love would help him heal.

Sirina widens her eyes at me and mouths, *What?* I shake my head and come back to reality.

Bad idea. Because then Mrs. Wainwright says, "But he did want me to call you." She pauses. "Look, Mabry, Nick's now a purple belt. He really needs to focus on that. We both think it might be time for you to take a break from each other."

"A break?" My mind starts going in all directions. "For how long?"

She sighs. "Mabry, he thinks you two should break up."

"Break. Up?" I croak. My heart seizes up with protest. I look at Sirina, who is statue-still and staring at me. "But—but. But, we're in love!"

"Oh, honey." Her voice delivers nothing but pity. "Bless your dear heart."

"He loves me!" I cry out. "He told me!"

"Well, okay," she says. "But he also loves karate."

"But what about the Cotillion?"

She seems a little surprised. "That—that's almost two months away. He's already asked you to the Junior Cotillion?"

"Well—" I start, and I suddenly feel like an idiot. But, I mean, once someone has professed love to you, shouldn't that go without saying? Of course he would ask me! *He would! He would!*

For a few awful seconds, nobody says a word and it feels like time has stopped, caught between my will to rewind it and its natural tendency to plow rudely forward, mowing down everything in its way.

I hear a crashing sound, which could be the actual sound of my heart breaking. But then Nick's mom says, "Oh, *no!* The cat just broke my coffee mug. I have to go. You'll be all right, I promise—you'll see. Good-bye, Mabry!"

My heart seems to stop beating, like it's been stabbed. Filleted. Maybe even julienned into long, thin shreds. And you know what happens when your heart stops beating. You die. You just up and die.

I'm aware that it's been about an hour, so I must still be alive, but I might as well be dead because my body feels like it's in a state of rigor mortis. Stiff and rigid and unmovable. Sirina tries to hug me, but I can't hug back. Hunter is also taking pity on me, nuzzling me with his snout, but I can't even reach out to pet him.

"I can't believe he had his mother call to break up with you!" Sirina says, for about the tenth time. "What kind of guy does that!?" She's fuming.

Apparently, a wonderful, beautiful guy with an enticing mysterious side. And promising bone structure. And indigo-blue eyes. Who might actually grow to be about six-foot-three if his pediatrician's predictions are right. But it's hard to even talk, so I guess I'll have to explain that to her later.

"Come on." She tries to pry me off the couch, but it's like I've been flash frozen in place. I don't budge. I *can't* budge.

"Let's go get ice cream or something!"

"Don't. Want. Ice cream," I manage to say. I also want to tell her how annoyed I am that she's trying to trivialize my pain with ICE CREAM! But I'm in too much agony.

She sighs and releases my arm. It creaks back into place.

"He's a jerk," she says, putting her hands on her hips. "A hot one, okay, but still a jerk."

"Not. A. Jerk."

"Seriously, Mabry! Come on!"

I stare ahead, staying stiff.

"Let's just do what we usually do. Ice cream. Come on, Mabry, don't you want a Blizzard?"

"My heart. Is a blizzard," I manage. And it is. It's like a Snickers bar being mashed up and ground up and blended into something frozen, by some heartless Dairy Queen clerk. A cold winter storm of pain and anguish. I'll never look at ice cream the same again.

"Well, it used to work." Sirina sighs. "I don't know why you care about some guy who just had his mom dump you. You should be outraged!"

"He's just confused, I think." I hug my knees in.

"Oh, I get it. This is about that phone call last week."

It was on Thursday, five days ago, just as we were getting off the phone. I'd taken a deep breath, squeezed my eyes shut, and said the words. *I love you.* And then he said them right back to me. Well, basically.

"No, Sirina," I say. "It's about being in love!"

8

"Mabry, he said, 'Me too.'"

"AND"—I look right at her—"*AND* the next day he held my hand when we walked between the P.E. hall and the arts alcove." Plus, he's the first guy who didn't follow my words with "Thank you," or "You're hot, too," or "I know." Or silence. Or "I'm moving to Canada." That happened once.

Sirina exhales loudly, clearly unconvinced. I guess it's hard to be very persuasive when you're in a fetal position. Besides, I know she's thinking she knows the drill. Mabry gets a boyfriend. Gets dumped. Cries. And does it all over again. Rinse and repeat. On the outside, I know it looks the same as it always does. But it's just not. He told me he loved me. Maybe not exactly in the traditional words, but at least he *agreed*. He was The First! He was *El Amor de Mi Vida*—the love of my life!

"What do you want me to do, Mabry? You're barely moving. Want me to stay or go?"

"Stay," I bleat.

"Okay," she says. Even though Sirina thinks this whole true love thing is stupid, at least she doesn't think *I'm* stupid. Just a little insane sometimes, or so she tells me. She sits back down on the couch with me. "Then will you at least do me one favor?"

"What?"

"Blink."

So I do. I not only blink, but take in a chestful of air, finally, bracing myself for what's to come now. The crying. And not the dignified, beautiful, clean cry that Cristina just pulled off. I try for that graceful cry, I really do—and I've had plenty of practice—but my messy, slimy tears always seems to wind up on sleeves, and sometimes, in especially bad times like this, couch pillows.

Sirina passes me a box of Kleenex.

9

Oh, Cristina. How do you love with such grace? You must not truly understand the pain, not as I do. The torment! The agony! *No, Cristina, no entiendes nada!*

Sirina stays until her mom calls and tells her she has to come home for dinner.

I go upstairs to my room and lie down. I must have fallen asleep, because Hunter nudges me awake and I sit up, coughing.

My nose feels stuffy. My throat feels swollen. I hear my brother's footsteps in the hall. "Aaron?" I call out to him. I use his real name instead of "A-Bag," which is what I prefer to call him. Of course, he started calling me "M-Hole" first, so I think he deserves that.

He pauses at my doorway. He's fifteen but acts twelve sometimes. "What's up, loser? Let me guess—malaria?"

See why I call him A-Bag?

"I don't feel good," I say.

"Well, Mom said to come down for dinner," he says. "She and Stephanie are waiting." He means Stephen, my mom's boyfriend, the science teacher. His name is pronounced like "Steffen" so my brother likes to call him "Stephanie" behind his back, and sometimes in front of it.

"Tell her I'm not hungry."

He nudges me and smirks. "He brought that pie he makes. That berry one? Yeah, he took it into one of his teachers' meetings, and it 'went viral.'"

Oh, yeah, that's a Stephen-ism. Something "going viral" means that people liked something, or that generally things went well. A-Bag and I, on separate occasions, have both tried to explain to him what it actually means, but we gave up a while ago. Now the way Stephen misuses the phrase seems almost normal, and I'm half-afraid that I'll go into school and use it wrong myself. (Q: How was your weekend, Mabry? A: It was pretty viral. Thanks for asking.)

I try to smile, but it's no use.

"Whatever, you're no fun," Aaron says, and leaves.

A minute later, there's a "Shave and a Haircut" string of knocks on my bedroom door. Stephen. Of course.

"Come in," I say in my most unwelcoming tone.

The door opens. "Hey there, kiddo!" he says. He puts his hands in his pockets and rocks back and forth on his feet. "What's the four-one-one?"

I take a stiff breath and say flatly, "That's the number for information." I can't help it. Sometimes I like to watch him squirm.

He makes a gaspy laugh and says, "No, I mean—that's a—uh, a little joke." His laugh comes to a wheezy end. "I mean, what's going on up here? I hear you're not feeling well?"

"I'm not."

"Well, I hope you feel better soon," he says.

"Thanks."

He smiles and nods, and turns toward the door. Before leaving, though, he turns back around and says, smiling, "Wanted to make sure you weren't just up here hangin' ten."

It's another one of his jokes. One that he uses ALL THE TIME, like, anytime my brother or I are a little late to dinner, or have slept in late. You know that phrase *surfing the Internet*? Well, apparently *hangin' ten* is an older term that meant surfing—like, your *ten* toes are *hanging* off the surfboard. So, in his strange little science-teacher mind, *hangin' ten* means "surfing the Internet," and it's very, very funny. IN HIS OWN MIND.

11

"I'm definitely not hanging ten," I say.

He gasp-laughs again and leaves, with a little forehead salute.

A little later, my mom brings a grilled cheese sandwich up to my room and says, "You want to talk about it?"

"You wouldn't understand," I tell her.

"I might."

"Have you ever really been in love?"

She pauses. "Well, yeah."

I roll my eyes. *Well, yeah* isn't a yes. *Well, yeah* is wearing fleece pajamas and watching *Dateline* on the couch with a pointy-looking man in a bow tie. *Well, yeah* is going to PTA meetings and working in an office and buying in bulk from Costco. *Well, yeah* isn't really being in love.

She puts the grilled cheese on my nightstand and gives me a half smile. "All right, I'm going to bed. Eat your grilled cheese while it's still hot."

I look over at the sandwich. It's perfectly golden and crisp, and on a paper towel so it doesn't get soggy. I pick it up and take a big bite. And for a second, I'm full of appreciation for the *blah* kind of love that would make a mom cook a grilled cheese for her ailing daughter.

"It's good," I tell her.

She gives me a good-night kiss on the forehead and says, "I love you."

"Well, *duh*," I say, "I love you, *too*." But it's not nearly the same. It actually should be a different word. How are these different feelings all called *love*?

Right before I turn out my light, I send Sirina a text. *Good night, my little jazz-handed sea monkey.*

It's nice to know that she's the only person on earth who isn't going to ask what a jazz-handed sea monkey is. Our good-night texts are a tradition we started in sixth grade after one too many rounds of Mad Libs. They're random blends of adjectives and nouns that make no sense—just constant little inside jokes between the two of us.

My phone buzzes with her response. *Good night, my little coral-reef dancing queen.*

perder *to lose*

yo pierdo

tú pierdes

ella pierde

nosotros perdemos

ellos pierden

I t's the next morning. My mom is standing at my door, her arms crossed. "You think you have *what*?"

"A.I.W.S.," I say. I groan and roll over. "You look really small. I better stay in bed today."

She sighs. "And, Mabry, what exactly is A.I.W.S.?"

Of course she would ask that. *Of course.* "Alice in Wonderland syndrome," I tell her. I open one eye and reach for the glass of water on my nightstand, pinching at it with my thumb and index finger. "Why is my water glass so tiny?"

She raises her eyebrows at me. "I've never heard of such a thing."

"It's *real*!" I say. "Just Google it!" And it is—*it is*! Plus, the good thing is that you don't have to have a fever to have A.I.W.S., so it's not like she can prove that I *don't* have it.

But instead of giving me sympathy, she just starts bossing me around. "Mabry, get up, get dressed, and get ready for school."

"Mom, *okay*, listen. I probably just have a migraine." Here's what I know from experience: a claim of a migraine or strep throat or even a cold will buy you at least a day out of school, while, very ironically, a claim of an ailing heart—the *heart*, which you can't live without, which is the most important organ in the body—won't even get you a late slip.

But my mom just turns her head sideways and gives me that no-nonsense stare, like she is the Queen of the Whole World, or maybe even Señora Lomas from *La Vida Rica*, and I am one of her servants, who has no free will at all.

At school, on the way to first period, I run into my friend Amelia. She starts talking about the color she wants to paint her room. "It's kind of like purple, but it's not one of those pale purples—it's more like a blue-purple. It's called Mystic Moon."

"Uh-huh," I say. "Sounds nice." And it does. But I can barely focus on anything but the wreckage in my heart.

"GOR. GEOUS," she says, like it's two words. "But I'm a little scared."

"Why?" I ask.

"Well, come on, Mabry. *Purple!* It's bold, even for me. What if I totally hate it? I mean . . ."

She keeps talking but my ears no longer register her words. Instead, I see him, My Love, My *Nicolás*, moving—*gliding*—toward me in slow motion. I inhale a warm breeze. A bird soars behind him. I hear a piano playing gently. The breeze caresses his bangs from his face.

For that moment, the air catches as if it's been locked in my lungs, and our eyes meet as if they've been seeking each other through eternity, and—

Er.

Wait.

Not. As. Planned.

Instead of running toward me—as the music increases in pace and intensity, as the bird is joined by its mate—Nick *bolts*. He takes an immediate detour into the Teen Life lab, which *I know* he doesn't have until sixth period.

". . . was thinking about pink, but then I was like, pink, really? I mean, how old am I, four?" Amelia is still going, twisting her blond hair around her fingers as she talks.

"Right," I say, but it comes out a little garbled, because, of course, I am speaking through a crushed soul. I don't want to see Nick anyway. *I don't, I don't, I don't!* Okay, *I do.* But I shouldn't want to. I mean, you go out with someone for six weeks and think you know them, and suddenly, your future mother-in-law is calling you to break up!

Amelia looks at me. "You okay?"

I clear my throat. "I'm really sorry, Amelia. I sort of just saw Nick."

"Oh." She twists her face into a grimace. "Ugh. That's the worst thing about a breakup. Seeing the guy all the time afterward."

No, Amelia, I want to say. *The worst thing about a breakup is scraping your soul off the bottom of his shoe!* It's like we're living on different planets sometimes.

Our friend Jordan catches up to Amelia and me in the hallway. "Hey!" she says to us, all too cheerfully. Then she looks straight at me. "Uh-oh. What's wrong?"

"She and Nick are over," Amelia tells her.

"*What!?*" Jordan says. "Since when?"

"Since yesterday after school," I tell her.

"What happened? Oh my god, did he leave you for Ariana?" Jordan asks, meaning Nick's girlfriend before me.

"No," I say. "For karate."

"Karate? *What?*" This time Amelia does the drilling. "He actually said that?"

"Well, I haven't really been able to talk to him. I think maybe it's just what his mom wants him to do. She's the one who called."

"His *mom* broke up with you?" Jordan says, way too loudly. "What a wimp!"

"He's n-not—" I stammer. I haven't spent six blissful weeks in love with a wimp—there's no way! I mean, do wimps have those ocean-blue eyes? That slightly crooked but adorable smile? I think *not!*

"Yeah, he's such a baby," Amelia declares.

Jordan smiles. "Just wait till word gets out."

"You're not— *Don't say anything, please!*"

"Don't worry, Mabry," Jordan says. "This makes *him* look bad, not you."

"Yeah," Amelia adds. "You should totally be laughing at him."

"Just don't say anything. I don't want anyone laughing at him. *Please!*" I beg, but the bell rings and they scatter away too quickly. I'm left pleading for a mercy that will never come, like on *La Vida Rica*, when Irina was lost and stumbled upon a pack of wolves in the hills and was never heard from again.

At lunch, I find Sirina in the à la carte line. "My world is falling apart," I tell her.

A normal Sirina response would be to say, *Your world is not actually falling apart.* Instead, she just gives me this I-feel-kind-of-sorry-for-you look and orders a Chipwich from the cafeteria lady.

"A *Chipwich*? You're eating an ice-cream sandwich? Really?" I ask Sirina.

She looks at me. "Yeah, why not?"

I just shake my head. It's hard to feel like you're being taken seriously when you're pouring your heart out to a friend who's just sitting there eating a Chipwich, like it's a day at the carnival or something.

At our lunch table, Jordan immediately scoots over to make room for us, and Amelia gives me a pat on the back, which actually makes me feel a little *more* like a leper.

Sirina wedges in close to me and I open my lunch—pasta salad.

"He won't even look at me," I say as I stare into the chaotic, oily bunch of noodles.

"He's an infant," Sirina says.

"When Axyl broke up with me, I un-friended him," Jordan says. "You should do it first before he does it to you."

"But I could *never* un-friend him," I say. "He's *still* the love of my life."

Amelia chimes in. "You should just come in tomorrow looking all hot, and be like, *Whatever, dude, I'm over you.*"

I sigh and shake my head. No one understands. *No one!*

"Block him on your phone, too," Jordan says. "I blocked Axyl on everything. There was no *way* he could come crawling back to me. I didn't want to speak to him or see him or have anything to do with him—not if he was the last guy in the world."

She's such a drama queen sometimes. "I'd rather *die*," I say.

I'm still staring into my pasta, and no one's talking, but I can practically hear them all exchanging glances, their eyes inflating, their eyebrows shooting up into their hairlines. Sirina nudges me in the ribs with her pointy elbow. "They're *just* trying to help, Mabry," she says.

"I know." I exhale. "I'm sorry."

"He's a butthead," Amelia says.

"Don't call him that!"

Amelia and Jordan get up from the table, exasperated, and start to walk away. "Sorry," I call after them. To Sirina, I say, "I didn't mean it to come out like that. I just—I just want him *back*." My eyes brim with tears. I try not to blink.

"Hey, Mabry?"

"What?"

"You, my friend, are the poster child for misery."

I sigh and poke at a noodle with my fork. "I can't wait for you to fall in love so you know what it feels like."

Sirina looks at me for a second. Then she shakes her head and looks away and says, "The way you're acting, I wouldn't wish it on my worst enemy."

We finish lunch. Or rather, I finish staring at mine, and she polishes off her Chipwich. "Sorry," I finally murmur.

"I know, me too," she says.

And just as we're about to leave the cafetorium, she says, "But, Mabry?"

"Yeah?"

"You *are* driving me crazy."

I'm kind of stunned. I really have no idea what to say to that, but just then, Mrs. Hurst, the nutrition manager, starts screeching about how we all need to return our trays and pick up all remaining food and "food waste" from our tables and UNDERNEATH THEM and get headed to our fourth-period classes. She says it with such urgency you almost feel like you must spit out anything in your mouth just to follow the rules. So, luckily, I don't have to say anything to Sirina right now.

At the end of the school day, I see *Mi Amor* again. Through the crowd of faceless faces, he is sailing toward me. My breath catches in my throat for a second. I feel like I am about to drown.

He will save me. His hand will grab mine, and he will sweep me out of this mighty middle-school ocean.

Nicolás! My heart calls out to him.

And it appears as if he hears my heart. Because his sparkly blue eyes meet my emerald-green ones. I open my mouth to say his name, to ask if we can just talk—and then, out of nowhere, A SHARK ATTACKS.

A shark by the name of Patrick Hennessey. Who is usually more of a minnow than a shark, but today he might as well be a great white.

"Nick!" he calls out. "Downstairs. You coming?"

"Wait up!" Nick calls back. He bolts past me.

I am Cristina aching for Luis. I am Andres pining for Consuelo. I am Elisabet yearning for Cristof. I am devastated, alone, abandoned. A washed-up shell piece on a remote island beach. The piece that winds up jabbing you in the ball of the foot, and then gets cursed at and thrown back into the ocean.

"Mabry, *Maaaay*-bry." Sirina puts her hands on my shoulders and steers me toward the locker we share. "You're standing there like a statue from a Greek tragedy. You look ridiculous."

I sigh. "Let's just get this day over with so we can go home and watch *La Vida Rica*."

"Oh, my little *pobrecita*," Sirina says, rubbing my shoulder.

Then we hear, "Girls?"

We turn to see Mrs. Neidelman. She's in charge of the Hubert C. Frost Middle School news blog, *The Vindicator*. I'm a reporter and Sirina's both my editor and photographer. It's something we've been working on together since we got "redirected" from the drama club last year. Well, since *I* did. I still remember Jessica Morgan's snotty little face when she told me, "This is the drama club, not the *melo*drama club." And then Mrs. Neidelman *just happened* to ask me if I could help out by writing for *The Vindicator*. "Anyone as passionate as you are, Mabry, would be an asset to our team," she'd said. And Sirina quit the drama club and came with me.

Mrs. Neidelman clasps her hands together, like she can't quite contain her excitement. "Well, I'm so glad to have run into you girls. I have a last-minute request."

"Sure," Sirina says, way too quickly. She wants to become a news editor or a photojournalist for real one day. But working on *The Vindicator* isn't as much fun for me as it is for her. I mean, the interesting stuff is not what's going on in the classrooms and on the fields—it's the stuff that happens behind the bleachers, under the stairwells, in the hidden alcoves. The stuff that Mrs. Neidelman won't let us write about.

"There's a band rehearsal in the cafetorium. Would you mind snapping some photos? Maybe write a blurb about the concert next week?"

I sigh. No bleachers. No stairwells. No alcoves. No janitor's closets.

"Yeah, okay," Sirina says.

Mrs. Neidelman looks right at me. "Now, I know this isn't the most exciting thing, but it's been a slow news week"—as if there's ever been anything *but*—"and, Mabry?" She looks at me and gently clears her throat. "Well, this will be good for you. You know how I love your, uh, *flair*, but this is good practice for just sticking to the facts, okay, dear? The who, what, where, when. Just some nice, basic reporting." She gives me a cautious smile.

I tell her okay, but as soon as she's down the hall, I mumble to Sirina, "Nice, *boring* reporting."

"Boring," Sirina says, and laughs. "Okay, Mabry, that's one thing you will never be."

"Welcome, ladies!" Mr. Greer, the band sponsor, greets us with a radio-active dose of enthusiasm as we enter the cafetorium. His smile spreads his mustache wide over his upper lip. "Urine for a real cheat!"

Or at least that's what it sounds like he says, but it's hard to hear anything over the squawking trombones, the farting tubas, and the kazoo-like screech of a flautist in distress.

Sirina smirks at me. "Some 'treat,' huh?"

"Treat?"

"Yeah, what Mr. Greer said. 'You're in for a real treat.'"

"Oh, right," I say.

I follow Sirina closer to the stage, so she can get some shots.

"Hey," I tell Sirina. "Any closer and our eardrums might actually burst."

"Fine, I'm sure we can leave if it becomes medically necessary," she says, and takes a couple shots.

"Wonderful, boys and girls. *Just* wonderful," Mr. Greer calls out, his hands pressed to his heart. "But let's try that 'Hero's March' once more."

And the band plays on. It's bad enough that my face starts to squeeze and pull in all sorts of directions on its own. When the music finally stops, Sirina looks at me, amused.

"Can we leave?" I ask. "I think it's already becoming medically necessary."

But the soloists are about to start, and Sirina shushes me. Mr. Greer calls Kipper Garrett up front. Kipper's this shy kid in my biology class. He's kind of short and square-shaped, which seems to bother everyone but him. Some of the guys make fun of him—not just for how he looks, but for the off-brand shoes he wears, or for the thermos he brings in his lunch. But it never rattles him. It's like when he was little, his dad told him the sticks-and-stones rhyme, and it's stuck with him ever since.

"Kipper will be playing a lovely rendition of Bob Marley's 'No Woman, No Cry,'" Mr. Greer tells us.

Kipper steps forward in his slightly-too-long black pants. He wipes off the reed of his clarinet, places his lips on it, and closes his eyes.

I brace myself. Sometimes you just want to go up to kids like Kipper, give them a little knock-knock on the head, and say, *Are you trying to make it that easy for those jerknuts? Are you aware that you're practically serving yourself up to them on a silver platter? Because even though their teasing doesn't seem to faze you, it makes the rest of us feel pretty bad.*

But when he starts playing, I stop feeling sorry for him. He's good. I mean, *really* good. The music he plays is like eardrum balm. Sirina takes a few closer shots of him, and when he's done, she claps. I do too.

Mr. Greer announces Kailey Kinnell next on saxophone. She is whomping out something that might be "When the Saints Go Marching In," but it sounds like the mating call of a whale with sea pox.

Sirina turns toward me. "Maybe we can do a little write-up on Kipper? He's pretty good. What do you think?"

"Remember, we're supposed to be keeping it as boring as possible," I joke. Sort of.

"Well, he's got talent. Plus, he's nice. Maybe he deserves a little attention. Remember when Amelia didn't have money on her lunch card?"

He'd been standing right behind Amelia in the lunch line when she tried to run her card and it came up with a zero balance. And he'd just given the cashier his card and told her to put Amelia's lunch on it.

"I remember," I say.

"And in P.E., when he has to choose a team, he always picks the kids no one wants—and he picks them first. Anyway, why not, you know? It's kind of nice when you can use the power of the press for good."

Kailey finishes up, and we have to clap for her, too, and Mr. Greer calls up the third soloist. Colby Ahrens steps up front and positions his flute, but the sound that we hear is something that even the worst flautist in the world couldn't achieve.

EEEEEEE. The mechanical scream of an alarm, not too far away.

Crash + Burn

CRAAAAASSH!

The window shatters with a sound so sharp and ringing that it overwhelms his senses, leaving him feeling like his ears have been stuffed with cotton. Before the last of the glass finishes its *tink* to the ground, Thad tucks his bleeding fist farther up into the sleeve of his sweatshirt and rams his left hip against the emergency exit leading out to the school's back field. An alarm cries out, and for a second he freezes. *Go, GO,* he tells himself, and falls forward into a run. He flies right past the new rubber track at a pace that he's sure would make any P.E. teacher proud.

Anger is like a high-octane fuel. He feels his heart pounding too high in his chest, his breath too full in his lungs, but he can't stop now. *Nick Wainwright, you smear.* Thad runs even faster.

He reaches the woods, his path now full of rocks and trees. He trips on a root, and finally feels the pain in his right hand. For the first time, he looks back. The school is in the distance; there's no one chasing him. His scalp feels itchy with relief, and his breath slows some as he trots along the winding path.

A pebble jabs through the sole of his shoe, and he hops around, letting out a few pent-up words—words he can't get away with at home, words that feel good coming out. But then a thought makes him suck the words back in—practically gasp them into his lungs. He's left something behind. He'd been so angry, he must have run right past it. It's still back there, somewhere. Hopefully not too close to the window he just punched out.

His skateboard.

Crap. Crap. Holy, holy crap.

It was an old board, but it had belonged to his father. He can't go back for it without getting caught. It's just another thing he has to say good-bye to.

doler *to ache*

me duele

te duele

le duele

nos duele

les duele

The *EEEEEEE* noise continues. Mr. Greer starts shooing everyone toward the exits.

"But it's not a fire alarm," Colby says, still standing at center stage with his flute. "That's just one of those emergency exit alarms. And anyway, there's no smoke."

"Colby, you'll have your chance," Mr. Greer says. "But an alarm's an alarm. Let's move, boys and girls!"

We file out of the cafetorium with the band. When we get outside, Sirina huddles close. "Look." She shows me a shot of Mr. Greer overreacting to the alarm. His eyes are wide, his mouth is open. His arms are outstretched.

"That's funny," I say.

"Oh, come on, Mabry—then laugh, okay? Laugh!"

27

"I would, if such a thing were possible."

The alarm continues. Everyone's getting restless. A piccolo player starts chasing around a horn blower, and some shrieking begins, and a tall bassoonist bumps into Sirina, nearly knocking the camera out of her hands.

"Watch it!" I yell, momentarily happy to have an outlet for my terrible mood.

Sirina looks at me. "Hey, we have everything we need. And school's already over. Let's just go."

It seems like anywhere I go, I feel restrained, confined, a prisoner to heartbreak. "Fine, let's go home."

"No, not *home*. Let's go for ice cream."

"I told you ice cream's not going to help this time."

"Mabry, listen to me. You need to get over him. If you can't do it for *you*, do it for me. Your best friend. Who knows what's best for you."

"Well, I *love* him, Sirina. It's *real*. What am I supposed to do?" I ask her.

"How long have we been friends, Mabry?"

"Forever," I say. Well, close enough—it was really the third day of kindergarten. On that day, she fell down while standing in the play-ground line. Her eyes rolled back into her head and her body started shaking and twitching. Some people screamed, some people laughed, but I knelt down right next to her and held her hand. It wasn't because I was so great or anything. It was because I was struck with guilt: she had been right behind me in the lunch line earlier. There were two Jell-Os left—one red, one green—and I was definitely eyeing the red. *Cherry! Yum!* But then I saw it—a fly landing right on the red Jell-O's whipped-cream center! I had looked around and realized I was the only witness. So despite wanting the red, I chose the green, secretly leaving her with only the contaminated option.

And there, on the asphalt, in front of my own eyes, she was dying, and I was sure it was my fault. *Sorry, sorry, sorry,* I whispered to her, under all the commotion. Soon after, she was diagnosed with epilepsy, which she now takes medicine for. It took me three years to confess to her the true story behind my playground compassion—but by that time, we'd already decided we were fated to be friends forever.

"Yes," she says now, with all the authority of Someone Definitely In Charge. "We've been friends a long time, a very long time. So now you're going to trust me when I tell you what you're supposed to do. You're supposed to close your mouth and stop talking about *Nick Wainwright*"—she says his name like it's a dirty word—"and keep putting one foot in front of the other. Until we get to the mall. Dairy Queen awaits."

"But I—"

"Uh-uh!" She wags her finger. "No talking. Just walking."

I try to remind her that it's useless, but she puts her fingers on my lips and clamps them together.

"Now, the next time that mouth opens," she says to me, "it needs to be for the sole purpose of shoveling in a Blizzard."

"You can talk now, Mabry," Sirina is saying, now that I don't want to. We're at the mall, having our therapeutic Blizzards, and, for this moment—this fleeting moment—I'm free from the torment of heartbreak.

She continues. "Now, *this* is love. In food form."

Oh, Sirina, I think, *if only love were that simple.*

I finish off my Blizzard. I not only finish it, but scrape the bottom with my spoon, and lick the edges. And when the ice cream rush just abandons me, like *Nicolás* has, I sink back down into the same old Heartbreak Hole.

"What do you want to do now?" she asks.

"I want to figure out why every guy I've ever gone out with has broken up with me. I mean, I've been dumped *nineteen* times since fourth grade."

Sirina is excavating the creases in her Blizzard cup with the corner of her spoon, apparently looking for any remaining pieces of Heath bar that could possibly be hiding.

Finally, she says, "Maybe it's because sometimes it seems like all you care about is guys, and *loooove*." She drops her jaw and actually rolls her eyes when she says The Word. "It's a little *weird*."

You know how most of the time when your best friend uses this word to describe you, you're doing something like mixing Sprite with root beer and pretending it tastes great and she's laughing and using the word *weird* in a way that makes you feel special? Funny? Appreciated? Unique?

This is not one of those times. No. When she uses it this way, I start to feel embarrassed.

"Am I that bad?"

Her eyebrows lift apologetically, and she tries to smile and make it better. The fact that she says nothing more gives me all the information I need. And *then* some.

"Fine. I'll swear them off. No more boys." Then I have an idea. "Would you kill me if I asked my mom to send me to an all-girls school?"

"With a knife," she says.

"I'm serious," I say. And I'm starting to think I might be. I picture Hermana Ampuero, the nun on *La Vida Rica*. Well, she wasn't always a nun. In fact, she used to have a boyfriend—okay, three—before she was a nun, when she was just a gorgeous stiletto-wearing nurse. But after she accidentally put her cheating lover into a coma by breaking a bottle on his head, she moved to Suelo and took her oath.

"Well, I just don't think that would work. You'd be plotting your escape in two days."

She's probably right.

"You know what I think?" she continues. "I think you should stop idolizing Cristina. I mean, look at Mariela! She's the one breaking hearts, not sitting there, like Cristina, sobbing all the time, like some sort of victim."

"*Victim!?*" I say. "Cristina is, like, *the lady hero of love.*"

"Then why is she so miserable all the time?"

"Because—" I start to answer, but realize I don't have anything good to say. "She's, like, you know . . ." But my voice sort of trails off.

"At least Mariela doesn't sit around feeling sorry for herself."

"Well, that's probably because she never gets her heart broken in the first place," I say. "*She's* the one doing the damage."

"Even better," Sirina says. "See? You could learn a lot from her."

For few minutes, I think about it. How *would* a Cristina, such a devoted woman, suddenly become a heartbreaker like Mariela? I mean, it just might not be possible. *It was a good idea, Sirina,* I imagine myself telling her, with a mournful look in my eye. *But you just can't make a fruit out of a flower.* That's what I'll say. *A fruit out of a flower.* I like that.

Soap + Water

*K*nock. *Knock.* "Are you okay in there?" Aunt Nora asks from the other side of the bathroom door.

"I'm *fine!*" Thad's words come out tight, a little angry. How the heck can such tiny little bubbles cause so much pain? He's glad at least the cuts have stopped bleeding.

Aunt Nora doesn't seem convinced. "I heard a *swear* word. It was loud enough to hear in the kitchen, you know."

Thad lets go of the breath he's been holding in. "Sorry. I didn't mean to yell." He turns on the cold water and sticks his hand back under the faucet for a moment of relief.

"*Thad?*" she says. "What's going on?"

"Nothing," he calls out. "I'm just cleaning up some cuts on my hand."

"What kind of cuts?"

"*Scrapes*, I mean." That sounds better. He's gotten plenty of those lately.

The knob twists, but he's locked the door. He doesn't want her to see his hand and freak. Make him go to the doctor. Or worse, the hospital. If he never meets another doctor in his life, he'll be happy. He's sick of the blues and greens of hospital scrubs. The tubes everywhere. The beeps and buzzes of the machines. The patterns on the wallpaper that will be etched into his retinas forever. And he's pretty sure he'll feel a gagging in his throat at the sight of arranged flowers for at least a decade. Why do people send them anyway? They just sit there, demanding attention, and then they *die*. How does that make anyone feel better?

"I'll be out in a *minute*!" he says.

"What are you cleaning the scrapes with?" she asks.

"The stuff in the brown bottle."

"Hydrogen peroxide?"

He glances at the label. "*Yes*, Aunt Nora."

"And make sure you wrap your hand with gauze."

"I *know*. It's not like I haven't gotten scraped up before." Which is true. Since he started skating two months ago, he's gone through two rolls of gauze. But these are much more than scrapes. These are wounds.

"How bad is it?"

"*Don't worry*!" Thad says. He knows that telling Aunt Nora not to worry is like telling a bear not to crap in the woods. "It's not bad, okay? I'm still alive."

She hums out an exhale.

Thad looks in the mirror and scowls at himself. It's not Aunt Nora he's mad at. It's Nick Wainwright.

The floor creaks as Aunt Nora walks back into the kitchen.

He waits until he can hear the clang of the dishes, and slips into his room.

There's sixty dollars in the drawer of his desk. He'll have to say good-bye to that today, too. He gets the cash out of his father's old wallet and slips it into his pocket.

He passes Aunt Nora in the kitchen on his way out. She's standing at the stove, stirring a pot of soup.

"Hey, wait," she says, trying to get a good look at his hand. "That's a lot of gauze." Her eyebrows lift.

"Well, I'm not Tony Hawk or anything just yet. It'll heal." He gives her his half smile and changes the subject. "How's Mom?"

"She's okay. She's sleeping."

"Good," he says. "I'll sit with her when I get back."

"You just got home. Where are you going now?"

"To the mall."

"Again? You were just there a couple days ago!"

He shrugs. "I like it there. And anyway, I have to get something."

She looks at the clock. "Well, *I* have to leave for work in two hours."

"I'll be back by then, okay?"

She studies him. "What do you need to get?"

"A new skateboard."

"You broke the skateboard, too?" She looks at him with new worry. "How bad *was* this fall?"

"I didn't break it," he tells her. "I lost it."

"You lost it? Where?"

Thad cracks a smile. "If I knew that, it wouldn't be lost."

Aunt Nora sighs, a slight look of surrender on her face. "I have to go shopping on Sunday. Maybe I can pick one up for you then."

"*Noooo.*" He shakes his head. "Sunday's a long way off. And anyway, you can't just 'pick up' a skateboard, Aunt Nora. That's like me 'picking up'"—he waves his arm toward her—"I don't know, *shoes* or something for you."

She smiles and looks down at the thick black shoes she wears to her cashier job at the Buy-It-All.

"Thirteen years without a skateboard, and now you can't live a couple days without one?"

Thad shrugs. "I need to get around."

Her eyebrows lift. "So, did you get around to making it up to school today?"

He forgot that he'd told her he was thinking of going up there after classes let out. An unofficial tour, just to check it out without any teachers or principals or counselors breathing down his neck.

But he definitely doesn't want to tell her about what happened when he did.

"I *told* you what I did. I fell off my board and I scraped up my hand." He tries to turn it into a joke. "Those are my accomplishments for the day."

She sighs and turns back around to stir the soup. Over her shoulder, she says, "I think it'll be good for you to be back in school."

It was actually something he had been kind of looking forward to. Kind of. Not being the new-old kid, and all the questions that come with that, but just pretending to have a normal life, if that was even possible anymore. But after today, he's fine with staying right here. Here and the mall, places that feel safe. That's good enough. His world definitely doesn't need any Nick Wainwright in it.

"I *am* in school," he tells her. "Mine just requires a username and password."

"But I thought you were ready to enroll here at Frost. Your old friends would probably love to—"

"Well, I'm *not*." He surprises himself with his sharp tone. "Sorry," he says, immediately regretting it. These surges of anger take some getting used to.

She gives him a soft look. He's been getting a lot of those soft looks lately. He's not sure he deserves them. In fact, he's pretty sure he doesn't, especially after today.

"Anyway, you and Mom still need me around during the day," Thad says. He knows she can't argue too much with that. "I better go now, so I can get back in time for you to leave."

She relents. "Okay, fine. But be quick. And maybe you should get some of those gloves while you're at it."

"Gloves?"

"I'm sure they make them. To protect your hands when you skateboard?"

Skate. But he doesn't bother correcting her this time. "Good idea," he says.

Actually, it's a great idea. Covering his hands means covering the key evidence that he broke the window. *Brilliant* idea.

He's almost to the door when she adds, "Oh, you know? Maybe someone'll return the skateboard to you."

Sure, Aunt Nora. Some nice man in a blue uniform. Driving a fun car with a siren.

He hopes he never sees it again in his life, because with his luck, it's already in the evidence room at the police station. He doesn't know what kind of crime he committed by punching out a window on school property, but he's pretty sure it's something punishable by law.

But he just shrugs casually and says, "Yeah, maybe."

"Don't lose hope," she tells him. "It's definitely possible, you know. It was your dad's, from when he was about your age."

"I know."

"Well, our mother marked everything with our names when we were young. Even our *socks*." She laughs. "So who knows? It may make its way back to you."

And then a memory jars him. In his mind, the memory is like an old photo, stuffed in the back of an album. A little blurry, a little off-center. And in that memory, on the underbelly of the skateboard, just behind the back wheels, in faded black marker, are the tiny blocklike letters: *Bell*.

His dad's last name. *Thad's* last name.

Oh.

Crap.

herir *to injure*

yo hiero
tú hieres
ella hiere
nosotros herimos
ellos hieren

As Sirina and I are finally surrendering our Blizzard cups into the recycling bin, I feel a vibration through the tile floor under my feet and hear a whir of wheels approaching. A kid on a skateboard almost sails by, but comes to a skidding stop in front of us and steps off the board with a graceless thud, almost falling.

He is kind of tall, and he looks skinny and loose-jointed under his blue sweatshirt and jeans. He's wearing a baseball cap backward over his shaggy brown hair. My head can't place him, but my guts seem to recognize something about him immediately, and they squeeze together tightly in a protective huddle.

And then he speaks—*"Mabry Collins?"*—and I suddenly know why all the air feels like it's being vacuumed out of my lungs.

It's Thad Bell.

Thad Bell. *My very first love.*

Thad Bell. *My very first heartbreak.* It involved monkey bars, a fall, and a permanent scar on my soul. And it was the day before Valentine's Day.

Sirina squints as if trying to recognize him. He is a different version of the Thad Bell I used to know. It's as if someone took his fourth-grade picture and stretched it out, scuffed it up, and dulled the brightness out of his gold-brown eyes.

"And Sirina, right? It's me, Thad Bell. You guys remember me?"

My mind goes back to fourth grade. We'd just finished a section on Europe. I was hanging upside down on the monkey bars, trying to keep my shirt tucked into my pants. He walked up to me. I was happy to see him—I smiled, and I wondered if it looked like a frown since I was upside down. You know that saying—"a smile is a frown turned upside down"? Well, then, I thought, the opposite must also be true.

But I was smiling, whether or not he could tell.

"Hey, Mabry," he said, lifting his chin a little. "What's Italy the shape of?"

We'd just learned this. "A boot!" I said, proud and smart, and thinking I was practically a genius.

"That's right. And that's what I'm giving you."

I swung a little from the bar, confused. "You're giving me some boots?" I pictured some cute white cowboy boots, like the kind baton twirlers wear.

"No, I'm giving you THE boot. We're over."

And then he walked away, leaving foot dents in the mulch.

And I fell, thudding gracelessly into the sand, like I had been dumped NOT ONLY by Thad Bell, but by the universe as a whole.

Here, now, I say, "How could I forget?" And not in a friendly tone.

"*Wow*, so," Sirina says, "this is crazy. What's it been—like four years?" She looks at me, like I'm who she's asking.

"I haven't been counting," I say in this very cool and tight-lipped way.

"Yeah, about that long," Thad says.

"Didn't you move away?" Sirina asks.

"Yeah, but we moved back a few months ago."

Sirina eyes his skateboard, which is tilted up under his foot. "Cool board," she says.

"Thanks, I just bought it like five minutes ago. I lost my old board. Sucks because it was my dad's."

"You lost your dad's skateboard and you broke your hand? Good going," I say.

He looks surprised, and then looks down at his right hand, which is wrapped in gauze. "Oh, that," he says, and laughs a little. "That's from earlier. Yeah. Just a few scrapes. I'm new at this. But I got some gloves now, so I can fall all I want."

Sirina laughs. I don't.

"So what are you up to besides learning how to skate?" Sirina asks him, a vast question I'm secretly curious to hear him answer.

"Today, just buying this board, but usually I'm here for the nachos," he says.

She laughs. "Seriously?"

"Yep. Burritos, sometimes. Most times."

"Don't get out much?" I say, meaning every bit of the bitter tone that comes across.

It doesn't seem to affect him. "Yeah, not so much."

"What about school?" Sirina asks.

"I'm just doing online school."

"Online school? Is that the same thing as being *homeschooled*?" she asks.

"Yeah." I snort. "What are you, Amish?" Despite my mockery, a fleeting image of Thad in an Amish Sunday suit flashes into mind. For a second, I'm intrigued. I wonder what it would be like to go out with an Amish guy. Would he pick me up in a carriage? Would we cause a scandal? Would my first kiss be stolen behind a barn? Would it cause a fight among his family, and if so, would he choose me over his Amish life?

"No, genius," Thad says to me. "*Online*. It involves a computer and, yes, electricity."

"I *know*," I say. "*Obviously*."

Thad blinks his eyes in this self-righteous way and looks at Sirina. "Am I—? Did I—? Have I—? Done something to her?"

"Oh, what, besides giving me a curse?" I say loudly.

He takes his foot off of his skateboard. "I, uh—I don't understand girl language."

"She's just—*gah*," Sirina says. I hear the frustration in her voice.

"Nineteen times, Thad Bell! And you were just the first!"

"I need, uh, maybe an interpreter?" He puts a question mark on it.

"You probably don't remember," Sirina says in this apologetic tone. "You dumped her back in fourth grade."

"Oh." Thad grimaces. "Sorry. I guess I'd kind of forgotten about that."

"Don't worry, it's just, she's—uh—had a really bad couple days. And she's taking it out on you instead of the person she *should* be mad at."

"He crushed my soul!" I cry out.

"Me? *I* crushed your soul?" Thad says. "I was *nine!*"

Sirina puts her arm around me, but says to Thad, "Not you. It's this guy Nick. He just—*you know.*"

"Wait—Nick Wainwright?" Thad asks.

"You remember him?" Sirina asks.

"*Oh*, yeah," he laughs in a not-happy way.

"HE IS MY DESTINY AND I LOVE HIM!"

"Mabry, come on," she chides me. To Thad, she says, "She's obsessed with this TV show, *La Vida Rica*—it's this Latin soap opera. That's why she sometimes sounds so crazy."

"It's not a soap opera. It's a telenovela. And anyway, Nick was the love of my life!"

"He dumped her for karate."

"Uh, lame," Thad says. "Really lame."

"*He* didn't dump me," I say. "Not really."

"Huh?"

Sirina makes a cringey face. "His mom did."

"Dude, *what*? You got dumped by somebody's mom? And you're practically crying about it? That's, like, classic!" Thad laughs.

"HE LOVES ME."

"Uhhh . . . Hmm," Thad says. He looks at Sirina with wide *has she gone crazy?* eyes.

"HE WAS GOING TO TAKE ME TO THE COTILLION."

"What's a cotillion?"

"The eighth-grade-graduation dance at our school. The Junior Cotillion. It's like she thinks she's going to marry the guy who takes her." Sirina sighs. "I just don't know what to do with her."

"Jeez. *Dude*. Tell her to stop falling for tool bags," Thad says.

"Can you *please* tell her how exactly to do that?"

He shrugs. "It's easy. You just . . . don't."

"Is it such a crime to love?" I ask. Very bravely.

Thad says to Sirina, "Does she really believe in all that?"

"Then lock me up!" I say. But they continue to ignore me and my torment.

Sirina sighs. "Completely," she says to Thad. "No matter what I say, all she cares about is getting him back."

For a second, Thad says nothing. He just stands there with this bug-eyed look on his face. Then he asks, "Getting him *back?*"

"Yep, that's pretty much it," she says. "Sick, right?"

But he's smiling. He looks at me. "Do you *really* want to get him back?"

"Haven't you heard *anything* I've been saying?"

"You want him to start calling you again?" Thad asks.

"Yes!"

"What? *No*," Sirina interjects.

"And texting?"

"Of course!"

Sirina glares at him.

"And . . . I don't know, what? Bringing you flowers and stuff?"

"With all my heart!"

"Seriously?" Sirina asks Thad. "What are you doing?"

"It's okay." He nods. "I think I can help." He leans against the rail overlooking the food court. "I know how a guy thinks. I know what a guy wants. I can help you get him back. He'll *fall in love* with you."

I ignore the ridiculous tone in his voice when he says The Words because I'm too fascinated with the idea of having Nick back. In Love. With Me.

"Wait," Sirina says. "That's a horrible idea. That's the last thing she needs. I mean, I know she sounds a little like a nut right now, but she's not, really. Well, not in a *bad* way. The guy doesn't deserve her!"

43

"Yep, I get it," Thad says. "That's why there's one condition."

"What's that?" Sirina asks.

"That she breaks his heart."

"Break his *heart*? I don't want to break his heart!" I complain.

"Wait," Sirina says. "Why do you want to help her break his heart?"

"Okay, obviously, I'm not a fan of the guy. I mean, I just—" He shakes his head. Then he looks up at Sirina. "I just think the guy's a complete *wipe*."

"He *is*!" Sirina says, sounding satisfied, finally, while my heart screams in agony.

"HE IS NOT!"

"And also, so say I was a jerk in fourth grade. Hey, Collins, let me make it up to you now. You can have him begging for you."

"Think about Mariela," Sirina tells me.

"Who's Mariela?" Thad asks.

"Just someone from *La Vida Rica*," Sirina tells him. Then she looks at me. "She's someone who Mabry could learn something from. Someone who wouldn't be crying over some guy."

I start to argue that you can't make a fruit out of a flower—or was it a flower out of a fruit?—but they both look at me like I should be packed into a straitjacket, like Elisabet when she was found living in her dead sister's husband's attic, so I just say, "What about the Cotillion?"

"Fine. You can lure him back. Let him ask you to that stupid dance. And that night—*bam!* You stand him up."

"That sounds like an *awful* idea," I say.

Thad looks down and shrugs. To Sirina, he says, "Oh well, I guess she likes crying her eyes out over *meatwads*."

"No, I *don't*!" I say immediately.

He steps on his board. "Ah, never mind. That's okay. I gotta go anyway."

"*Wait!*" I say. If it'll make Nick fall back in love with me, maybe I should go along with Thad's plan. For now. I see *Nicolás* and me together, admiring a rainbow. Looking up at the night stars, maybe sharing a wish *juntos*. Together. I see us running hand in hand on the beach. Laughing joyously in the rain.

Oh, my heart is so hungry for him!

So I say, "Okay."

"Great," he says. We exchange numbers and he says, "I'll be in touch." Then he takes off on his brand-new board. A little shakily, if you ask me.

"Hey! No skateboards!" the mall cop, Captain Jerry, shouts. He takes off on his Segway behind Thad, the swirling red light tailing him. But even though Thad looks a little unsteady, he's definitely fast—too fast for Captain Jerry, who circles back, points at us, and says, very sternly, "No. Skateboards!" again before rolling off.

"I hope he calls you soon," Sirina says. "Thad, I mean, not Captain Jerry."

"Sirina, are you really sure I should do this?" I ask her. "You *do* remember what Thad did to me?"

"Mabry," she groans. "Fourth grade was, like, a lifetime ago!"

"Wow," I huff. "Thanks for the sensitivity."

"Come on—we were kids!"

Oh, she's *so* forgiving. I sigh. "Whatever, Saint Sirina." Maybe *she* should join a convent instead of Hermana Ampuero.

"Mabry! Come on! Don't forget what I did when he dumped you!"

And I haven't. The day after Thad dumped me—Valentine's Day, of course—she gave everyone in the class a red, heart-shaped lollipop. Everyone except for him. He got a Dum Dum. At the time, it was a brilliant show of friendship and loyalty, the first of many. "I remember," I say.

45

"When have I ever let you down?" she asks me now.

"Never."

"Right. So listen to me, okay? You need to get over Nick no matter what it takes."

"I'll try," I say. And maybe I should. Maybe Thad can help me get my *Nicolás* back. And then the heartbreak thing? The standing-him-up thing? Well, once Thad and Sirina see us together again, they'll get over *that*. I'll make flowers-out-of-fruit out of both of them! I'll make them both believe in true love.

Peanut Butter
+ chocolate

ow, Thad thinks, gliding back home on his new skateboard. *That was easy. She walked right into it.* Here he's been wondering how he'd ever get back at Nick; and there she's been wondering how she'd ever get Nick *back.* It's like peanut butter and chocolate, as his dad used to say. A win-win situation.

Still, the girl is ridiculous. To be obsessing over such a smear. Wow. Nick hadn't been so bad in fourth grade, but he's definitely changed. It shouldn't surprise him. Everything's changed in those four years.

Everything.

Anyway, what is it with Mabry's insistence on this love thing? It's like believing in the tooth fairy. Santa Claus. Unicorns, even. He's glad he dumped her back in fourth grade. She was ridiculous back then, too, although he doesn't remember why he dumped her. Probably on a dare.

He's a sucker for those. He once ate a worm on a dare.

Although he probably shouldn't admit that. Especially if he's calling someone else ridiculous.

Thad sees an orange cone right in front of him. Crap. They're doing construction on the sidewalk—he didn't expect that. He has to skate into part of the street. A car honks at him. His muscles freeze for a second, and he almost loses his balance. He's embarrassed by his response, and by the prickly remains of fear that crackle in his fingertips. He shouldn't be scared of anything anymore—there's not a whole lot left to lose, and if he's going to lose anything else, well, then, *bring it on.*

He shrinks a little lower on his board. It's so different, this new world on wheels. Until you're on them, you never really think about where you can go, and where you can't. Better cross this route off the list—it's too rocky for wheels of any type.

He skates through an intersection—a four-way stop but no cars—and rolls back onto the sidewalk. He relaxes a little, and navigates around some crushed glass on the pavement. A car drives slowly by. Could it be an unmarked police car? A detective? He feels a queasy panic rise from his stomach to his throat. But it's just a man, a regular man, who doesn't give him a second glance.

He takes a breath and tries to reason with himself. So he punched out a window. Okay, on school property. Okay, on government property. What's the worst they can do? Arrest him? Maybe. Send him to juvie? Possibly. Or maybe they'd slap his family with a big, fat fine. Make them pay to replace the window. Great. Like Aunt Nora needs that.

Everyone should be glad that it was a window he punched out, and not Nick Wainwright, who deserved it a lot more than that innocent plate of glass. It's probably also a good thing that Nick was so amazingly clueless. That Nick hadn't realized Thad had overheard him, that Nick hadn't gotten a good look at him, or at least hadn't recognized him if he did. Otherwise, he'd already be in deep stew.

Another car heads toward him—a little blue Volkswagen bug, being driven by a blond lady with sunglasses. She smiles at him through the car window and he feels a sudden urge to impress her. He jumps on his board and does a switch stance—at least he thinks that's what it's called—left foot forward now. But the car drives on, and the left-foot-forward thing doesn't feel so good. He jumps and switches back, but his ankle gives way and he hits the pavement, his injured hand suffering another blow. He's not sure if he's mad at himself or at the laws of gravity, but he feels a familiar stab of injustice, and gives the pavement a good stomp with his foot like a stubborn four-year-old. He's thankful that no one is there to see his mini-tantrum, and gets back up and jumps on the board like it never happened.

Tricks are overrated anyway, he thinks. *So are people like Nick Wainwright.* He used to like Nick. They were on the same Little League teams back in third and fourth grades. They once went to a Star Wars revival together, Thad as Chewbacca and Nick as C-3PO. In third grade, Thad had spent the night at Nick's; that night the cat vomited up a mouse in Nick's bed. It was one of the greatest, most disgusting moments in each of their lives.

But today—well, Thad wouldn't have known words could hurt so much, especially coming out of someone he used to like. But maybe that's why they do feel so bad. You expect stupid crap like that from other people, not from someone you used to consider a friend.

And Nick used to be a friend.

Used to be. That phrase pretty much describes everything in his life.

He can't wait until Nick is put in his place.

He stands up tall and sticks his hands in his pockets. Just a nice, easy, casual zip home. Okay, a little wobbly, but who cares? Why not pretend he has nothing to worry about? He makes himself look bored again. No prob. No rush.

Except that he knows there probably is. He's afraid to look at his phone. Not just because he'll fall if he does, but because he's sure he's about fifteen minutes late. And Aunt Nora's waiting. He feels a wave of guilt about that—he told her he'd be home. But then, a stab of annoyance. He's thirteen—isn't he supposed to be out having fun anyway?

Part of him wonders what would happen if he were to just skate away into the sunset, but most of him knows that he's headed back home. Sunsets are probably overrated, too, and anyway, it's cloudy outside.

THE VINDICATOR

The Official News Blog of Hubert C. Frost Middle School

Band ~~Blows Hard~~ *Gears Up for Spring Concert*

~~If you 1) own earplugs; and 2) have absolutely nothing better to do next Tuesday night, then please be informed that~~ Bandemonium, the Hubert C. Frost Middle School Band, will be performing a collection of ~~ridiculous choices~~ *favorites* such as ~~the godforsaken~~ "Hero's March" and "Warrior's Dance" for the annual spring concert next Tuesday night, in the cafetorium at 7 p.m.

Math teacher and band leader Mr. Greer promises ~~free earplugs to first fifty attendants.~~ *that members of the audience will be in for "a real treat."*

The concert will include several soloists, including Kailey Kinnell on ~~dying whale~~ *saxophone* and *award-winning clarinetist* Kipper Garrett ~~on clarinet~~ (see profile below). ~~Who is actually pretty good. Seriously, you should take your earplugs out for him. He is magical.~~

The concert is free and open to the ~~pubic.~~ *public.*

51

Eighth-Grade Clarinetest ~~Better Than You Would Think~~ *Is an Award-Winning Musician*

~~You may not know it to look at him, but Kipper Garrett is practically a celebrity.~~ Since third grade, Kipper Garrett has racked up an ~~amazing~~ assortment of ~~trophies.~~ *awards, the latest being the County High Notes Winning Woodwind.* He ~~will probably be extremely famous one day, because~~ he practices at least an hour every day, and ~~on top of that, he's a really nice guy.~~ *credits his success to his mother, a clarinetist herself who studied with the famed German soloist Sabine Meyer.*

[click for more]

IN OTHER NEWS . . .

Study Finds There Is No Real Point to Being First in Line

A groundbreaking study out of the Hiram Macomb Center for Education shows that, despite popular belief, "line leaders" are no more likely to be successful than mid-liners. [click for more]

querer *to want*

yo quiero

tú quieres

ella quiere

nosotros queremos

ellos quieren

Walking into school the next morning, I see Abe Mahal in the center of a crowd. He's gesturing wildly and telling a story that I can't hear. I spot the back of Jordan's head and reach through the mob to tap her on the shoulder. She glances back at me and nods, holding a finger up to mean *one minute*. But Officer Dirk, the school security guard, doesn't give her that minute.

"DISPERSE, PEOPLE!" Officer Dirk says in his all-caps voice. For once, I am on his side. I only wish for some sort of human Drano. The crowd starts to shift and break apart, and Officer Dirk swats us all away like we are houseflies. Jordan adheres to my hand, and I pull her down the hall toward my locker, where Sirina is unloading her backpack.

"What's going on?" I ask Jordan.

"Oh my god. Somebody broke out a window downstairs yesterday after school. Abe was there when it happened."

"Who did it?"

"They don't know yet," Jordan says, her eyes wide. "They heard this crash and the guy just *tore off* through an emergency exit. But Abe said he heard there was a prison escape in Mount Claire yesterday, so"—she lowers her voice—"it's possible that a murderer was here. On. School. *Grounds*."

"So there's a *crime scene*? An actual *scene*?" I have a fleeting but thrilling fantasy that the producers of *La Vida Rica* have been asked to take charge of our school. There will be flower deliveries during algebra, ceviche for lunch, fitted P.E. uniforms! The health center will be staffed by stunning and elegant doctors, and nurses with white hats, and balconies will be installed on all second-floor classrooms, for both mad kissing scenes and the occasional brush with murder. And it will all be set near a beach.

Sirina looks at me, her eyes getting a rare sparkle of excitement. "Are you thinking what I'm thinking?"

It's probably not salsa lessons for P.E., I realize.

"The YoJo!" She grabs my hand and squeezes it.

The YoJo—the National Youth Journalism award—is something that Sirina has pined for since we started writing for *The Vindicator* last year. It's a biannual contest, and each December and June she sends in our entry. But with articles like "Hands Down, Single Mittens Most Common Items in Lost and Found" and "Ding Dongs Banned from Cafetorium After Fourth Microwave Explosion," we haven't had much of a chance.

Sirina continues. "This is the first newsworthy thing that's happened since we started school here. We could write an investigative series of articles! This could be our big break! Just think!"

And I *do* think. I think about Sirina and me onstage. The two of us smiling beatifically and waving to an adoring audience. Our long hair cascading down our backs. Our dresses, glittery. Our two hands together, accepting the Golden Plume.

"Should we talk to Abe?" I ask her.

"Mabry, Abe is the chief of the rumor mill. He's already talking about escaped murderers. No, remember what Mrs. Neidelman says. Facts first. Always start with the official sources."

I look over her shoulder. With only his loud voice, Officer Dirk is breaking apart the small clusters of people who are, undoubtedly, talking about the window-breaking incident. Or the murderer on school grounds. "Well, there's our official source now," I say.

We both move swiftly in his direction, dodging the crowds. "Officer Dirk," she says, "can you tell us what happened? It's for *The Vindicator*."

But the warning bell rings, so he just glares at us, as if the bell's spoken for him.

"I take it that was a no," I say as we turn and walk in the other direction.

"Well, okay, definitely bad timing, but this is so exciting!" she says before she dashes down the hall toward her first-period class.

"I heard it was Ms. Roach's pen pal from prison," Jordan says at lunch. "He got out of jail and decided to come surprise her at school. He asked her to marry him but she said no, so he broke the window and ran."

Sirina snorts. "Where did you hear that?"

"Madison told me," she says. "I think she heard it from Allie."

Sirina shakes her head, "Never mind. These are just crazy rumors."

"How do you know?" Jordan asks. "Maybe it's true. Hey, I should ask my neighbor. Her uncle works at the prison."

Amelia jumps in. "I heard that the guy might have been part of the Russian mafia—"

"No way!"

Jordan and Amelia continue to compare details, and Sirina turns to me. "So I went down to the part of the hall where it happened . . ."

She keeps talking, but my eyes bounce around the cafetorium, desperately seeking Nick. He's nowhere in sight. In his usual spot, about five tables over, Abe and Patrick are facing each other, crouching slightly, their hands held at sharp karate angles.

"BOYS!" Mrs. Hurst yells at them. "You will sit down and enjoy your lunch! No fighting in the cafetorium!"

"Hey, Mabry," Sirina says, tapping at my hand. "Would you *please* stop staring at your kung fu fighter and start listening to me?"

"I'm not staring at him. He's not even over there. I don't know where he is, which is crazy. When is he ever not with Abe and Patrick?"

"God, I hope that Thad can cure you of him," she says. "But right now, *I'm* your best friend, and I'm right next to you, and I need you to focus. We've got to get to the real story to even be in the running for the YoJo."

"Okay, you're right, I'm sorry," I say.

"I was telling you the hall was closed—the hall where the window incident happened. It's all coned off. Mr. Jenkins said it was a safety issue, but this is so crazy."

Then our conversation is interrupted by "Oh. My. Darling. *Clementine*." It's Amelia. She's been trying to make that expression a thing since sixth grade, but despite the fact that she uses it—and abbreviations of it—a million times a day, it hasn't really caught on.

We both turn. Amelia is staring up at Madison Buckner, who has stopped by our table to deliver some news.

"Are you serious?" Jordan says to Madison.

"What?" I ask.

Amelia answers. "Madison just said that she heard that the person who broke the window was that sub who always wears the man-clogs—remember him? Mr. Frick? Yeah, guess where he's been for the last three months. An asylum! *O.M.D.C.*"

At that, Sirina and I exchange a look that says *There she goes again.*

The girls make squealing noises, and I can't help but feel a little adrenaline rush.

"I have an idea," I say to Sirina, just above a whisper.

"What?"

"Finish your corn dog."

"That's your idea?"

"No, dummy." And then I lean in closer and say quietly, "Let's go check out the crime scene."

"But I told you—it's closed."

"Yeah, officially."

She glances around the room. "Like, sneak down there?"

I lift my eyebrows.

She smiles. "Very telenovela. I like it."

She takes the last bite of her corn dog and we get up from the table and carefully make our way toward the door. But our plan is almost scuttled at the cafetorium exit. "Hey! Where are you girls going?" Mrs. Hurst asks when we've almost escaped.

"Bathroom?" I say, but it sounds like a question.

"One at a time," she says.

"But—" I say.

"You." She points to Sirina. "You can go now. The other one will have to wait until the first gets back."

"Mrs. Hurst?" Sirina says. "She needs, uh, something that I have? In my purse? A girl thing?"

"You girls need to be prepared!" she says, and looks right at me. "Have a seat."

"Well, how am I supposed to be prepared when I've never had *it* before?" I ask.

"Oh," Mrs. Hurst says. Her stern look vanishes. "Your first?"

I nod.

She looks at Sirina and back at me. "Okay, just this once. And, honey?"

"Yes?"

Now she whispers, "Welcome to womanhood."

When we're free and into the hall, we can't help but laugh. I say, "I kind of feel bad about lying."

"I know," Sirina says. "Me too. But we won't be feeling bad when we win the YoJo."

We pick up our pace and run across the hall, down the stairs, and through the language corridor. We're almost to the crime scene when we turn the corner and I plow into a ribbon of yellow caution tape, pulling down an orange cone with it.

I am on the way to the ground when something pulls me back to standing. It is the mammothy hand of Officer Dirk.

"WHERE DO YOU THINK YOU'RE GOING," Officer Dirk asks, in his commanding way.

"Was that the window?" Sirina asks, pointing to a large space now covered in plywood.

"THIS HALLWAY'S CLOSED."

"But we're here for *The Vindicator*. Can we take a quick look? We'll be careful," Sirina assures him.

I feel the need to add to her plea. "*Please.* We won't touch anything. Cross our hearts," I say, drawing an X directly above what's left of my own.

"NO CAN DO."

Sirina keeps trying. "Well, if we can't go look at it, then can we please just ask you a few questions about the incident?"

His arms cross over his chest. "ONE. TWO. If I get to five and you're still here—DETENTION," he declares, and rudely skips ahead. "FOUR."

So we turn and run. Back around the corner. Back through the language corridor. Back up the stairs.

"Well, that was useless," I say as we reach the main floor. "We *could* talk to Abe, you know."

"Yeah, like *that's* reliable," she says. "That's like taking the low road."

Which may be right. But so far, it doesn't feel like the high road is getting us anywhere.

After school, Sirina and I are about to head to my house for some much-needed *LVR* when I see *Nicolás* down the stretch of the hall in front of me. But Jason Murray does, too. "Hey, Nick," his voice booms. "Your mom's outside. She's got a clean diaper for you."

And I have a sinking, weighted feeling. Word about his mom and our breakup has clearly gotten out.

I look at Sirina. "Did you hear that?"

But she seems to be focused on the YoJo roadblocks, and is

in no mood for any kind of sympathy. "Yeah," she says.

"Jason's such a bully!"

"He is, but it's like my sister warned me. She said three-quarters of the population of any given middle school, at any given time, is trying to get in touch with their inner jackass." She looks at me. "And, Mabry, before you go feeling all sorry for Nick, remember that only a couple of days ago, that statistic included him."

"But they're basically calling him a baby! Nick's not a baby, he's just confused. He doesn't deserve *that*."

She just rolls her eyes and says, "God, like I said, I sure hope Thad can cure you. I'm counting on it."

vagar *to wander*

yo vago

tú vagas

ella vaga

nosotros vagamos

ellos vagan

Aurelio is in the desert. He has been for five days—the words *Día Cinco* flash up on the screen. He's wandering and wandering, with no food or water. There's really no story line here, besides that. Each day, he gets a little more scruffy and rumpled, and a little more naked.

"How long are they going to drag this out?" Sirina asks.

I don't even try to answer. She's still grumpy about the YoJo obstacles, despite the gummy worms I've given her, and despite the fact that Hunter has chosen her as his favorite person again. He is curled up at her feet, and she strokes him with her fuzzy sock.

Aurelio is panting and fall-walking, a few steps in this direction, a few steps in that. Every now and then the camera flashes to a lake full of alligators, so I have a distinct feeling that's what awaits Aurelio.

Then the scene changes. We're watching Mariela again. Earlier in this episode, she visited her mother, who is being held in prison. Now Mariela's at the police chief's office. His feet are up on his desk, and he's smoking his cigar, making commands on the phone, but when the door opens and she saunters in, he looks up at her, holds his cigar in midair, and becomes immediately mute. The episode ends with the camera zooming in on her gorgeous face, which is doing all it can to look perfectly innocent.

My phone buzzes. Sirina picks it up and looks at it. "Who's 'Nacho Face'?"

I take it from her. "Hi, Thad," I say, putting the phone on speaker. "Sirina's here with me."

"So I don't get it—who's the old lady?" he asks.

It takes me a minute to realize that we're hearing the theme song from *La Vida Rica* in stereo. "You're watching it?"

Sirina's jaw drops.

"It just happened to be on," Thad says. "Plus, I wanted to see this Mariela chick."

"Okay," I say. He's watching my show! Maybe he's not so bad after all. "So, the old lady's her mom, Señora Trujillo. They locked her up because they think she stole a pig."

"A pig?" he asks.

"Yeah," I tell him. "But the thief was really this poor kid from the village. She was covering for him. She's a really nice lady, but she scandalized the town a long time ago, when she fell in love with a cartel guy and had Mariela. She was totally shunned. But now Mariela will do anything for her mom, and—"

"Yeah, yeah, all right, I get it," he says. "Anyway, ready to be a heartbreaker? I have your first assignment."

When I don't answer right away, Sirina chimes in, "Yeah. What is it?"

"I want to hear it from her."

"Yeah, I'm ready," I say, but it sounds wobbly and weak.

"Crap. You still think you love that wad, don't you?"

Madly. Deeply. But I can't say those words anymore. Even though I remain quiet, Thad seems to know what I'm thinking.

"All right, then. Pardon me while I projectile vomit," Thad adds. He makes some violent gagging sounds and says, "Okay. We're done here."

"Don't hang up," I say quickly. I remind myself that I need to do whatever it takes to get Nick to ask me to the Cotillion, even if it involves convincing Thad that I want revenge. "I'm listening."

Now Thad pauses. Then he says, "Sirina? Is this going to be a waste of my time?"

"No, no," she tells him, but looks at me, giving me quiet commands with her sideways nods. "She'll do it. She's in. Just be patient with her. It's just that she really believes in the L-word. That doesn't just change overnight."

"Collins? *Are* you in?"

They can't see the image in my mind. Nick and me dancing. Slow dancing. *Close* dancing. He dips me, then he spins me around and around and around and—

I take a breath and say it. "I'm in."

Sirina smiles at me.

"All right, good," Thad says. "Okay, here's what I'm thinking. First, I think Sirina was right. Mariela's got this thing down. She knows the difference between the real stuff and the quote-unquote love."

He makes love sound so trivial. Foolish. "'Quote-unquote love'?" I hear myself saying quietly.

"You know, the thing that passes for love in your world," he says.

63

Brutal.

"Glad you agree with me about Mariela," Sirina says. "Mabry needs to start channeling her."

"Yeah, Mariela's a good start. Collins, you have to get him to notice you in some new way—stop being so sappy and needy. No wonder the guy ran in the opposite direction."

"So I'm sappy and needy. *Thanks*," I say. "Thad, I have an idea. Why don't we just forget the plan? Why don't you just go ahead and give me a list of everything that's wrong with me. You'd probably *enjoy* that."

"I don't know what's wrong with you," he says. "I barely know you."

Ouch. Somehow that hurts worse. I mean, we have a history!

"So I guess those three weeks in fourth grade meant absolutely nothing to you."

He laughs—like he thinks I'm joking!

"Anyway, you'll be over this ridiculous idea of love soon enough," he says.

"You sound completely heartless," I tell him.

"Sometimes I wish I *were*," he says.

"What's that supposed to mean?"

"Nothing," he says. "All I'm saying is that the stuff you believe in, it's all dumb. Love is for chumps. You'll get that soon enough."

I fight the urge to put my hands over my ears and hum over his words. I reflexively look over to Sirina for support, but she's giving me this smug smile. It's two against one.

"Okay, fine," I say. "But just for the record, you are the enemy of all things beautiful and free."

"Aw, you got me where it hurts," he fake whines. "I better go cry myself to sleep." Then he makes his voice high and mock pleasant. "Buh-*bye* now!"

"Bye, Burrito Face," I say, even though he's already hung up the phone.

Hunter jerks his head up. He must smell A-Bag, because a second later the door opens. Hunter jumps up from under Sirina's feet and scurries toward the door.

"Hey, loser," Aaron calls out. "I'm home!"

"Hey, A-Bag," I call back. "No one cares!"

He comes into the room. "Oh, look, it's two of the three stooges!"

Sirina launches Hunter's tennis ball at him. Aaron twists girlishly to avoid the ball, but it hits him in the stomach.

"Smooth move, Ex-Lax," I say. It's the best I can come up with.

"You better be glad that didn't go through the window," my brother says to Sirina.

"Relax," Sirina says. "You know I have a better arm than you."

Aaron looks at me. "Seriously, M-Hole. *Mooove.*"

I look right back at him, defiantly. "We were *watching* my *show*."

But then Aaron threatens to fart us out of the room, so we leave in a hurry, with Hunter following behind us. There are very few things worth enduring the odious *Essence of A-Bag*.

Upstairs in my room, I say, "I don't know who was more obnoxious— A-Bag or Thad."

"Definitely A-Bag," Sirina says. "At least Thad has a point. Like I said before, Mariela's your woman."

"Yeah," I say, but kind of weakly.

She narrows her eyes at me. "Mabry?" She says my name slowly. "You're going to do this, right?"

"*Yes*. I already told you."

"Because I need my best friend back. I can't take it anymore, watching you get your heart broken over and over. For once, I'd like to see you claim your power." She is practically pleading with her eyes.

"Yeah, I know. I'm definitely in," I tell her, my eyebrows lifting. It'll all be okay, I tell myself. If she's my true friend, she'll be happy for me.

"Okay." Her face relaxes. "Come on. Let's see your best Mariela."

I glance up at the mirror across my room. What I see is a standard-issue eighth grader with skinny jeans, flip-flops, and a hoodie. "Well, problem one: I don't look like her at all," I say.

No. Mariela has the kind of infectious beauty you almost feel like you could catch if you look at her for too long.

"Well, maybe try acting like her. Act confident."

"But I don't feel confident."

"That's why it's called *acting*. Just try it."

"Seriously?" I ask.

"Yes, *seriously*. Don't forget—Mariela's a character on a TV show. She's a pretend person. That lady who plays her is *acting* a part. If *she* can do it, you can, too."

I look at myself in the mirror. My shoulders are hugging inward, protectively. I relax them a little and roll them back, which, even though it makes me feel a little taller, also makes me feel a little exposed. But Sirina says, "Good," so I take a breath and try to go with it. I realize that I haven't been breathing deep enough—that the air is stuck in a small area in my lungs, and when I breathe deeper, I feel better. I smile at Sirina in the mirror.

"Better," she says, smiling back.

I put on a little mascara. It can't hurt. I lean my head over and fluff my hair out, then whip my head up and check myself once again.

"Good. That's much more Mariela," Sirina says.

I turn all the way around and peek at my reflection over my shoulder. If I hold my eyebrows at just the right level, and angle my head in just the right way, and position my hands on my hips, well, it's almost convincing.

Sirina studies me in the mirror. I turn and look directly at her.

"Well, *hello*, heartbreak," she says in a smoldering voice. "Thy name is Mabry."

And then we start cracking up, and it feels good enough that when I catch a glimpse of myself in the mirror, looking satisfied, looking—I don't know—maybe a little bit powerful, it starts to seem possible. For a second, just a second, I wonder what being a heartbreaker would feel like. Victorious? Triumphant? Maybe you can make a fruit out of a flower after all.

Sirina stays for dinner. Stephen's eating with us tonight, too.

My mom's a lawyer. She's always busy, and as far as I know, Stephen's the only boyfriend she's ever had. My brother and I don't even have a father—I mean, technically, we do, but my mom never met him. She chose him from a piece of paper at the New Beginnings Fertility Clinic, so it's hard to think of my father and not picture Flat Stanley, the traveling piece of paper from a book my mom read to me when I was little.

Flat Stanley's name was John. He was a graduate student in engineering; his ancestors were German and Dutch. That's about all we know about him. Surely there must have been more exotic choices—a Tahitian island gentleman, perhaps, or an Argentinian cattleman, even. Or—*oh!*—an Egyptian prince! But, no. She basically chose a version of

Stephen. Well, you could say that my mom definitely has a type, despite not having a romantic bone in her body.

The topic of the night is, of course, the Case of the Broken Window and the investigative series we'd like to write. We're filling them in on the rumors—the ex-con pen pal, the murderer, the man-clog-wearing substitute teacher—and the fact that Officer Dirk won't give us any info.

"Well," my mom says, "the school probably just doesn't want to add to the hype. It can be a distraction."

"But the rumors *are* a distraction," Sirina says. "And there are so many stupid ones out there right now."

"Oh! You know what I heard?" Aaron says. His eyes are big, like he's just bursting to tell us some sort of secret.

"What?" I ask.

"I heard that it was this guy serving time for some computer crime. An old boyfriend of Mrs. Vander-Pecker."

"Our principal?" It's hard to imagine, but I do try.

"Yep. But he was released after ten years in the joint. And his first stop? To see her. But then, guess what?"

"What?" I ask.

"He saw your face, and he was so grossed out that he just threw himself out the window!"

"Oh, *shut up!*" I say, irritated not just with him, but with myself, for allowing him to get to me.

"Aaron!" my mom practically whines.

He just laughs.

My mom shakes her head at him. To us, she says, "I'd be careful about listening to the rumors."

"Well, what do you think happened?" I ask.

"There's clearly not enough evidence to know with any level of certainty at this point," my mom says. "But I'd say that it probably wasn't a premeditated act. It sounds like it was some kind of emotional outburst. Someone was upset about something."

"A crime of passion!" I say. So *La Vida Rica!* "So you think it could've been over a broken heart?"

"How would that make sense?" Sirina says, and laughs. "A broken window for a broken heart?"

"Let me take this, Ellen," Stephen says to my mom. To us, he says, "You see, kids, relationships can be very complicated. That's why there's a Facebook status for it."

A-Bag grins. "Ah, *this* from a man who has eighteen 'friends.'"

"Aaron!" my mom says, annoyed. "Go finish your dinner in the kitchen."

"Aw, it's okay, Ellen," Stephen says. "He's just razzing me."

My brother looks too happy as he pops up from the table and says, "Sayonara, suckers!"

My mom changes the subject by asking Stephen about what's happening at his school, which starts a brain-numbing flow of words like *curriculum* and *budget* and *superintendent*. There is nothing intriguing or exciting about any of these topics, and it's all a little hard to endure, especially when there's a crime of passion underfoot.

After dinner, I walk Sirina to the door. "Shoot me if I ever get that boring, okay?"

"Can't we just settle for a slap?" she asks. "A vicious one?"

"Deal," I say.

I watch her get into her mom's car, and wave as they drive off.

Good night, my lily-spattered organ-grinder, I text her after I can no longer see the car.

She writes right back. *Good night, my maple-syrup moist towelette.*

Fire + sky

That's been staring at his computer screen off and on for the last few hours. It's the first ten equations of his algebra work. It *always* seems to be the first ten equations of his algebra work. He's been in a mood all day—restless and annoyed. Not even watching her stupid show, which was laughable, could snap him out of it. The only character that seemed to have a brain in her head was Mariela. He doesn't know much Spanish, but there was enough kissing and shouting and embracing and sneaking around to figure out basically what was going on. And come on, it's all predictable anyway.

So I was kind of a jerk on the phone with her; so what? Thad wonders if he should send her a text or something to make up for it. Not with an actual apology, but something like *Let's meet at the mall next time. I'll buy you a burrito.* Some type of peace offering.

But then she may ask why he was such a jerk anyway—and then what will he say? That he's been on edge since he broke the window, worrying about the cops showing up at his house? No, wait—that he's been on edge for six whole months, since his life exploded?

That today is his father's birthday, and it's the first birthday his dad never got to have?

That thought is like a knife in the gut.

He makes himself look back at his computer screen, but it's filled with stuff he just doesn't understand. He lets out a frustrated growl and throttles the air in front of him, then gets up from the desk.

In the kitchen, Aunt Nora's sitting at the table, a stack of papers in front of her. "Something wrong, hon?"

"I hate algebra," he says. Somehow that's easier to say. "I *hate* it. It royally sucks."

"Well, maybe it'll be better in a real classroom—"

"No, it won't," he says. "There's no way you can take the suck out of algebra."

She sighs and goes back to the papers.

"Is Mom awake?"

"Yeah," Aunt Nora says, and looks up. "But wait—I need you to do me a favor."

"What?"

"Try not to bring your mood in there," she says, nodding in the direction of his mom's room. "She's kind of in a funk today, too."

"Okay," Thad says, and exhales hard.

He walks into the room. She is lying on her side away from him. "Hi, Mom."

"Oh, hey," she says, lifting her head, and attempting to roll over to her back. He sees her struggling and steps toward the bed, wanting to help her.

"No," she says, waving his hands away. "Let me try on my own."

He steps back, watches her wriggle around. His throat tightens so much that he has to look away just to take his next breath. His eyes settle on the wheelchair. It's folded up in the corner—she hasn't used it today.

"Okay," she says, facing him now, a little more upright.

He tries to ignore the fact that her legs look twisted.

"Would you mind rearranging my pillows?" she asks.

He's relieved to have something simple to help her with, something like pillows. He plumps them up and stacks them under her head.

"Perfect," she says, smiling at him. "Hey, how's your hand?"

"It's good," Thad says. He's been taking good care of it, keeping it clean and covering it with fresh gauze. Wearing the gloves whenever he goes outside of the house. There's *no way* he's going to end up in the hospital.

"Can I see?"

He holds his hand where she can see it and unwraps the gauze a little. His knuckles look like a road map. There's an interstate etched across the thumb side of his fist. She cringes.

"It's fine. It doesn't really hurt," he tells her. Which isn't really true—his hand *does* hurt sometimes. But there's Tylenol in the bathroom cabinet. And at least if he keeps this wound clean, it'll heal. It's the invisible ones that are harder to treat.

She asks for her hairbrush. He doesn't want to watch it fall from her hands, or see it get stuck in her hair. That's torturous. So he says, "I can brush it, Mom."

She gives him an amused look. "You want to brush my hair?"

"I—I mean, I can." He stares at the bedside table.

"I've got a few tangles."

"Yeah." He smirks. "That's why I'm offering."

She gives him a tiny smile. "Okay."

He gets the brush from the top of the dresser, where Aunt Nora must have left it, and moves the chair toward the head of the bed. He starts to brush her hair close to the ends, like he's seen Aunt Nora do. He works on a small tangle right above her shoulder, being overly gentle, afraid to hurt her even just a bit, afraid of the pain in his right hand if he were to squeeze the handle of the brush too tight.

And then she says, "You think—I don't know—that he's celebrating somehow?"

"Dad?" he asks, his brushing hand momentarily paused. Sometimes she seems like a little kid. Just how is his dad supposed to be celebrating? He's a box of ashes. A box of ashes that cost ten dollars and seventy-two cents to ship. His mom doesn't know that part—Thad signed for the delivery on his own. He just opened the door and there was the mailman, ringing the doorbell, holding a box. Just like any other box. And a Harriet Carter catalog—the place that sells things like toilet paper cozies. Thad had accepted them both together, his head swimming.

"Yeah. What do you think he's doing?"

Sitting in the front closet, in a black box, that's what.

But he thinks about what Aunt Nora said—about not bringing an attitude in with him. And his mom's smiling now, sort of. Thad can't see her face from where he stands brushing her hair, but he can see the rise of her cheeks, and feel the burdensome, overwhelming, helpless wave that sometimes hits him. He wants to keep her smiling. So he keeps brushing and says, "Probably eating cake."

"Yes!" she says. "He's definitely eating cake."

"And maybe hanging out with Michael Jackson."

"Michael Jackson?"

"I don't know a lot of dead people," Thad admits.

Then he has an idea. "Hey, Mom, Aunt Nora's not going to work till late. Want me to go to the store and buy a cake?"

"Oh, I—" She sighs. "That sounds fun, but honestly, I think I'm pretty tired. I'm sorry."

"That's okay," he says, putting down the brush, although he can't help feeling a little disappointed.

She pulls the blanket up to her chin, and he notices her feet are covered up, too. He doesn't want them covered up—he wants to see her wiggle her big toe. Both big toes, maybe. It could happen.

"Mom?" he says. Maybe she'll try, just for him.

"Hmm?" she says, like she's too tired for words.

"Never mind." He gives her a kiss on the forehead and leaves the room quietly. On the way back to the kitchen, he pauses at the front closet and stares at the louvered door. Behind that door, on a shelf, the Box of Dad sits.

Happy birthday, Dad.

This is the problem with love—real love, not the stupid make-believe stuff that Mabry passes it off as. On a good day, it can wind up in a wheelchair—on a *good* day. On a bad day, it can end up in a box that costs ten dollars and seventy-two cents to ship.

cortar *to cut*

yo corto

tú cortas

ella corta

nosotros cortamos

ellos cortan

In the morning, there's no sign of Sirina at school. I study my new Mariela face in the tiny mirror on the inside of the locker door, brush some of the mascara flakes from my cheeks, and try that whole *heartbreak, thy name is* thing silently. It feels tinny and hollow without her. *¿Donde estás, Sirina? ¡Donde estás!* I finally pull out my phone and call her. It's an illegal act here at Hubert C. Frost, but it's like when, on *La Vida Rica*, Rafael had to steal food for his starving children. Something that has to be done.

"Why are you calling me?" she asks, panicked. "You're going to get caught!"

"Where are you?" I hope to hear that she's just running late, because a day of school without Sirina is a day of unbearable loneliness.

"I had one of those auras," she says quickly. "I'm fine; my mom's just being paranoid and wants me to rest. I'm just going to stay home and eat Jell-O."

Jell-O. It's an ongoing joke between us—ever since I made the Red Jell-O Confession. But I find it hard to laugh right now, because I always worry when she has an aura.

The auras are part of her epilepsy. They used to come right before a seizure, but she hasn't had one of those in almost a year. I try to remain calm. She hates it when I get too anxious about it—she tells me my stress is contagious. So I ignore the ambulance sirens and hospital scenes that are blasting through my head and say, as reasonably as possible, "But you're okay?"

"Yes! I don't need you to start worrying, okay? Look, I did everything I could to come to school today, but my mom is just being a total nut. And we seriously don't need to get on the wrong side of Officer Dirk right now, so I'm going to hang up before you get detention."

And she does. I feel as alone as Graciela when she was lost in the forest and living in a cave. I try to remind myself that I've been through worse, such as the four weeks last summer that Sirina went off to her epilepsy camp, leaving me lonely and miserable, a shell of myself. Even though it was nearly impossible, I *somehow* did manage to stay alive. So I should be able to handle one day without her.

I look down at my purple tunic. I look down at the heels I borrowed from my mom's closet. And suddenly I feel like an eighth grader in costume instead of the Mighty Mariela I was last night. It's like without Sirina, I have no Mariela powers at all.

Amelia's my lab partner in second-period Biology. Despite my saggy, soggy, heavy heart, today's The Big Day. Today is The Day We Dissect a Worm. I've prepared for this day. I've said good-bye to my last enjoyable gummy worm. I've come to terms with the idea that I will cut into the flesh of a real being. I've even thought about whether I should have whooping cough today or not, and have decided that I should not. For today is a rite of passage.

Also, turns out I was vaccinated against whooping cough.

Other people are naming their worm things like Pepe or Brutus, or even Bait, but Amelia decides we should name our worm either Pat or Terry, because it's both a boy *and* a girl. I don't like either choice. "How about something like Kai or Drew?"

She makes a face and considers my suggestions, then declares our worm Dylan. "So, do you want to watch or cut?" she asks me.

Cristina would watch. But *Mariela*—now, *she* would cut.

So I say, "Cut." I put on my gloves and stand over the worm.

"Now," our teacher, Ms. Frederick, says, "as you begin your dissection, think precision. Steady hands. Remember, class, you are not cutting into a Hot Pocket. You are performing surgery on a delicate and lovely creature."

I hold my hand out. "Scalpel," I say to Amelia. She looks at me strangely, but hands over the knife, and I slice carefully into Dylan. This is no butter knife. And I see it for myself. Five tiny little hearts.

"Look!" I say to Amelia. "Isn't this amazing?"

Amelia leans over to look closely, then recoils. *"Ew!"* she says. "Gross! What is that?"

"Dylan's hearts," I say. "They're fascinating."

"Honestly, Mabry, you're the only person I know who would think worm guts are 'fascinating.'"

Kipper, sitting across the lab table, glances at me shyly. "My worm has some dirt in its crop." Then he smiles. "Her name is Glenda."

"It's not a *she*," Amelia corrects him.

78

"Kipper's just getting all excited about the girl parts!" Brian Stead, his lab-partner-slash-bully, says, whooping with laughter. The other guys around us laugh and bump fists, until Ms. Frederick tells them, in teacher language, to shut up.

Kipper looks up at me and smiles with quiet dignity. I smile back. Sirina was right. He did deserve some positive press.

In the stretch of hallway visible over Kipper's shoulder, I see *Nicolás*. He walks slowly, and his face is blotchy and almost as red as his sweatshirt, like he's been crying. The teasing must still be going on. It's like someone's picked a little scab off my heart and it's bleeding again.

I force my attention back to the gentle Dylan and his various and magnificent parts.

It's a bit ironic. You always think of love conquering all. But I'm starting to wonder if that's true. I mean, just look around the room of one-hearted, mean-spirited creatures like Brian, cutting open the bodies of *five*-hearted, *gentle*-spirited creatures like Glenda and Dylan.

Forget doves. Why isn't the worm the universal symbol for love?

I make a quick stop to change at my locker between fourth and fifth periods. As I'm changing out of the heels and into flats, a boy voice says, "Heard you're doing an article about the crime scene."

I spin around. It's Abe. Patrick stands just behind him.

Abe continues. "Dude, you should talk to us. It was *manic*."

"What happened?" I ask. I know Sirina wouldn't approve of me talking with the rumor mill, but what else do we have at this point?

"Okay," Abe says. His head bobbles and his eyes are wide. "So we were downstairs, just, you know, practicing fight moves—"

"Yeah," Patrick says, crouching suddenly. "*Hi-yah!*" He completes a series of stiff hand movements that seem to go on way too long.

"So you two were doing karate when this happened?"

Abe says, "Yeah, well, Nick too, and we—"

"Wait. Nick?" *My* Nick?

I have a memory flash from Wednesday, the day it happened. The same day as the band rehearsal. Abe calling Nick to come downstairs. Nick running right past me without even a moment's glance. My heart pangs now just as it did then.

"Yeah, we were doing some fierce spin kicks—"

Patrick snorts out a laugh. "Yeah, I got Abe in the cojones!"

"Yeah, dude, I still owe you one!" Abe says, and makes a false kick in the general direction of Patrick's pants, while Patrick squeezes his knees together and squats.

Mere children. Both of them.

"Anyway," I say.

"Anyway, so then we heard this loud crash. Dude, it was, like, *really* loud."

"Yeah, it was like a *cannon*," Patrick adds.

"So I looked over and saw the guy who broke the window. He was huge," Abe continues, "like a giant, and I was like, 'One step closer, dude, and I'll open up a can of roundhouse on your—'"

"No way, you said that?" Patrick says, in sincere amazement. He holds his fist out for a bump.

Abe looks at me, and back to Patrick, his head bobbling a little. "Dude, you were there!" He looks back at me and sighs, flustered. "I *did* say it. He probably just didn't, you know, hear me."

"Okay," I say, "so what else? Can you give me a description?"

"Oh. Yeah." Abe brightens back up. "Okay, so I stand on my left leg," he says, demonstrating. "And then I bend my right knee and bring it up—" He looks like a dog about to pee on a fire hydrant.

"Abe? I mean a description of the guy who broke the window. Not the can of roundhouse."

Patrick cackles.

"Oh," Abe says, putting his leg back down. "I mean, the guy looked huge."

"What else?"

"Humongous," he adds.

"Like the Hulk," Patrick says, holding his arms out wide.

"Can you give me any other details? Like his hair? His eyes? Anything like that?"

"Um." Abe bites his lower lip and looks toward the ceiling. "Well—it happened so fast."

I wait a moment, but he doesn't offer anything else. "Okay, well. Then what happened after the guy broke the window?" I ask.

"I mean, so, like, me and Patrick—"

"We're not idiots—we took off," Patrick interrupts.

"Dude, we didn't 'take off,'" Abe says, impatient. "We went to find Officer Dirk! You make it sound like we ran away!"

"Well, we didn't want to get *blamed* for it," Patrick says.

"What about Nick?" I ask.

Abe shrugs. "What about him?"

"Did he run off with you?"

"We *didn't*," Abe seethes, "*run off*. We went. To get *help*. Big. Difference."

"Yeah, and Nick couldn't keep up with us. We were like bullets. *Pyooooo*," Patrick says, his finger ripping through the air in front of him.

"Dude," Abe says, slowly shaking his head. "Just. Shut. Up."

I realize I've got to interview Nick. Even if I wasn't already dying to talk to him, I need him for this story. But then I remember that it's pretty much impossible to interview someone who has been avoiding me at all costs. So I ask Abe, "Can you get Nick to call me?"

Abe looks at me. "You don't need me. Just call his mommy," he says, and he and Patrick crack up. I start to point out that Nick is one of his best friends, but Abe's already tuned out. He and Patrick start karate-chopping themselves away, until Abe cripples Patrick with the crotch-kick payback he's been waiting for.

escribir *to write*

yo escribo
tú escribes
ella escribe
nosotros escribimos
ellos escriben

I am a sharp-dressed reporter with shiny hair and a cinched-waist dress. He is a tousle-haired eyewitness to a terrifying crime. We meet in secret, in a back alley, behind the lavandería. *A nightgown, drying on a line, flaps in the breeze. "Tell me what you know," I say.* Dígame. *He looks into my eyes—deeply in them—and he says, "Mi* querida, *my darling, I will tell you anything."*

The final bell has just rung and I'm hiding in an empty classroom across the hall from *Nicolás's* locker. Okay, so I'm stalking him just a little bit. I'm not nearly as bad as Elisabet, who I've seen in an episode lying in wait, carefully watching for her dead sister's husband, *from underneath his own bed.*

It's just that every time I see Nick, it's like trying to corner a squirrel, so I'm going to have to catch him off guard. Okay, fine. Like Elisabet.

And then he appears! He's still a little blotchy, like he was earlier, and his hair looks barely brushed. Even so, my lungs inflate and every noticeable cell in my body goes on high alert. I make myself wait until he's opened his locker and is reaching for something from the top shelf before I tiptoe out of the classroom toward him.

But then—*oh no! No!*

Our eyes catch in the reflection of the mirror glued inside his locker door.

His head whips around.

"Nick." I try to speak calmly. "I mean no trouble." Which, it hits me, are EXACTLY the same words Elisabet used. "I'm doing a story for *The Vindicator*," I say quickly. "About the window incident? I talked to Abe and Patrick. They told me you were there."

"Oh. Yeah." His eyes dart around, like they're trying to escape from mine.

I look over at the empty classroom. "Can we go in there and talk for a few minutes?" I do my best not to sound like a smitten girl who is practically *weak* with love.

He hesitates, but then nods, shuts his locker, and follows me.

I sit down at a desk, and he finds a desk away from me and begins tracing his finger over a carved-in *T*, while my heart cries out silently. *Estás tan cerca, pero tan lejos.* You are so close, but so far away.

But I gather myself, remembering Mariela.

"So," I say. "You, Patrick, and Abe were downstairs."

"Yeah, well, we were practicing karate moves. Down by the mechanical arts room." He looks at the wall as he speaks to me, and I jot down his words in my notebook. "Patrick meant to kick me but he ended up accidentally kicking Abe in the—well, you know. We were kind of joking around and then we heard the window break."

"They said they went to get help."

"Well, they just went running off in the opposite direction. And I—I mean, I looked up and saw someone for a second, but the guy tore off. He had a sweatshirt on. It was blue, maybe. Or black. One with a hood, so he was kind of shadowy. It was hard to see."

I write it down. "Abe and Patrick said he was huge," I tell him.

"They barely saw him. But he was tall, I guess."

"So what did you do?" My heart starts to crawl out of the little pit down deep in my chest. "Did you give chase?"

"Do what?"

"Give *chase*? Like, run after him?"

"I mean, not exactly. The guy flew through the emergency exit. He set off the alarm."

"You mean, before you could get to him," I prompt.

"Um." He leans back in his chair. "Sort of. Yeah."

So courageous!

"How far did you chase him?"

He sucks his lips in, activating a little dimple-like dent in his left cheek. My heart squeezes.

He smacks his lips apart. "Um? Not too far, because Officer Dirk came down and cleared the area."

"Did you see where he went after he went through the door?"

"It looked like he ran for the woods."

You are so brave, my love. My unsung hero. You are brimming with valor.

"What?" he asks.

"Oh! Nothing," I say, suddenly aware that my thoughts were trying to make their way toward him. Like my heart. "I mean, wow. Running after him."

"Oh." He lets out a little panting laugh. "Well, I mean, I didn't exactly . . ." He shrugs, smiling shyly, still avoiding my eyes.

A bell rings—the one that rudely demands that you leave the building, after you've been required to be there all day.

He shuffles in his seat. "I better go," he says.

"Just one more question," I say. "What was going through your mind?"

His eyes shift left.

I try again. "I mean, Abe and Patrick just took off in the other direction. But not you. Why not? Was it because of a sense of school safety? Justice?"

His eyes shift right. "Yeah, I guess. I mean, I didn't want anyone to get hurt or anything." Then he looks at me, as I commit his words to paper. "But I really better go. My mom—" His voice skids on the word, and he cuts himself off. "My *ride*'s probably waiting."

We stand up to go, and I say, "Maybe you would have caught him if Officer Dirk hadn't gotten in the way."

"Yeah. *Maybe*."

"Well," I say to his bouncing-around eyes, "thank you. And let me know if you think of anything else—"

"Like what?" he asks.

"Like a more detailed description of the intruder." I think about *La Vida Rica*. When Paolo was robbed by a road bandit, it took about four episodes for him to recall exactly what happened and realize the man behind the kerchief was none other than his own half brother, Roberto! "Sometimes more details come to you afterward."

He nods. And we part ways. I turn around to see if he's watching me, but he's not. But I could swear he's walking a little taller.

Maybe Kipper Garrett isn't the only person who deserves a little positive press.

I go straight to Sirina's house after school. She answers the door in her pajamas, eating a pickle, a copy of *Mental Floss* in her hand.

"You look like you're on vacation."

"More like house arrest," she says, standing back for me to come in.

"How's the aura?" I ask as we go into the kitchen.

"Totally gone. It was barely there in the first place. Remind me not to tell my mother next time, unless we're doing standardized testing, okay?" She says this purposefully loud enough for her mother to hear.

"I heard that!" her mom calls from the living room.

"Anyway," Sirina says to me, sitting down on a stool at the island. "What did I miss? Any developments?"

"*Actually* . . ." I smile.

"Mabry, *what*?"

"I got the story!"

"Officer Dirk *talked to you*?" Everything on her face lifts upward. Her eyebrows, the corners of her mouth, her cheeks.

"Well, no, but—"

Her thrilled face melts into annoyance.

"You talked to Abe," she says. Her voice flattens with disappointment.

"No, listen. Abe and Patrick came looking for me. For us. They heard we were working on the story. They were all like, 'Yeah, you should have been there!'"

She snorts. "Let me guess. They pulled out all their Bruce Lee moves and scared the intruder out of the school?"

"Yeah, kind of."

"See? That's why I didn't want to give them the satisfaction in the first place!"

"But, hang on, they told me something else."

"No *doubt*," she says.

"No, listen," I say. "They told me Nick was there. He was with them."

"Oh, great. So it was the whole trifecta. Okay, so what did they do? Did they organize a warrior army against this poor criminal? Did they save the school—no, wait, *the world*—from the wrath of this killer? We're still talking about a killer, right?"

"It was basically the Incredible Hulk," I tell her, smiling a little.

She smirks. "Okay, well, at least this is entertaining. What else happened?"

"Oh, you know, some roundhouse kicks and stuff, but it was hard to get any information about what really happened now that they're all down on Nick."

"They are?"

"Well, you heard the diaper comment yesterday," I say.

She shrugs. "Yeah, well, that was from Jason Murray. He's just as bad as Brian Stead. But Abe and Patrick? His *friends*?"

I nod. "Yeah, them, too. I asked them if they could get Nick to call me—you know, as a witness—and they were like, 'Oh, just call his mommy.'"

"So are you going to?" she jokes.

"Ha-ha," I say. "I already talked to him."

"*Mabry*," she whines.

"Before you try to shame me, listen. This is actually where the story starts." I smile. "While Abe and Patrick were running away, Nick practically chased the guy down."

She looks at me skeptically. "Chased?"

"Well, I mean—"

She rolls her eyes. "So what do we actually have for this story besides the Incredible Hulk and your hero?"

I pull out my notebook. "Are you ready to get to work?"

She pauses. "Well, we can start—but I still want to get something from an official source."

"Well, fine, you can wait for that 'high road.' But *that* hallway's closed." I look at her. "And at least the low road's wide open."

That night, after we've finished the article, my teeth are brushed, and I am in bed, I text her. *Good night, my jujitsu justice angel.*

And then I get her message back. *Good night, my spork-wielding heartbreaker.*

THE VINDICATOR

The Official News Blog of Hubert C. Frost Middle School

~~Hero Walks Amongst Us~~
Hooded Stranger Breaks Window in Language Arts Hall, Runs

On Wednesday, at approximately 3:30 p.m., ~~a violent giant~~ *an intruder* broke a window in *the easternmost corner of* the language arts hall. *Eyewitnesses allege that* a man in a hooded sweatshirt drove his fist through the window, shattering the glass, and then ~~ran out of~~ *exited* the building through a nearby emergency door, setting off an alarm within the school.

The key witness, ~~a valiant and brave~~ eighth grader ~~named~~ Nick Wainwright, ~~chased~~ *saw* the trespasser ~~down the hall while help was summoned. The subject~~ disappeared into the woods behind the soccer field.

Wainwright describes the man as ~~massive and hulking.~~ *tall.* He reports that the man was wearing a dark-colored hooded sweatshirt. ~~We should all be proud to go to school with such a hero, who was able to keep us safe through this harrowing event.~~

When asked why he ~~gave chase~~ *didn't flee the scene with two other students who had been present at the time of the incident,* Wainwright ~~acknowledged a sense of justice and safety, and~~ said "I didn't want anyone to get hurt."

After-school activities were temporarily suspended while the ~~scene of the crime~~ *area* was cleared.

The motive for this ~~vicious outburst~~ *incident* is unknown. ~~, but most likely, it was a crime of passion.~~

~~Jordan Sweeney reports that her neighbor's uncle, who works at the state prison, said a murderer did in fact escape the prison on Monday. There is the possibility of a connection to the crime.~~

Further information and/or reports of suspicious activity can heretofore be reported to ~~Sirina Fein~~.

school administration
—Mrs. N.

IN OTHER NEWS . . .

Lunch Workers "Horrified" by Inappropriate Use of Puddings and Jellied Desserts

A team of cafeteria ladies, led by lunch supervisor Mrs. Teagen, declared strong disapproval for students' varied abuse of desserts, following incidents in which Hayden Dunlop placed a glob of butterscotch pudding on a tissue after a staged "sneeze," and Nolan McRae began "oozing" green Jell-O from a pretend neck wound. Teagan instituted a mandatory recall of all [click for more]

morir *to die*

yo muero

tú mueres

ella muere

nosotros morimos

ellos mueren

"**Y**ou did *what*?"

It's Saturday, and Thad and I are at the mall for our first official heartbreaker meeting, and he's been shoveling in chips with bean dip for the past five minutes, *with his skate gloves on*. But now he looks at me, a chip paused in front of his mouth.

"I interviewed him for *The Vindicator*. About the biggest news that's ever happened at our school," I tell him, then ask, "Don't you ever take those stupid gloves off?"

He doesn't answer. He just puts the chip down on a napkin and wipes some of the dip off his gloved hand.

"I can't believe you eat with those things on. I hope you wash them."

He closes his eyes and takes a deep breath.

"What's your problem?" I ask. "You told me to get him to notice me in a new way. That's exactly what I did."

"I wasn't thinking *that*, though," he says. "I was thinking more like you were going to do the Mariela thing."

"Well, I did, but I still couldn't get him to talk to me!"

"So you got him to talk to you about this whole stupid window thing?"

"It's not a whole stupid anything. I mean, for one, it's our chance to win the YoJo!"

He squints. "The YoJo?"

"The Youth Journalism award. It's like the Pulitzer for middle-school news reporting. I mean, this is the first exciting thing that's happened in our school in, like, ever, and we're writing an investigative series—"

Thad's eyes roll to the ceiling.

"And for two, it's an actual crime, and he was the only real eyewitness."

"Eyewitness? What do you mean, 'eyewitness'?"

"Nick saw the guy who broke the window."

Thad studies me. "Yeah, well, what exactly did he see?"

"Well, I mean, okay, so not a lot. A guy in a sweatshirt."

"Right. So it doesn't sound like Nick saw much of anything."

"Well, at least he didn't run away like the rest of them. And you know, sometimes people piece things together later. They remember details."

He closes his eyes. "No, no, no, and no," he murmurs. He shakes his head and repeats it again. "No, no, no, *no*, and no. Okay, change of strategy."

"Great," I say, and don't mean it.

He looks right at me. "Are you listening to me, Collins? Ignore him. Leave him alone. That's your next assignment."

"So first I was supposed to get his attention. Which I *did*—"

"Not exactly the way I was thinking."

"Well, but, I did. And now all of a sudden I'm supposed to ignore him?"

"Yeah, 'cause you're, like, totally going in the wrong direction. You're like three degrees from being a stalker."

"No, I'm not!"

"Where do you think he is right now?"

"Karate," I blurt out *waaay* too fast.

Thad lifts his eyebrows.

"I'm just *guessing*!" I attempt.

"I bet you know what he was wearing to school Thursday, two weeks ago."

"Oh, *yeah*? Well, he wasn't in school on Thursday two weeks ago. He was out with a cold," I say.

Thad's face is smug.

Um. *Yikes.* Maybe he's right. "But I am *not* a stalker!" I say.

"No, you're right, you're not. Just close. Three degrees from it."

"Okay, shut up, Mister Helpful."

It's not that I'm angry—I'm just a little, oh, I don't know, *horrified*. Maybe I'm like Hilda, the woman who was once secretly in love with Luis. She spent several episodes following him around the town and plotting a way to get rid of Cristina. I get a shiver. I am freaking myself out.

"*Dude,*" he says. "Come on, stop looking like that. I just meant it seems like sometimes you get, you know, *obsessed*."

"I prefer to call it *intense*."

"Yeah. Intense, okay? Let's call it that."

"And *focused*," I add.

"Okay, fine. That too. Look, it's not always a bad thing. If Nick was, like, I don't know, a lost bag of gold, you'd totally find it. And you'd be a millionaire."

Well. He *is* like a treasure to me.

Thad continues. "But the problem is, he's not a bag of gold, he's just a bag of—"

I narrow my eyes. "What's your problem with Nick anyway?"

"I told you—I think he's a wad."

"But why? What has he done to you?"

"Collins, drop it, okay?"

"But you seem to—"

"Okay, let's just say he stole a Star Wars figurine from me back in fourth grade."

"Are you kidding me?" I snort.

He puffs out his cheeks with an exhale. "Maybe it's a guy thing. Anyway, laugh if you want, but he's going to be laughing at *you* soon. All you're doing with this news stuff is bringing attention to him. It's a total one-way street."

"Well, *Luke Skywalker*, I got him to notice me for something other than my *sappy* self, as you put it, and I got him to talk to me. Don't those two things have to happen if"—*he's ever going to fall back in love with me*—"I'm going to get him to ask me to the Cotillion? So I can break his heart?"

"Yeah, but you can't just chase him down like that. I mean, sure, maybe if all you care about is your yo-yo thing—"

"The *YoJo*," I correct him.

He shrugs. "But not if you care about getting back at him. I mean, the way you're going, he's going to break your heart in half all over again."

I do care about the YoJo, but I also care about winning Nick back. And I also care about my poor heart, and not letting it get broken again.

"Look, Collins, you're going to have to backtrack. I mean, you can't do anything to change what you've already done. So now you have to ignore him for a while. Don't screw it up this time."

Ignore him. "I don't like this assignment," I say. "I liked the first one better. I was kind of getting the hang of Mariela."

"Well, you can still do that," he says.

"Okay, good."

"*While* you ignore him." He goes back to his bean dip.

"For how long?"

"Till he starts looking for *you.*"

Right now, I can't really imagine that happening. But it's happened before, so it can happen again, right? I look over at Thad and it hits me. I'm taking love advice from someone who has just polished off some refried beans and is now licking the plastic container clean. How did it ever come to this?

He looks up and catches me staring at him.

"Aw, Collins, don't look at me like that. You're not hopeless. You just got to break your bad habits. From what Sirina says, you could fall in quote-unquote love with a paper bag if it looked at you the right way. Which explains your whole obsession with Nick." He pauses and then says, "Hey, you know what you need?"

Yes, I do know what I need. I need to be with the love of my life. I also need salsa lessons. And a C+ in history wouldn't hurt. But I just say, "What?"

"A burrito," he says, eyeing the Macho Nacho kiosk. "I promised you a burrito."

"Well, I don't want a burrito," I say. *I just want Nick.*

"But you *need* one at a time like this," he says. "And anyway, like I texted you, I'm buying."

"Okay, fine."

It's a big, ugly, graceless type of food, but I *am* a little hungry.

Thad orders us two massive burritos the size of our forearms. "I don't think I can eat all this. We should just split one," I say.

"I'm not sharing."

"But you just had all that bean dip!"

"That was just a warm-up," he says, "an hors d'oeuvre."

Thad plops the foil-wrapped burritos on the not-so-clean table. They land with heavy splats, and Thad goes to get extra hot sauce. When he comes back, he says, "You didn't have to wait for me."

"I wasn't waiting for you. I was waiting for a fork and knife. And a plate."

He laughs. "Seriously, Collins? You really don't know how to eat a burrito?" He rips into the foil and starts with a massive bite.

"I know how to eat a burrito," I say, "with *manners*. What kind of burrito did you get me anyway?"

"Seafood," he says.

"Seafood?"

"Yeth," he says, and opens his mouth to display all. "See? Food!"

I close my eyes before they burn out of my head. "You're so obnoxious! What are you, six?"

He takes a swig of his Dr Pepper and clears his mouth and says, "*You're* obnoxious. Just eat and stop being such a snob."

"I'm not a snob!" I say.

He dips his burrito into a mound of hot sauce. "You're acting like one." He makes his voice mockingly high and, for some reason, British. "*Where's my fork? And don't give me a salad fork! Where's my fancy, fancy napkin?*"

"I didn't say that!"

He shrugs.

"Well, okay, fine, if I'm a snob, you're a pig." I try to rip open the foil like he did, and take a massive bite. Through a full mouth I say, *"I'm Thad Bell, I'm such a man. Stuffing my face."* I take my burrito and dip it into his hot sauce. *"I like lots and lots of hot sauce because I'm such a big, big pig man."* And then I take a big bite. *"Yum, yum, yum!"* I say as I chew like a rabid animal.

And then I nearly die, because it feels just like heartbreak, if you could take all of the emotional stuff out of it and just leave the physical torment.

The hot sauce is *hot*. My entire face heats up, including my earlobes, and the backs of my eyes burn. Searing pain fills my throat and chest. I gasp and grab for his Dr Pepper. I take a big sip, which only intensifies the burning feeling. I start to cough. Thad runs off—*of course!*—and then he has the nerve to come back with a bowl of chips! *Oh, yes, pleeeease, sit down and enjoy some refreshments while I asphyxiate,* I would say if I could actually talk.

But he pushes the chips in my direction. "Here. This helps."

I'll try anything at this point. I take a bite of one and the burning in my mouth starts to subside.

"Dude," he says, and starts to laugh, "that was pretty impressive."

I narrow my eyes to slits. It's a nice, threatening look, I'm sure of it.

"Hey, what's that?" he asks, eyeing the neckline of my sweater.

"What?"

"I think you just grew some hair on your chest."

Horrified, I look down quickly, before I realize it's just a stupid joke, and not a very original one. Still, it kind of surprises me that I feel a little thud of disappointment when Thad pulls out his phone and looks at the time, and says, "Dude, I gotta go."

"You do?" I ask. He's already gathering his trash. "Hey, next time, you want to meet somewhere else? You can come to my house or something. Or I can come to—"

"Nah. Here's good. Anyway, I gotta go. I'm late."

"For what?"

"For home," is all he says.

"Oh," is all I say back. Then he skates off, breaking all the rules—not just of the mall, but of proper etiquette in general.

"Rude!" I call out, but he's long gone. A woman passing by shoots me an offended look. "Sorry, not you, ma'am!" But then I notice the ma'am is actually a sir. And then I see Captain Jerry appear on his Segway, and the *sir* approaching him, and I realize it's probably a good idea for me to go home really fast, too.

Windows + Doors

Thad checks for police cars or other out-of-place vehicles sitting outside the town house when he comes home. It's only been a few days since he broke the window, but today he's extra nervous, now that he knows Mabry's trying to investigate the "crime scene," as she calls it. It's like the air has been trapped high in his lungs and he hasn't really exhaled for hours, not since he amazingly derailed her with the lie about the Star Wars figurine. *Did she really believe that?*

But the coast is clear. Even from outside, he can hear the comforting whistle of Aunt Nora's teakettle. It makes him relax a little. The door is unlocked, so he goes right in, happy not to have to fish the keys out of his pocket.

She is at the table, stirring some honey into her tea.

"Hi, Aunt Nora."

"Hi, hon," she says. It's her day off, but she sounds tired. *Over* this day, like she sometimes says.

"What are you up to?" he asks her.

"Well, I have a friend stopping by soon."

Somehow he never really imagined Nora having friends. Not that she wouldn't. Just that she's so busy. Working here or working at the Buy-It-All. But always working.

Thad takes off his skate gloves and unwraps the thin layer of gauze.

Aunt Nora's eyes go to his uncovered hand. She winces. "It still looks pretty rough."

"It's better," he says as he reaches for the milk. "I'm taking care of it." He pours himself a bowl of cereal.

"You don't have to eat that standing up, you know," she says.

"I was going to take it to my room."

"Why would you do that?"

"So you can hang out with your friend."

"Well, I'm sure he'd love to see you. He was asking about you. He knew your dad."

He? Thad's spoon stops in midair. He'd been picturing two middle-aged women sitting down for tea, not a visit from a man.

"Your friend knew dad?" Thad asks.

"They were good friends when they were kids," she says. "We all went to school together. But I haven't seen him or talked to him in, oh, about ten years."

"And he just contacted you out of the blue?"

"Pretty much. Said your dad's been on his mind. He wanted to know how he could get in touch."

Thad swallows the cereal too hard, and it travels down slowly, scraping the sides of his throat.

Aunt Nora starts to tear up. Thad puts his spoon down and regrets every gaping mouthful of the cereal. It sits heavy in his stomach.

He takes a seat at the table. "So you had to give him the news?"

She nods. A tear slips to her cheek, and she wipes it away with the side of her hand and laughs. "Just look at me! Fine company I'll be."

He laughs, too, thankful to have something to laugh at, something to loosen the tightening feeling behind his own eyes.

"Anyway," she says, a little watery. "He'll be here any minute."

Thad doesn't want any tears of his own to slip out in front of anyone, let alone a stranger. "I really should go to my room. I have school stuff."

"Oh, Thad, just stay for a few minutes, okay? That's all. He'd like to meet you. You're half your dad, you know. All the good parts." She looks at him with birthday-cake eyes that are soft and sweet and hopeful.

The good parts. He feels a jab of guilt. Where are those good parts? Nothing about him feels good anymore. No. Everything about him feels as broken and sharp as the glass he shattered. *He* should be wrapped in yellow caution tape.

"And anyway," she continues, "it'd be nice for you meet him, too. He's a security officer at the school."

The cells in his body start to pulse with alert, as if an alarm has been pulled somewhere inside. *Waaat! Waaat! Waaat!* He sits upright. *Security officer. School.* The words bounce around in his head as he struggles with the proper emergency response. His mouth drops open and words jump out. "Uh, can't, no—"

But the doorbell rings, and the sharp sound zips through his spine, cutting his words off like the edge of a cliff.

"Oh, hon, relax," Aunt Nora says, getting up from the table. She's no doubt confusing his real anxiety with the anxiety of going back to school.

But Thad can't relax, not with his internal security system bleating *Danger! Danger!* As soon as she's out of the kitchen, he jerks to standing, his chair toppling over, his thigh knocking the table a few inches off center. That'll leave a bruise.

He hears them talking. "Dirk! You look so good."

"NORA! GREAT TO SEE YOU." His voice is louder than any person's should be. It's like his volume has been turned up to eleven.

"Come in! Please!"

"LOVE TO."

He hears the whooshing sound of a jacket against a sweater. The squeezy breaths of an embrace. The gentle *thwack-thwack* of the friendly back pats.

"Can I get you some tea?"

"HERBAL IF YOU HAVE IT."

Thad's muscles unfreeze and he rushes toward the back of the house, to his mom's room. He cracks open the door. She's sleeping.

"Thad?" Aunt Nora calls him. "Where are you?"

He can't hide. He looks down at his hand, bare without the skating gloves. If this school security officer doesn't already know that he broke the window, this will definitely give it away.

Thad jams his hands into his jeans pockets and walks out slowly.

"Hi," he says. The man's eyes are too light blue, like an interrogation light is shining through them. His face is fleshy and heavy. His nose points downward, the corners of his mouth droop toward his chin, his eyebrows are low. Everything about him seems weighted down.

"THADDEUS," the man says.

Thad pulls his gaze away, settling his stare on a square shape in the linoleum floor. He wonders what will come next. *Thaddeus Bell, you have the right to remain silent.*

But the man says, "OFFICER DIRK MEADOWS HERE, BUT CALL ME OFFICER DIRK. IT'S AN HONOR TO MEET YOU."

Thad's eyes flicker back up to the man's, and then straight down again.

Officer Dirk extends his right hand.

Crap.

So much for hiding his scraped-up hand. He thinks about bolting again, but knows it would make things worse. Might as well face reality.

He draws his right hand out of its pocket. But before he can reach it toward its fate, Officer Dirk's hands clap into his shoulder blades, pulling Thad into him. It takes him a second to realize this is a hug.

"YOU LOOK JUST"—the loud voice cracks right into Thad's ear—"LIKE HIM."

And just as soon as the hug has started, it's over. He leans away from Thad, takes a sniffly breath through his nose, and asks Nora about that herbal tea.

Aunt Nora smiles. "Peppermint or lemon ginger?"

"DEFINITELY LEMON GINGER."

"Well, have a seat."

Officer Dirk pulls a chair away from the table and swings it around. He sits down, straddling the chair, and looks up at Thad, who is standing hesitantly on the other side of the table.

"WHAT ABOUT YOU."

Thad pauses. He looks over at Aunt Nora.

"Oh, Dirk, I can never get him to drink tea."

"NOT EVEN WITH HONEY."

Even Officer Dirk's questions sound like proclamations. Thad wonders how he gets through life without question marks. Does he declare directions when he gets lost? Does he command friends to come over, women to go out on dates with him?

Nora laughs gently. "Nope, not even with honey."

"I HEAR YOU'RE COMING TO SCHOOL SOON."

"Oh." Thad stiffens. The answer, he's decided, is no, but he gets the feeling that may be the wrong one. And *maybe* is too wishy-washy for this Proclamation Man. And *yes*? Well, that's just a bold-faced lie.

Aunt Nora bails him out. "We've been talking about it." She brings two teacups over to the table. "Now, speaking of school"—she looks at Thad—"don't you have some work to get to?"

Relief. "Yes!" He knows he sounds way too happy about school-work, but he's grateful for this exit. Suddenly he feels exhausted. "Well, nice meeting you," he says to Officer Dirk, dipping his face a little.

Officer Dirk nods. "A PLEASURE."

Thad turns to the stairs.

"HEY, THAD."

Is this the moment he springs it all on him? *I know what you did,* he'll say in that eighteen-point-font voice.

Thad turns back to face him, but moves in slow motion.

Officer Dirk's searing eyes lock on to Thad's. He takes a sip of his lemon-ginger tea. And says, "SEE YOU SOON."

And even though Dirk's voice is as PA-system as ever, his words are subtle.

Does he know?

Oh, he knows. He's got to. Those eyes. That look.

Thad goes upstairs to his room. Despite the chatter downstairs, and the occasional statement of laughter—a practical war cry of "HA, HA, HA" over the tinkling giggles of his aunt's—he's worried. He doesn't know—in his head, that is—that Officer Dirk knows what he's done, but he feels it in the center of his stomach.

It's just a matter of when the guy will strike.

ver *to see*

yo veo
tú ves
ella ve
nosotros vemos
ellos ven

For the first part of the next week—three whole days!—I heed Thad's advice and go Nick-less. I avoid his locker hall. I make sure to take different routes to my classes, which involves me being two minutes late to Biology for two consecutive days, and getting a detention warning for the criminal act of Being in Love. Okay, technically, it's tardiness, but there would be no tardiness if there were no love, at least in my case.

And then Nick happens to walk into my class as I am drawing a penis.

Maybe I should state it this way: *Girl, 13, Suffers Coronary Attack While Diagraming Anatomical Penis During Family-Life Education Unit. Services to Be Held in Cafetorium After Final Bell on Wednesday.*

Of course, I am not the only person drawing a penis. We are all drawing penises and THIS IS FOR A GRADE. Anyone caught laughing or expressing merriment of any sort is immediately sent to the back of the room, so the only people currently located in the regular part of the room are me (because I'm too mortified to laugh); Kipper, who is his usual serious self, tackling the assignment with earnestness and a mind for science; and Ti-Ti, a new student from Vietnam who doesn't yet understand *this kind* of English. She's innocent and sweet, and seems to think we're still studying worms. If only, Ti-Ti. *If only*.

So, Nick walks into the room, and Ms. Frederick looks up. "Can I help you with something, Nick?"

"O-oh, I—" he sort of stutters, "I'm looking for my jacket. I think I left it here last period."

Brian Stead belts out a laugh. "Your last period? Did you also leave your tampon?"

The class erupts in laughter, and Ms. Frederick stands up and starts yelling how the HUMAN REPRODUCTIVE SYSTEM IS A BEAUTIFUL THING and that if Brian thinks Nick has a period, then he really should be paying attention in class, which only makes the class laugh louder. Nick shrinks a little more in the front of the room.

And then Charlotte Wang says, "Shut your traps, you guys."

And Parker Berry says, "Yeah, seriously."

Shut up. Yeah, seriously. It's been five days since the article about the window was posted. Could this be the power of the press at work? After a full week of hearing him being teased, these words are like the social equivalent of being elected class president. Or treasurer, at least.

And Abby Newton holds up a black jacket and asks, "Is this it?"

Nick nods, and goes to the back of the room to collect it from her.

And Brian says, "Check the pockets!" just loud enough for

everyone to hear. But then his words are followed by an *"Ow!"* Brian rubs his ear and turns around. "You flicked me in the ear," he says to Charlotte, who sits behind him.

"Well, leave him alone. *You're* the big baby," Charlotte says to him as Ms. Frederick starts yelling that ANYONE WHO CANNOT GET ALONG WILL BE SEPARATED and I look at Nick. The fact that someone stuck up for him—flicked Brian's ear on his account, even—seems to be setting in. He looks surprised, almost hopeful.

His eyes meet mine, and there's a flutter of a smile on his face before he's hurried out of the classroom by Ms. Frederick.

The power of the press. It's happening! Take that, Jason Murray. Take that, Abe Mahal.

At lunch, I see Nick sitting at the end of his old lunch table. There's an empty seat between him and Abe, but at one point, when Abe gets up for something, Patrick slides his tray toward Nick so that he can grab a few Tater Tots.

So it may not be the offering of a firstborn, like when Raquel brought her baby to her childless sister, Gisel, so that, after years of feuding, Gisel could raise him as her own. But still, it's an offering, if not a truce.

I nudge Sirina. "Patrick just gave Nick a Tater Tot!"

She looks at me, tucking her chin back. "Okay, well, I just gave Jordan a Dorito, so . . ."

"Ha-ha," I say.

"Oh, guess what? *O.M.D.C.*, I thought I saw Ariana checking Nick out today," Amelia says. Which isn't helpful.

Ariana. I seethe inside. I look at Sirina for help. For *strength.*

"So what?" she says. "Maybe people are starting to be nice to him again. Since the article came out. Unintended side effect, I guess." Then she looks right at me. "It was unintended, right?"

"Pretty much," I say.

"What does *that* mean?"

"I mean, it was nice to be able to give him some positive press. It's no different than what you did for Kipper."

"Yeah, but I've never been quote-unquote in love with Kipper!"

She's saying that now, too?

"Well," I say. "He was our key witness. I'm just saying, I'm glad it helped a little. I hated to see him suffer."

"Well, you better get over *that* soon," she says, her forehead crinkling. "You haven't somehow conveniently forgotten about the plan, have you?"

"*Noooo*," I say. "It would be kind of hard to forget that I'm supposed to break Nick's heart, Sirina."

Or at least go along with the plan until I have Nick back for good. Until Thad and Sirina are finally happy for us—until they finally believe in love. Without quotation marks.

After school, Sirina and I are walking to our locker when we spot Nick down the hall.

"Is he—" I stop so quickly that someone almost knocks me over from behind. I don't know if what I see is real or just a mirage, like the ones Aurelio sees of his lost love, Ana, while he's out there in the desert. "At our locker?"

"He is," Sirina says. "It's like he's waiting for us. I wonder what he wants."

To tell me he's made a big mistake? That he still pines for me? That he meant every single bit of that "me too"?

When he sees us, he stands up a little straighter. "Hey," he says, as we approach. He looks right at me. "Can I talk to you?"

Of course of course of course! says my heart.

But wait.

Ignore ignore ignore, says Thad's voice in my head.

Gah. This is too hard!

"It's about the article," he adds.

Oh. The article. Right. So, not undying love after all. I deflate.

But Sirina looks alert. "What about it?"

"I remembered some more details, like Mabry said I might." He looks at me. "I thought we could talk again."

Just then, Abe turns the corner, circle-kicking in our direction. When he gets close, he crouches, circling his rigid forearms in front of his chest. Then he wails *"Eeee-yaaah"* and lunges forward into a high kick.

"Dude," Nick laughs nervously. "Awesome."

"Yeah, well, come on, then," Abe says. We hear Patrick's warrior cry from somewhere not too far away. "Dojo's in the math hall today."

"Cool. I'm coming." Nick breaks into a grin and bursts forward in a run. Then, as if just remembering us, he turns around. "Sorry," he calls to me. "I'll find you tomorrow."

I watch him go, allowing myself to luxuriate in his words. They echo through me. *I'll find you tomorrow, I'll find you tomorrow.* That's what his lips said. But I'm pretty sure I felt his heart add, *because without you, I'm lost.*

Sirina looks at me with disapproval. "Oh my god, you're swooning. You're actually *swooning.*"

"What?" I say, like it's ridiculous. "I am *not.*"

"You are. It's a good thing he ran off so quickly. You're being so obvious right now."

I start to defend myself, but she says, "Don't worry, Mabry. I can read you. I know you're trying."

I am? I almost ask, but instead say, "You do?"

"Yeah, I don't think you said a single word to him. You totally ignored him. Good job." She squeezes my arm. "I know it's not easy."

I give her a little smile. She has no idea how not-easy it is.

buscar *to look for*

yo busco

tú buscas

ella busca

nosotros buscamos

ellos buscan

That afternoon, I sit down at the table in front of Macho Nacho with Thad and steal a chip, dipping it into his bean dip.

"Would you like a chip?" he asks sarcastically.

"Sorry," I say, even though I'm not really. "Guess what?"

"Hmmm." He tilts his head to his shoulder. "You've recently discovered a huge wart on your pinkie toe?"

I just look at him.

"No, you've recently discovered a huge wart on Nick's pinkie toe? No, wait! The finger he uses to pick his nose!? Does he still do that when he thinks no one's looking?"

I blow out a breath and stare at the ceiling.

"Am I close? Hot or cold?"

"Ice-cold," I say. "You know, it's really hard to give you good news."

"Good news?" he asks. "Does that stuff still exist?"

I ignore him. I plant my hands flat on the table and lean forward. "I did what you said. For three days, I ignored him like crazy. But today, he practically hunted me down."

"What do you mean 'hunted you down'? For what? Your pelt?"

I roll my eyes. "He just wants to talk some more."

"About what?"

"Well, he says he remembered some more stuff, you know, about the window incident, but maybe that's just an excuse. . . ."

He is staring at me, his chin jutting forward and his eyes all buggy. "What?"

"No way. You're killing me, Collins. Don't do it. You just can't."

I let my mouth drop open. "What are you talking about? How am I supposed to"—*win him back*—"break his heart if I can't even talk to him? And don't forget, you said I only have to ignore him until he starts looking for me."

He begins to shake a little, like there's some sort of tiny earthquake going on. It takes me a second to realize it's just his heel bouncing up and down under the table.

"Anyway," I say, "I need to talk to him. Don't forget, I need him for the YoJo."

"Yeah, that's what's ridiculous. You and Sirina think you're going to win some award for a news series about a broken window? Come on, Collins. Write about something that matters."

"Like what?"

"Like a zillion other things."

"Well, it's the most interesting thing that's happened. I mean, I know they're probably rumors, but what if it *was* a murderer who broke the window? It's actually true about the prison escape—my friend Jordan's neighbor's uncle works at the prison, and he said so!"

He exhales and looks up at the skylights in the ceiling over the food court. "The guy's just using you and you're totally letting him."

"Just admit, for a second, that it's possible that he misses me."

"He hasn't even had a chance to miss you. Until you started writing about him, he was running down the halls to avoid you, right?"

"Right," I grumble.

"And he has to really miss you if you want him to . . ." He looks at me. "Do I have to say it?"

"Yes," I say, slightly enjoying his discomfort. "You do."

He makes quote marks in the air with his fingers. " *'Fall in loooove'* with you and ask you to that stupid dance." He puts his hands down and shakes his head. "Just, like, for a while, pretend he doesn't exist. Make him wonder, *Where is she? What's she doing?*"

I sigh. Would he wonder those things? *Could* he wonder those things?

Thad continues. "In fact, here's your next assignment: find a replacement for Nick."

"A replacement?" I ask. For Nick? *There's no such thing.*

"Someone else to talk to. Just enough to make him a little jealous."

Jealous. Okay, if I really were Mariela, this wouldn't be hard. But no matter what I do, in my heart, I'm a lot more like Cristina, devoted and loyal, pining after Luis, wanting nothing more than his safe return.

"I don't really like anyone—" Thankfully, I stop myself before I accidentally add *else*. "Not in that way."

"You don't have to 'really like anyone,' genius. It's just a game, like the rest of the love stuff you believe in."

I ignore that comment. "Hey, what about you?"

"What *about* me?"

"You could meet me after school, like, right after the bell rings, and maybe—we could stand by his bus and, I don't know, laugh, and maybe for like two seconds, we could hold hands—"

He is shaking his head very fast. "Nope. No way. There's *noooo* way that I'm going to your school."

"Fine, somewhere else, then. I pretty much know where he is at all—" I drop that sentence like a hot potato as soon as I realize that I indeed *do* sound like a stalker.

"Nope. I'm good here. And it doesn't really matter, because I'm not *that* guy."

I exhale loudly and slump. It's not like I *wanted* to laugh and flirt and hold hands with Thad, but if it could somehow bring me a step closer to Nick—well, then, I'd suck it up and do it.

Oh, Nicolás, my Nicolás, no matter how it looks, everything I do, I do for you.

"Look, Collins, this really shouldn't be that hard." He looks away and shakes his head. "For one, Nick's a tool. There are lots of other tools around to choose from. And for two, you may be a total head case, but you're not *totally* disgusting to look at."

Wow. Thad Bell. Calling me not totally disgusting. I'm almost touched—that's got to be his version of a compliment.

"Okay, I'll try," I say. "But we're supposed to talk tomorrow. He said he'd find me."

"Well, don't be alone when he does," Thad says.

"I'm hardly ever alone," I say. "I'm with Sirina, or Amelia, or Jordan."

"A *guy*, dummy. You need to start talking to other *guys*," Thad says, sounding exasperated. "If Nick feels like he can't have you back, he'll want you back even more. It's like that saying: 'You don't appreciate what you have until it's gone.' It's totally legit."

"Oh, *jeez*. You're just *so* much wiser than your years," I joke.

But Thad doesn't laugh. He just puts on this weird, tight smile, and looks away.

"Come on," I say, stepping on his toes under the table. "What do you appreciate now? *Chewbacca?*"

"Huh?"

"Chewbacca! Or was it Darth Vader?" I tease. "The figurine Nick stole from you."

He turns back to me for a second, like he's holding his breath.

"What?" I ask.

He still doesn't answer.

Just as soon as I think I've hurt his feelings in some strange and unknown way, he breathes out a gust of air and says, "No, you know what I appreciate now? Screaming Yellow Zonkers."

"What are *those?*"

"They were like popcorn with sugar. Yellow sugar. They were my dad's favorite. I always thought they were kind of gross. But you know what? You can't get them anymore. They stopped making them. And now, sometimes I just really want a Screaming Yellow Zonker."

I just stare at him.

"*What!?*" he asks with annoyance.

"So, what, I'm supposed to be a Screaming Yellow Zonker? *Really?*"

"I'm just saying, I'd take a Zonker over a burrito any day. And you know how much I like burritos, so . . ."

I narrow my eyes at him and he narrows his back at me, and then it turns into a full-fledged stare-off. For a full minute. Then two. And then I forget to keep count. It's a vicious eye-lock, and it's starting to feel so strong that it's even getting to *me*. Finally, his eyes snap away.

"I won," I declare.

"Only because you were about to suck my soul out through my eyeballs," he says back.

I laugh. "Maybe I already did."

"My soul yields to no one," he says back, with a little smile that—for just a brief millisecond—gives me a jolt or a pang of something. Like something stirs under my rib cage. And then I remember with relief—the *bean dip*. It's just the bean dip.

"So, what does he eat now?" I ask.

"Who?"

"Your father. Now that he can't have those Zonker things."

"Oh," he says. "Right." He turns his head and squints a little, like he's trying to focus on something in the distance. I look in the same direction, but only see the usual shops and signs. Then he says, "Nothing, I guess. That's what dead people eat."

"Oh!" Dead. Oh no. *Oh no.* I feel a flurry of panic. You'd think after all the telenovelas I've watched, I'd be used to death. But I'm not. "I'm sorry! I really am! I—uh—I didn't know."

"I know you didn't. No worries," he says, shrugging.

I feel awful. How does someone's dad just die? Poisoning? Murder?

He seems to sense what I'm thinking. "Car accident," he says, very plainly.

I study Thad's face for any sign of what he's feeling, but the only thing that really stands out is some dried frijoles near his chin.

"Stop admiring me," he says.

"I'm not! I was just—"

"I'm kidding, doofus." He gets up. "Anyway, I gotta go."

"Okay. I'm sorry, though, about your dad."

And then he takes off. Watching him leave, I feel like I've opened up a puzzle, but can't find the corner pieces. Or that I've put on my favorite coat, but one of the buttons is gone.

Wheel + Axle

Thad is staring at his mom's big toe. They're both staring at it. She's pulled the sheet up so her slightly puffy foot sticks out at the bottom of the bed. It reminds him uncomfortably of one of those dollar-store Halloween props—usually a disembodied hand.

"Hang on," she says. "I did it earlier when the therapist was here."

Thad stares at it harder. Maybe he can will it to move. He's read about people who can bend spoons with their minds, so maybe if he tries hard enough it'll work.

"It's so frustrating," she says, and she lets out a big sigh.

"Want to try pressing into my hands?" he offers.

"Sure," she says, sounding tired.

He puts his palms on the soles of her feet and presses gently into them. Sometimes he can feel her press back, just a little. Sometimes he's not even sure if she's actually moving her feet, or if it's just the intention he feels—hers or his own. Today, he doesn't feel any pressure back.

"Thanks," she says, signaling she's had enough. "Sit down and talk to me. How was your day?"

He shrugs. "I don't know."

He knows it's vague, but he really *doesn't* know what to make of this day at all. Each day that he's not caught, both the relief and the anxiety build. It's like a game of dodgeball—the longer you stay in it, the higher your chances of getting blasted in the nuts.

She looks at him expectantly. "Well, what did you do?"

He goes back to his conversation with Mabry. *I told someone that Dad died,* he thinks. But the words stick in him, and he knows that's where they'll stay. He doesn't like to talk too much about it. It's not that he's in denial; it's just sometimes kind of nice to try to keep his dad alive in some way, if only in someone's imagination.

But today, he surprised himself by telling Mabry the truth. *What was that about?*

"Well, you had to have done *something*," his mom says, teasing a little. "Come on, make me feel like I'm part of the world."

He smirks. "Well, big excitement."

"Oh yeah?"

"I took my algebra quiz."

She lifts her eyebrows. "And?"

"I got a B," he tells her. Actually, it was a C, but close enough. Besides, next time, it'll be higher. He doesn't want to keep worrying her about his grades.

She holds up her hand, but it's slow and stays low. Then she puts it back down. "I was going to say *high-five,* but . . ." She laughs uncomfortably. "That's great. I'm proud of you."

He smiles and cracks his knuckles.

"Did you go to the mall again today?"

"Yep."

"You must like it there."

He does like the mall—not just the face-stuffing business that happens at the Macho Nacho. It's just nice to be surrounded by stuff that doesn't matter. It feels *safe*. Clothes, jewelry, shoes, massage chairs. Little kiosks of things like socks, or smoothies, or sunglasses. There is never anything life-or-death about socks, or smoothies, or sunglasses. Or eyebrow threading, whatever that is.

And then there's Mabry, of course.

Wait, he thinks. He wants to take that thought back. Yes, there's Mabry, but it's not really *her* that he likes. It's just the things she says sometimes, her weirdness—it's ridiculous. He's *amused*, that's all.

"Yeah, it's okay," he tells his mom.

It. Not *she.*

He feels his mother's stare, and it brings him back to the room.

"You're smiling," she tells him, a smile starting on her own face. "So maybe today was better than you're saying."

"Oh." He laughs, surprised. "Nah, it was okay. Nothing special. How was *your* day?"

She moans. "Oh, you know. The doctor. The therapist. Nora. What would we do without Aunt Nora?"

Seriously. What would they do without Aunt Nora? Without her, he'd be stuck here at home almost all the time. Just the thought of it makes his ribs feel like they're squeezing toward each other, compressing his lungs and making his heart work ten times harder. How would he even function without Aunt Nora?

Thad realizes his mom has spoken to him, but he's been too lost in his secret panic to hear what she's said. "What, Mom?" he asks.

"I said, 'Probably eat a lot of peanut butter and jelly.' I was answering my own question," she says, still smiling. "Play that game you like—what is it? Tankie?—and hang out at the mall."

And then guilt punches him in the gut. His sweet mom. She would do anything she could for him, *willingly*, and yet there are days, many of them, when he's tempted to chuck his phone off the escalator and order a second burrito. Maybe watch a basketball game at the RadioShack, bounce on some mattresses at Sears. Be where things don't matter for an extra hour or three. "Maybe if we get a ramp, I could take you sometime," he offers.

"To the *mall*?" she asks, like he's suggested they go snowboarding on Mount Everest.

"Well, yeah, the *mall*. You know, that big place down the street that sells socks, and cinnamon rolls, and earrings, and . . . and cheese *fundue*," he says, smirking. She used to love the cheese "fundue" at Schatzi's.

"Maybe someday," she says.

At the mall you can do almost everything on wheels. Buy things, eat things, hit every level, every kiosk. Even the bathrooms are fine on wheels. Maybe things could start to feel almost normal again.

Like she said, maybe someday.

She looks back at her foot. "Okay, I'm ready to try again."

Thad stands up and moves to the end of the bed. He narrows his eyes and cups his hands in the space around her feet, staring down through the center. "I'm beaming some extra energy," he jokes, sort of.

"Great. I can use all the energy I can get," she says.

So they both stare at her left toe. And stare some more. And then it starts to wiggle, just a little bit.

Yep, he thinks, smiling at his mother, *it's amazing the things you appreciate once they're gone.*

atraer *to attract*

yo atraigo
tú atraes
ella atrae
nosotros atraemos
ellos atraen

The next morning at school, I pass by Colby Ahrens. He gives me a little wave and a smile. I start to smile back normally, but then I remember I'm supposed to be finding someone to make Nick jealous. So I give him a look that I hope says *Come hither. And* stay *hither.* He gives me a look back that pretty much says he thinks I'm crazy, and then, in an obvious panic, he speeds down the dead-end cultural studies hall and finds a tattered-edged poster of a German castle, left over from International Awareness Week, to stare at.

In English, I try to throw Adam Dorner a glance or two. He used to like me, for about a week back in seventh grade. Adam's usually good for at least an ego-boosting smile or something, but today he's not looking anywhere near me. I guess I do that more than once or twice, because Mr. Bonna notices and yells out, "EYES FRONT, MISS COLLINS!" That's how he says it. Mortifying.

In the hallway between second and third periods, I make eye contact with Matt Hajib. Then I guess I make the mistake of trying to wink at him, like Mariela would, forgetting completely that I don't know how to wink. Whatever happens on my face ends up having the opposite effect, as later in the morning, during P.E., he trades me off the basketball team for Grace Wong—and Matt used to write me love poems! (Okay, it was only once, and it was in sixth grade, but still, it was a love poem . . . although I didn't really know it at the time. He wrote I had *cut* his eye when I was most certain I did NOT. Later, I found out he meant *caught* his eye. He also said my skin lit up like a Chinese lantern, and that was weird.)

I duck into the bathroom just before lunch, and when I come out, I nearly walk right into Michael Dorchett, throwing myself off balance.

"Whoa, there," Michael says, laughing a little. He steadies me, his hands on my shoulders.

"Sorry about that."

"No worries," he says. Our eyes meet. "Be careful." He seems slightly amused.

"I will," I say. And since he's still looking at me and holding my shoulders, I go for it.

I give him a smoldering smile. I'm pretty sure it's smoldering. Or sizzling, maybe? Anyway, something that could burn.

"Mabry?" He lets go of my shoulders. "Are you okay?"

Not exactly the response I was going for. "I'm fine," I tell him, trying to maintain my composure. I notice the corner of his collar is folded under. I reach over and start to smooth it out.

He steps back, his hand going to his collarbone. "What's wrong?" he asks.

"It was just—your collar—"

"I'll get it," he says, and rushes down the hall.

Sirina walks over. "What were you doing?"

"Flirting?"

"Mabry, that wasn't flirting. *Harassing*, maybe," she says, "but not flirting. What's happened to you?"

"Oh," I sigh as we start walking toward the cafetorium. "I don't know. I guess now that I'm supposed to be flirting with the whole wide world and making Nick jealous, I've completely forgotten how."

"Yeah, and speaking of Nick, where is he? He owes us some news."

"I haven't seen him yet," I say.

"So no news? Really?"

"Other than that I've completely lost my touch? Nope."

"Well, what's he been doing? Too busy kung fu fighting? Come on," she says as we walk into the cafetorium. "Let's go find *him*."

I grab her hand and pull her to our table. "I can't. That's pretty much the opposite of Thad's rules."

"Yeah, normally I'd be all over that. But when the YoJo's on the line?"

"Don't forget, I'm supposed to be a heartbreaker," I say, unpacking my lunch. "To quote Thad, 'You don't appreciate what you have until it's gone.'"

"Yeah, I get that, but we have to have the story," she says. "I don't even care that I'm your editor. *I'll* interview him."

"Wait!" I say, before I can think. "You don't even *like* Nick!"

"So?" she says. "What does that have to do with it?"

Technically, it shouldn't have anything to do with it. A journalist is supposed to be neutral. But it has *a lot* to do with it, as far as I'm concerned. Will Sirina even ask the right questions? Or will she just make him sound like a dork?

"What's wrong?" she asks. "It's like you're having some sort of telepathic communication with your spinach salad."

"I'll do it," I say. "I'll interview him."

She studies me. "What about Thad? What about his rules?"

I shrug. "You're my best friend. He's . . ." I stop. None of the words going into my filter sound right. *He's just a guy. He doesn't matter. He's not.* So I finally say the one thing that feels true. "He'll be fine." After all, he's been through a lot worse.

But I hardly catch more than a glimpse of Nick, and the whole day goes by without *him* finding *me*. The truth is that if I were a lost treasure, he'd be a penniless fool.

I drown my sorrows at home with *La Vida Rica*. Mariela has already slipped the key to her mother's jail cell out of the back pocket of the police chief, during an embrace. Now she is sneaking down the jail corridor dressed as a prison guard. Upstairs the chief has realized his keys are missing. My phone buzzes, but I let it go to voice mail. Thad or Sirina or my mom can wait.

But when Mariela finds the cell—*empty!*—and the credits begin to roll, I pick up my phone to see who's called. And I see something that almost stops my beating heart.

It was *Nicolás*.

I stare at the little missed-call icon that appears at the top of my screen and think, *Great. Just great. Now what?*

Do I call him back?

Of course, dummy, I hear Sirina's voice in my head. *We have an award to win!*

Fine, but don't come crying to me when you're scraping your coronary artery from the tread of his Air Jordans. That's Thad's voice.

"Grrrr," I say to the empty room. This is all too much.

I'm on the verge of calling Nick back (Sirina wins) when his name lights my phone up again. Technically, I answer it successfully. But socially, it's an epic fail, because the words out of my mouth are, "It's *you!*"

"Oh," Nick says. "Hey."

"*Hi.*" My voice comes out like a satisfied sigh.

"Can you talk?"

"Sure," I say. I can't help but add, "I thought you were going to find me in school today." *So we could look deep into each other's eyes. Maybe graze fingertips.*

"Well, I *was* looking for you," he says.

"You were?" *Yearning for me, maybe? Pining for me, perhaps? Say it, say it!*

"Yeah, but I just wanted to catch you alone, and you never were."

Darn you, Thad Bell! All this work to try to get him jealous only ended up keeping him away!

"Sorry about that," I say.

"No worries," he says. He makes this little laugh-like noise that he does. Over the phone, it sounds a little like a dog panting, but it gets me right in the left ventricle. *I miss him.* "Nick?"

"Yeah?" he asks.

"Have you—" *Have you missed me?*

But Thad's voice from inside my head keeps the words trapped in my new brain-to-mouth filter, which is growing thicker all the time. *Dude. Pathetic.*

"Have I what?" Nick asks.

"I don't know—never mind."

"Okay." *Pant-pant.* "So, you were right. I remembered more details. I have a better description of the guy."

I feel an emotional thud. Oh, right. The article. That's all he's interested in.

Nick and true love. Sirina and the YoJo. If you put those two things on a seesaw, I don't want to admit which one would be dangling in the air and which would be scraping the sand. I think about Sirina, and try to keep the seesaw balanced. I reach from the couch to my backpack and get ready to take notes. "Go ahead. What did he look like?"

"Well, he had that hoodie on, that sweatshirt. I think it was blue, and his face was kind of shadowy."

"Like, shadowy in what way? Like, sinister shadowy?"

"Well," he says, "I guess it was just kind of dark-shadowy."

"Could you see his hair at all?"

"It was under his hood, but I think it was brown."

"How about his eyes? What color were they?"

"They were brown, too. Definitely brown."

"Small and beady?" I ask.

"No, uh, I don't think so. Just brown eyes, that's all."

"Nothing interesting about them?"

"What do you mean 'interesting'?" Nick asks.

"Like, different in some way. Were they hazel, or just brown?"

"What's hazel?"

"Never mind," I say. "What else did you see? How about his nose? How sharp and pointed was it?"

"I don't think it looked sharp and pointed."

"Well, what *did* it look like. Round? Potato-like?"

"It was pretty straight. But it was still kind of hard to see."

"Because of his sneer?"

"Sneer?" Nick says. "No, I don't think he was sneering. He kind of looked surprised maybe?"

Surprised at your bravery. Your strength.

"Any defining characteristics?" I ask.

"Like what?"

"Like a huge growth, or maybe a skull-and-crossbones tattoo. Something like that."

"I—I don't think so. Sorry."

"No, that's okay. These are just things I have to ask. As a reporter." A sharp-dressed reporter with shiny hair, I remind myself. "So, how massive was this guy?"

"He was tall, but actually kind of skinny."

"What? Are you sure?"

"Yeah, I'd say skinny. *Ish*." He pants again. "But it was hard to tell with those baggy clothes. He looked like he was about our age."

"But he must have been strong," I say. "I mean, he had to be pretty strong to punch out a window in the first place. And fast, too, to get away from you."

"Oh," he says, and laugh-pants. "Yeah, maybe."

"And dangerous."

He pauses. "Maybe a little."

"Well, Abe and Patrick ran, so it must have been kind of scary."

"Oh, yeah," he says. "Okay, maybe he did look a little dangerous."

Oh, my warrior. My valiant, valiant man.

"Well, do you have everything you need?" he asks.

Everything but you, *my love. El guardián de mi corazón—the guardian of my heart. Everything* but.

I just say, "Pretty much."

"Awesome," he says. "When will the next article be posted?"

"As soon as possible," I say.

"Yeah, cool. That other one was *great*," he says, and pants again.

I realize that although I'll be making Nick happy, and Sirina, mostly, too, Thad won't be pleased. Not right away. But for now, two out of three isn't bad.

I call Sirina when I get off the phone with Nick. "I got the next part of the story," I tell her.

"What'd he say?"

"Brown hair, brown eyes—"

"That sounds like half the guys in school. What else?"

"He said the guy looked dangerous."

"Dangerous," she repeats. "Okay, let's get this thing written tomorrow. Somehow. You can show me your notes. But I'm starting to think there's a bigger story here."

"What?"

"Well, why aren't we getting any cooperation from the school? I mean, Officer Dirk's a complete roadblock. I'm going to have to talk to Mrs. Neidelman. Maybe she can make Dirk talk to us. It's like he has a personal vendetta against us winning the YoJo."

"Yeah, but I'm not surprised," I tell her. "It's like he has a personal vendetta against *life*."

Before I silence my phone for the night, I text her. *Good night, my rhinestone-studded sea urchin.*

Good night, my orange-peel toe sock, she writes back.

THE VINDICATOR

The Official News Blog of Hubert C. Frost Middle School

~~School Hero~~ *Witness* Describes Intruder, Window Breaker

TRESPASSER LOOKED "DANGEROUS"

While motives surrounding last week's school intrusion and broken window remain unclear, ~~school hero~~ *key witness* Nick Wainwright, ~~who bravely chased the perpetrator down the hall,~~ came forward with additional details about ~~this vicious crime.~~ *the incident.*

According to Wainwright, the ~~The criminal~~ *suspect* appeared to be male, and in his teens, with brown hair and brown eyes. *Though no estimate of his height was given,* Wainwright described the suspect as tall, with a thin build. He wore *loose-fitting clothes*, a pair of ~~baggy~~ jeans and a blue ~~hoodie~~ *sweatshirt with a hood.* Wainwright added that the suspect "looked dangerous." ~~Which seems very true, as it's known that Abe Mahal and Patrick Hennessey ran cowardly from the scene.~~

School officials were approached for comment multiple times, but are at this point uncooperative and unwilling to provide additional details about the incident. Further information and/or reports of suspicious activity can heretofore be reported to Sirina Fein.

Please see me. I have a fun event for you to cover!!!

Trust-Fall Injuries on the Rise

Following reports of increasing injuries, school officials have banned the practice of the trust fall, a traditional bonding experience in which a student falls backward into the arms of fellow pupils. While wrist injuries have historically been associated with this common team-building exercise, school nurses have seen an alarming surge of knee and shoulder injuries from students who mistakenly fall forward. Peer mentors, who rely on the trust fall for [click for more]

sonreír *to smile*

yo sonrío

tú sonríes

ella sonríe

nosotros sonreímos

ellos sonríen

"Tell me you're just messing with me," Thad is saying. I'm sitting on a bench; he's been balancing on his skateboard in front of me, hands in his pockets, but now steps one foot off and steadies himself.

"Well, I tried your plan, but it didn't work."

"You tried to make him jealous?"

"Yeah, I did."

"And how did you do that?"

"I flirted. With *boys*."

He looks at me like he wants to laugh, then sits down at the far end of the bench.

"Okay, so maybe I'm out of practice," I say. "Anyway, it backfired.

Every time he tried to find me, I guess I was too busy trying to flirt. It just kept him away."

"And so you just ditched the plan and wrote another story about him? 'Cause that's what it is, Collins. It's a story."

"It's not about *him*, it's about the window."

"I bet you made it into another Nickfest."

"Um, *hello*? He's the key witness. And we need the information. Sirina's going to die if we don't win that YoJo."

"Would you stop with the article? Nick's just using you to make himself look good, Collins. What's the big deal about a broken window anyway? It's not like a government conspiracy."

"But that's the thing. It could be a *school* conspiracy," I say.

"Oh, right," he says. "The infamous Hubert C. Frost Middle School conspiracy. Come on, Collins, be real. I'm sure there are better things to write about."

"In this town? Like what?"

"Like, I don't know, important things." He shrugs and looks away. "Or unfair things. There are lots of things that are unfair."

He starts to get that jumpiness that he sometimes gets, like when he was talking about his dad. He picks at the seam of his skating gloves. He wiggles his foot so fast that he has one of those personal seismic events of his.

I decide to save him from it. "What?" I smirk. "Like the fact that the Macho Nacho charges an extra fifty cents for black beans?"

"Yeah, that's a good start," he says, half smiling.

"Or maybe that there's a stolen Princess Leia figurine out there somewhere?" I snort. "I bet it was Princess Leia."

"Fine, Princess Leia." He stands up. "Come on."

I stay seated. "Where are we going?"

He pulls me off the bench. "We're getting you some practice."

He starts steering me to the overlook. We get to the rail and he surveys the food court below. "Okay, that one, that one, or that one?" Thad asks, pointing his finger at different guys below. "If you could go out with any of those chumps, which chump would it be?"

"None of them," I say.

The truth is, the only chump I want is Nick. And— *Wait!* He's not a chump at all.

Thad hangs his head in disgust. "I knew it. Okay, I *really hate* that we have to do this," he says with mock sympathy, "but let's pretend Nick is on *La Vida Rica*." Only he says *La Vida Rica* with a ridiculous accent, trilling the R, so I know he's making fun of it. "Give him a role. What would he be?"

I try to imagine it. I give Nick a little more height, a few muscles. And then I remove his shirt and put him outside somewhere. A beach. *La playa.*

"He's a lifeguard," I say. "He just saved a life. A little boy named Juanito."

"Okay, so Juanito is swimming around in the ocean, and let's say Nick sees a shark. So he dives in and saves the kid from the shark."

I smile. *La Playa Peligrosa.* A telenovela set on a dangerous cliff-side beach. I could get into that.

"Except here's the thing, Collins. The good news is that he saves the kid's life, but the bad news is that he gets chomped by the shark himself. He's swimming to shore with only one leg. And, yada, yada, yada, throw in a few episodes so we can see him writhing around, and finally, boom! He's dead."

Stop! Stop!

"Okay, I get it," I say, trying to be cool about it. "Nick's not here. That's all you had to say."

"So, now that that's settled and Nick's out of the picture, which chump would you want?"

I huff. And look at the selection of boys. They all seem so scrawny and unheroic next to Nick, especially in that lifeguard scene—*my* lifeguard scene, not Thad's. But finally I focus in on one guy who has nice shoulders and brown hair, and there is nothing too upsetting about the arrangement of his facial features. "The one in the gray shirt."

"Okay. Target identified. Now go get his attention."

"Okay, how?"

"Well, first, maybe lighten up a little."

Easy for him to say! He hasn't lost the love of his life! But then I remember his dad, and feel immediately awful.

"Oh," I say. "Okay, I'll try."

"Start by maybe smiling."

"Okay. Like, what kind of smile?"

He throws his palms up. "What do you mean, 'what kind of smile?' How many kinds are there?"

"A hundred and twenty-six, I think."

"A *hundred and twenty-six!?*" Thad laughs. "You're crazy."

"No, there's actually scientific research. And think about it: Let's see. There's the Carmela smile—the way she'd smile at her baby before Hilda stole him; or the ghost-of-Arabela smile, which is kind of sad; or the Cristina smile, not that she's smiled much since Luis was kidnapped; or the—"

"Stop. Just stop. The Mariela smile, I guess. I'm sure she has one."

The Mariela smile. So *sultry*! So *torrid*! *Am I even brave enough?* "Are you sure?"

"Let me see it."

"*What?* No!"

"Come on!"

"No *way*!"

"You're chicken."

I am. But I say, "I am *not*!"

"So let's see."

I study him. "You won't make fun of me?"

"Who, me?" he jokes. "Okay, I promise. I won't."

So I take a deep breath and turn forward, away from him. I close my eyes and try to summon Mariela. The vixen. There's a lift to the left corner of her mouth. Her eyebrows stay steady. Her eyes could start a fire. Okay, okay, I think I've got it.

So I turn my head with my Mariela smile oozing onto my face.

And cause Thad to have a conniption. He laughs so hard that a sputter of snot bursts out of his nose.

"You said you weren't going to make fun of me!"

"I—" *Guffaw. Guffaw.* "I know! I'm not—" Hyena laugh. Coyote laugh. "Making fun of you!"

I stand up and grab my purse, but Thad jumps up and clutches the corner of my sleeve. "I'm sorry!" He is still recovering. There are tears in his eyes. Of course. The insensitive wretch.

I ask, "Are you done with your animal sounds?"

"Animal sounds?"

"YOU SOUND LIKE A MOUNTAIN ANIMAL!"

Another laugh tries to escape his measly little body, but he catches it before it does. "Okay, Collins, I'm really sorry."

It actually sounds like he means it.

We stand for a second in silence, my arms crossed over my chest, him rubbing the back of his neck and having the decency to hold his laugh in.

Finally, I ask, "Was it really that bad?"

After a minute, he says, "Kind of, yeah."

"Oh. How bad?"

He breathes in and looks up. "Hmm. Well, you looked like—I don't know—I'd have to go with a half-asleep fire-breathing dragon."

"*What!?*" I cry out, but then I can't help it. Even though I'm slightly fuming, like an actual dragon might, I break into a laugh. "You are so ridiculous!"

He doesn't say anything. Just stares at me with a halfhearted smile.

"What?" I ask.

He looks away and shakes his head.

"*What!?*" I say again, frustrated.

He glances back at me. "Nothing." But then he looks at his shoes. "I was just thinking. You know, maybe your real smile is good enough."

Good enough? "What's that supposed to mean?"

He shrugs. "I don't know. I think it's fine."

He turns and I see the tips of his ears are pink. Oh. My. Gosh. Thad was being sweet. I'm not exactly sure how to handle this.

But I don't have to, because he says, "Well, go on. Your target awaits."

"Do I really—?"

"Go, or I will lean over the rail here and start announcing to everyone in the food court that you've been dumped nineteen times. And the last one was done by someone's mother." He looks at me. Walks to the rail. And takes a deep breath in.

"I'm going, you nut job!" I say, and speed-walk to the escalator.

I turn around. He's watching.

I get on the escalator and look up. He's still watching.

I wait for a bolt of lightning to hit me or something, but all that happens is that my feet land on the food court floor. I look up and see

Thad riding the escalator after me. He points his fingers to his eyes and then right at me to let me know he's watching.

I feel my heart beating in my chest. *Mariela powers activate!*

I walk toward the Cinnabon, where my target is. Now that I can get a better look at him, I'm even less sure about this. I watch him compress his Cinnabon into a dense patty and shove it into his mouth.

Um. No.

I look back toward the escalator, but there's no sign of Thad. I wonder if I can just bail.

But.

I take two steps in the direction of the nearest exit and hear from behind me, "Going somewhere?" A hand is laid on my shoulder and I freeze.

"Thad, don't make me . . ." I start.

He steers me in the direction of my target. I try to twist my way out of the path, but it's harder than it should be.

"Hi," Thad says as we approach the very stunned gray-shirted guy. Whose lips are coated with cinnamon sauce. "My friend here wanted to meet you."

I try not to act embarrassed. This, of all things, wouldn't embarrass Mariela. This is child's play.

"Oh. Hi," the guy says. "What's your name?"

I look at Thad. He widens his eyes and gives me a teeny, tiny nod to coax me on.

"Mariela," I say, and smile in a way that I hope isn't too dragonlike.

"Oh," he says. "My name's Eric."

"Enchanted to meet you," I say.

But then Eric asks me if I want to hear a riddle.

Thad looks at me expectantly. I look from him to the guy, who suddenly strikes me as a lot younger than his height suggests. "Where do you go to school?" I ask.

"Prestwood," he says. It's the name of the elementary school—*our* elementary school, the same elementary school where Thad dumped me on the playground.

Okay, this is *literally* child's play.

"Oh, that's great," I say, turning back into a very embarrassed Mabry. "But we better go."

"What about my riddle?"

Thad lets him tell it—(Eric: "If there are three oranges and you take away two, what do you have?" Thad: "I don't know, what?" Eric: "Two oranges, Einstein!")—and then we say good-bye, and as soon as we're on the other side of the escalator, the back of my hand shoots out and hits Thad in the shoulder.

"*Ouch,*" Thad says, but he's obviously more amused than hurt. "How was I supposed to know he was ten? Is it somehow my fault that his mom feeds him steroids for breakfast?"

I'm annoyed. "Isn't it time for you to go home?"

And he takes his phone out of his pocket and trips a little as he says, "Crap. Well past," and takes off without saying good-bye.

"Oh, is it half past burrito o'clock?" I call after him. And then louder, I yell, "You're so predictable!" It's like the guy will turn into a freaking pumpkin if he's a minute late. I make a point to give him a hard time about this. He certainly deserves nothing less.

Lost + Found

Thad's never late. Well, rarely. Three times max, and that includes today. Not bad for almost four months of such a tight curfew. *Curfew* seems like such a strange word for it. Like some minor nuisance that everyone his age has to cope with. No, *cutoff* is more like it.

As he gets closer to home, he has his usual panic. Will the cops be there? Did he just spend his last few minutes of freedom with *Mabry Collins? Seriously?*

But by the time he skates up to the town house, the only alarming thing he sees is Aunt Nora, standing at the window, surveying the street, like she's looking for him. He's not sure who he's most annoyed with—himself, for disappointing her, or everyone else, for expecting so much out of him.

He opens the door and goes in, and Aunt Nora stands by the sink now, wiping down the already clean counters.

"Sorry I'm late," he murmurs to her.

She looks over at him and softens. "It's okay, hon. I was just getting worried."

"Yeah, I know. Sorry," he says again.

She walks by and gives his shoulder a squeeze. "It's fine. Now, I have to run, and your mom's taking a nap. But wake her up in about fifteen minutes—she didn't want to sleep too long. She's just tired today. I think physical therapy wore her out."

"Okay."

"She had a little soup and rice—about a half cup of rice." Nora brightens.

"That's good."

"It is. You hungry?"

"I'll make something."

"Well, the soup might still be warm," Aunt Nora says.

Thad watches as she goes over to the stove and lifts the lid. He sees that the soup is green. Split pea. *Heave.* And it's starting to turn solid. *Retch.*

She sighs and turns the burner back on. "Sorry, it just needs a minute."

He'll turn it off and put it away the second his aunt leaves, but he doesn't want to tell her that. She seems to think pea soup is a perfectly normal food, and nothing at all like demon vomit.

"All right, Mister Man, I'm off to work." She smiles at him.

Sometimes when she smiles like that, he wants to hug her, but he'd never admit it. Aunt Nora looks like the word *warm* sounds. No sharp edges. He just says, "Okay, thanks."

At the door, she puts on a sweater and wraps a scarf around her neck. It's lopsided, which makes him feel kind of huggy again.

Jeez! he reminds himself. *Stop!*

She points to his mom's room. "Ten minutes, don't forget to wake her up."

"I won't."

And he doesn't forget. He doesn't have a chance to forget. Because in *five* minutes, when the pea soup burns at the bottom of the pot and he's on his second peanut-butter-and-jelly sandwich, the smoke alarm goes off.

He calmly resets the alarm with the end of the wooden spoon—it's happened before—and douses the soup pan with cold water in the sink. He won't need to wake his mother now—she'll be up like the rest of the block. All the neighbors are probably rolling their eyes. *Thad's cooking again,* they're probably saying.

The doorbell rings.

Thad groans. Must be the lady next door making sure he's not about to burn down the entire row of houses.

He storms to the door and whips it open, saying, "Everything's fine." But the last syllable gets caught in his windpipe because suddenly everything's *not.*

He is staring into the chest of Officer Dirk.

"THADDEUS."

Thad steps back. "Uh, hi."

"IS NORA HERE."

"No," he says, scanning the parking area in front of the houses. At least there are no flashing blue lights out there. No handcuffs in sight. "She just left for work."

He's holding a manila file in his hand. "I HAVE SOME PAPERS FOR HER."

Papers? Is a warrant considered a paper? His foot feels like jiggling, but he's standing on it.

"I can—take them for her?"

"I HAVE SOMETHING FOR YOU, TOO."

His mind starts going in eight different directions. How much trouble could he actually be in? If a public school is government property, has he committed some sort of crime against the government? Could he be an enemy of the state? He had posted a question anonymously on a message board, asking the world what happens when you punch out a window at school. He got lots of different answers, but the one that sticks out in his head is the one posted from someone in prison: *A good friend will tell you to tell the truth, but a great friend will stand next to you while you lie.* But what if you have no friends at all—good, great, or otherwise—except for some crazy girl? What then?

He realizes that Officer Dirk is just standing there outside the doorway and he doesn't seem to want to go away. And he's pretty sure he shouldn't be rude to someone like him—after all, his fate might be in this man's gigantic hands.

"Do you"—*please say no, please say no, please say no*—"want to come in?"

"WOULD BE GREAT."

Thad steps aside and Officer Dirk wipes his feet off carefully on the doormat, then steps inside and heads right to the kitchen.

What now?

"Do you, uh, want a Yoo-hoo?" Thad asks.

"NO."

"Or some water?"

"NO THANKS."

Thad hopes he doesn't have to offer him herbal tea, like the kind he drank with Aunt Nora. He doesn't want to stand around avoiding eye contact while waiting for the water to boil, for the tea to steep in the mug.

"Thad?" He hears his mom calling. Her voice is so quiet that he's pretty sure Officer Dirk hasn't heard it.

"Be right there," he calls back. He looks at Officer Dirk, accepting just a fleeting moment of interrogative eye contact, and says, "That was my mom. She's calling me."

Dirk nods, even though Thad worries Dirk thinks he's making it up.

He goes to the back of the house and peeks into the door. "Mom?"

"Hi, sweetheart. Is everything okay?" she asks. "It sounds like there's a lot going on out there."

Yeah, no doubt. The smoke alarm. The doorbell. And she can't even hear his own personal security system screaming that something's not right. "Everything's fine. I just burned some soup and someone came to the door."

"Oh. A neighbor?" she asks.

He opens his mouth to tell her the truth but then just nods his head. "Yeah, but no worries."

No worries. Yeah. Right.

"Okay, sweetie," she says.

He pulls the door closed again and walks back into the kitchen. Officer Dirk has his arms crossed over his chest. He's leaning on the counter, with that same heavy expression on his face as always. The manila file lies on the counter next to him. Thad never knew that a file folder could appear so menacing.

"YOUR MOTHER."

Thad waits for him to continue, but then realizes it's another odd Dirk-like statement-question, which translates loosely into *Was that your mom?*

"Yeah, she's—"

"NORA TOLD ME."

Dirk leans forward and places his heavy, monstrous hand on Thad's shoulder, which makes Thad suck in air and hold it in his lungs.

Finally, Officer Dirk removes his hand and picks up the folder.

"I'LL LEAVE THIS HERE FOR YOUR AUNT."

Thad nods.

"BUT THERE'S AN ENVELOPE IN THERE FOR YOU."

"Okay."

"IT MIGHT . . ." Officer Dirk shakes his head. "WELL, I HOPE IT WON'T BE TOO UPSETTING."

Oh. Okay. There it is. Thaddeus Bell, please report to juvenile hall at eight a.m. tomorrow. It could be that. Or maybe not. He's not sure of much at this point. Except for the fact that he's not in the market for anything upsetting.

Officer Dirk stands up straight. For a second, it looks like he'll go for another one of those sudden-attack hugs, but this time he just nods. "GIVE NORA MY REGARDS."

Sure, Thad thinks, *whatever regards really are.*

He walks Officer Dirk to the door and locks it behind him. Back in the kitchen, he glances at the folder. Whatever's in there, it can't be good. He puts it with a stack of papers on a shelf behind the table. Not exactly lost, but hopefully never found.

encender *to light, to turn on*

yo enciendo

tú enciendes

ella enciende

nosotros encendemos

ellos encienden

It's Monday, and I'm at the lunch table waiting for Sirina, who's in the toxic-food line. Jordan's blabbering on about *The Biggest Loser*, and although I couldn't care less about what she's saying, I turn to her and try to pretend I give a hoot, like Amelia apparently does. But I guess I fail at it, because Jordan finally comments on the fact that my eyes are visibly glazing over.

"Oh, sorry," I say. "I just don't watch that show."

"Yeah, now you know how I feel when you start talking about your telenovelas," she says.

I guess I do, then. "Sorry," I say. I stare at my chicken Caesar salad until Sirina sits down. She's got a Chipwich, a bag of Bugles, a roll of Donettes, and a Slim Jim.

"Holy cow," I say.

"Yeah, rough day. The worst," she says. "I tried to talk to Officer Dirk, but he just brushed me off *again*. And so I went to see Mrs. Neidelman, to tell her I'm getting nowhere with him. She just shrugged it off, and said maybe I wasn't catching him at the 'right time.' Like, when is the 'right time'? Never?"

"Did you tell her we wanted to enter it for the YoJo?" I ask.

"Yeah, and she was like, 'Oh, yes! The *YoJo*! Speaking of, the Spirit-leaders are performing at the Goat Festival in Wheatland this Wednesday!' Like she thought *that* was YoJo-worthy." Sirina throws her hands up. "*Clearly* the woman has no real journalistic background."

"What are we going to do?" I ask.

"I have no clue, but we have to think of something. I mean, if this case is stalled, then so are we." She sighs, and then adds, "I know I've been down on Nick, but so far, he's the only source we've got."

"Yeah, I guess so," I say, and smile weakly.

She gives me a tired smile back, then starts in on her Chipwich. Jordan and Amelia pull her into their *Loser* discussion by telling her that her lunch choices would be grounds for dismissal on the show.

And I look up from my romaine, and when I do, I see Nick staring at me. He looks away when our eyes meet, then back to me again. For one second, then two, then three. Three full seconds! And I'm pretty sure it's not just a look. It's like the look Hermana Ampuero gave the doctor she used to work with when he came to find her in Suelo. It's a Meaningful Gaze.

I try to explain this gaze to Thad at the mall later, but (no surprise) he doesn't get it. He keeps pretending he's trying to understand, but all he's really doing is using it as an excuse to make really stupid faces at me.

"Is this a *Meaningful Gaze*?" he asks. We're sitting on a bench, and he twists sideways, lowers his eyebrows, and looks over his shoulder at me.

"No," I tell him.

"How about this?" He turns back around and lets his head drop to the side. He opens his eyes as wide as they can go, and lets his tongue dangle sideways.

I swat at him.

"Oh!" He jumps up. "I know. How about this?" He puts one foot on the bench, then puts his elbow on his knee. He raises his hand and rests his chin lightly on his gloved knuckles, gazing like a presidential candidate into the distance. *Wistfully.*

"You're not even looking at me. Just stop," I say.

"I'm just trying to understand," he says, smirking.

"No you're not. Anyway, you're starting to look like an idiot."

"Just starting? I can do better," he says.

"Sit. Down." I say. "I didn't come here just so you could make fun of me."

"Oh, you didn't?"

"*Oh, Thad, you're so, so funny,*" I say in a mocking high-pitched voice.

He laughs, but then sniffs some air through his nose and scratches his ear in a way that makes me think he's a little embarrassed. I kind of want to enjoy his embarrassment and maybe even start making fun of *him*, but whenever I think about his dad being dead, I feel like I should be nicer to him.

"Okay, sometimes you *are* funny," I tell him.

He looks at me suspiciously. "You know what I don't get?"

"Yeah. A lot of things," I say.

He just shakes his head. "No. I don't get why we're even having this conversation. You were supposed to be making him jealous. And now, what are you telling me? That you failed *again*?"

"Or that I succeeded. In flirting," I say, a little smugly.

"You weren't supposed to be flirting with *him*, Collins. Not yet."

I throw my hands up. "Isn't the important thing for this plan to work that I get him to like me again?"

He shrugs and looks away. "I think the more important thing right now is that you stop liking him so much."

For a second, I'm panicked. *Does Thad know? He better not!* So I pretend-knock on the back of his head. "Hey, nut case. Who said anything about *liking* him? *Now* who's getting sentimental? Don't you remember I'm supposed to snare him? And break his heart?"

He turns back to me and narrows his eyes. "Quick. Tell me three things you don't like about him."

"What? *Why?*"

"For your own protection," he says. "This is your next assignment. It's easy not to crush on someone when you can focus on their flaws. So, now—*quick*. Give me three things you don't like about him."

"Three?" It seems like an impossible task, but just to cover for myself, I laugh-snort and say, "I could give you *twenty* if I wanted to."

"I'll settle for three," he says.

"All right, okay." I do the snorty laugh again. "Fine, I'll tell you."

"So you said."

"Well, okay, here you go. I don't like his mother, for one," I say.

I mean, what kind of mother-in-law would she be? Constantly hovering. Minding everyone's business. I could live without that.

"That's more about *her* than *him*."

"Okay, fine. I don't really like his haircut," I say.

"He's a Bieberhead, right? You agree?"

"Hardly ever. But fine, I'll give you that."

149

"Come on. Say it," Thad says, cupping his hand behind his ear. "I want to hear it."

I lower my gaze at him.

"*Saaay* it."

I exhale. "Fine." Through tight lips, I say, "Bieberhead."

"What? Who?"

I let out a frustrated breath. "Nick Wainwright is a Bieberhead," I finally say, just to shut him up.

Thad throws his fists up in victory. I roll my eyes.

"Okay, what else?" he says. He is enjoying this way too much.

Gah. What don't I like about Nick? I've spent so much time thinking about what I like—no, *love*—about him, it's hard to say. Then something pops in my head. His ears. His tiny ears. It's like they're stuck in fourth grade and haven't caught up with the rest of him. "His ears are small."

He laughs. Or channels a coyote. It sounds about the same. "Good. Baby ears. Keep going. More flaws, please."

"You said three things," I remind him.

"Yeah, and you said you could give me twenty."

"I don't feel like it."

Thad exhales through his mouth and sweeps his hand through his hair. "Well, there's a lot I don't like about him. *A lot*," he says, looking at me.

"Have you even seen him since elementary school? You hardly know him anymore!"

"And you know what?" he says. He seems a little upset. "You hardly do, either."

I should argue with him—after all, Nick was my boyfriend for six weeks! But I also kind of don't like seeing Thad upset, not in this way. So I say, "I did see him pick his nose once."

This seems to satisfy Thad a little. His mouth almost stretches into a smile, and his eyes seem wider, quicker. "So he *does* still do that."

"Well, I just saw it once," I say. "He didn't know I was watching."

"Still counts. Okay, that's a good one. A public picker," Thad says. He turns to me and squints his eyes a little. "Hey, speaking of flaws, did you know that one of your ears is a little higher than the other?"

Great, I think. *Welcome, new insecurity! You will be in good company! There are lots of experienced insecurities that have been eagerly awaiting your arrival. Have you met Unibrow? Or Man Knuckle? Or Toe Hair? And, yeah, how about the Double-A Twins—oh, you can't see them? Don't worry, no one else can, either!*

"Well, you're like Edward Scissorhands, wearing those stupid gloves around all the time."

"Awesome." He scissors his hands toward my head, making some sort of monster-y hissing sound.

"It's *not*," I say, scooting away. "It's creepy."

When he finally stops and looks away, I put my hands over my ears. Does one feel higher than the other? Is it the left one or the right one? Or maybe it's the earlobes! I feel them. Oh my god, one is bigger than the other. And here I've completely decorated them with earrings, drawing even more attention to this horrible flaw!

Nick turns to see me grasping my ears. "I was totally kidding," he tells me.

"You were?"

"Jeez, Collins," he says, flopping his head to one side. He blows out a sigh and adds, "Well, me and my creepy scissor hands better head out. See you next time."

"Why don't we meet somewhere else? Don't you get tired of the mall?"

"Nope," he says, and skates off. *Whatever.* I watch him go. He's getting pretty good. Not that I would ever tell him that.

And then I think of another Nick flaw. I bet Nick can't skate like Thad. But that will have to be one to keep to myself. It's hardly a real flaw anyway. I mean, I still haven't learned how to salsa dance, and I sure hope no one's holding that against me.

22

Crime + Punishment

When Thad gets home, Aunt Nora's practically pacing.

"I'm glad you're here—she's been in her chair for almost three hours now."

"Three *hours*?" He hadn't even realized he'd been out that long.

"She got into the wheelchair when the therapist was here, and she wanted to stay in it for a while after the therapist left. But I can't get her back out of it alone."

He stumbles over a couple excuses about losing track of time. The truth is that he wasn't careful enough—that he didn't want to have to keep track. "I'm sorry," he says.

"It's okay, hon, let's just . . ." She motions for him to follow her.

In his mom's room, he sees her in the wheelchair, her head leaning to the side. It gives him a strong and sudden ache. She just looks so small. So frail. So helpless. Tears push upward, but he squints them back.

"Mom?"

She opens her eyes and lifts her head, and in a groggy voice says, "Oh, good. You're home."

Thad gets behind the wheelchair and places his hands under his mom's arms. Nora scoops her forearms under her knees. "One, two," Nora counts, "three!"

They sweep her onto her bed, Nora making a tiny grunt, Thad not making a sound at all, not even a breath.

"So tired," his mom says.

"You can get some real rest now," Nora says.

Thad tries to help Aunt Nora put the pillows just right and arrange the bed, but she shoos him away.

"'Night, Mom," he says.

"Mmm-hmm," his mom hums, too tired for actual words.

He goes out to the kitchen and grabs a Yoo-hoo out of the refrigerator. He takes a swig.

Aunt Nora appears, her hands on her hips. "No way, uh-uh, not before dinner!" she says. It's more of a scold than the usual good-natured badgering.

"Okay, calm down," he says, his hands lifted in surrender.

"Have some plain milk instead," she says, and blows some air out of puffed cheeks.

Okay, she's definitely annoyed.

He opens the refrigerator and puts the bottle back in. "I didn't know you were waiting. You could've called me."

"I *did.*"

Whoops.

Did he even check his phone at all?

Nope.

He sighs. "I'm sorry. I guess I was"—*having fun for once; pretending this new life wasn't waiting for me, counting on me*—"distracted."

"It's just hard, you know." She looks like she might cry.

Oh no.

He doesn't know what to do. His eyes dart around the kitchen and land on the kettle. He guides Aunt Nora to a chair at the table and fills up the kettle with water. She sniffles. He brings her a paper towel. "Peppermint or lemon ginger?" he asks, words he knows she likes.

"Peppermint, please." She looks up. "With honey?"

The water boils and he pours it into two cups. He sits down at the table with her. She looks up at him. And smiles. Finally. Thank god she smiles.

"Well, look at *you*," she says. "*Actually* drinking tea."

"It can't be that bad," he jokes. He swirls the tea bag around his mug, watching the hot water turn greenish-brown.

Her eyes rest on the shelf behind Thad. A stack of mail sits unopened. A useless phone book. And the folder. The manila folder.

"What's that?" she asks, jutting her chin in its direction.

"What?" he tries.

"That file folder. Behind you."

"Oh," he says. *What now?* "I don't know."

"Where'd it come from?"

"I think"—his back straightens—"that guy—"

"Dirk?"

"Yeah, I think he dropped it off."

"Well, why didn't you tell me?" she asks, but doesn't wait for an answer. "Here, hand it to me, hon."

So he does. He crosses his foot over his knee and lets it bounce under the table. He watches her face. It doesn't crumble, but her mouth tightens and her eyebrows pull together and she says, "We need to talk about this. These are important."

"Okay." He braces himself. "What is it?"

"Your enrollment papers."

Relief.

"Well, Thaddeus, what do you think?"

"What about Mom?" *What about days like today, when she's stuck in her wheelchair?*

"We'll . . ." She takes a breath and looks away. "We'll figure that out. We will. But I need to know. Are you ready to go to school?"

Yes. No. He's not sure. He's not even sure they'll allow him in once they figure out he broke the window. If they haven't already figured that out. Maybe this is his punishment—mind games. "Can I think about it?"

"Thad." She tilts her head. "The longer you take, the harder it is to get back into the routine."

"I know, I just . . ." His voice trails off, and she lets it. She's opening the envelope.

She pulls something out and stares at it for a full minute.

His foot stops jumping.

Her face crumbles. She blots her tears with the paper towel he gave her earlier. She pushes the envelope across the table to him. Inside is an old photo. Two young boys, maybe ten years old. They've just caught a big fish. One of them holds the fishing rod; the other holds the line. They are both squinting in the sun and smiling.

Officer Dirk. And Thad's dad.

His face feels wet.

He was warned.

llamar *to call*

yo llamo
tú llamas
ella llama
nosotros llamamos
ellos llaman

On Thursday, Sirina and I are on our way to our first-period classes when we see Officer Dirk. He's leaning against the doorjamb, sipping something from a mug and listening to Ms. Roach. She's moving her hands around and smiling as she talks.

"Holy *something*. That's the most relaxed I've ever seen him," Sirina says, motioning for me to follow her. "Come on, maybe he won't be a jerk in front of Ms. Roach."

When he sees us, his already stern face hardens. It's like watching a regular stone turn into granite. I start to slow down but Sirina pulls me along.

Ms. Roach stops talking and looks at us.

"Do you have a few minutes, Officer Dirk?" Sirina asks.

He looks at his watch. "EIGHTY-TWO SECONDS."

Ms. Roach excuses herself and ducks back into her classroom.

"Well, I need more time than that. Can we schedule something? To talk about the window?"

"OH. I HAVEN'T TOLD YOU."

A few of those seconds are eaten up by the time it takes for us to realize he's asking a question rather than making a statement.

"Well, no, you haven't, but we were hoping—"

"MAYBE THAT'S BECAUSE IT'S NONE OF YOUR BUSINESS."

Sirina shrinks. The warning bell rings. Officer Dirk's granite face softens back into its usual stone, and he walks away.

"I'm sorry," I say. "I don't know what's going on."

"I don't, either," Sirina says. "But I do know one thing. This doesn't end here."

Later, as we are being herded into the cafetorium for an anti-bullying assembly by a group of rude teachers ("Left! *Left!* Not right! Didn't you learn the difference in kindergarten!?"), Nick spots me. He stops and holds his hand up in a stiff wave, disrupting the line and earning a scolding by Ms. Hilliard, the P.E. teacher tasked with managing the lines into the cafetorium ("I said go! *G-O!* It's pretty simple, folks!").

Nick gets back in line and scampers off, no doubt embarrassed. But when we get weaved into the seats, I see his tiny ears two rows up. And when Ms. Hilliard barks "No changing seats!" from the back of the room to some kid who apparently wasn't happy with his original seat assignment, and everyone cranes their heads back to see who this poor and slightly dumb soul might be, our eyes connect. You can almost hear the clink of our eyes locking.

And suddenly his eyes seem too close together.

Get out of my head, Thaddeus Bell. Get out.

Then Ms. Hilliard yells again. "I said stay there, didn't I?" And I notice a strange gap between Nick's side teeth.

Wait. That's what I notice first, because stupid Thad Bell has poisoned my thoughts. But then I realize that Nick—my *Nicolás*—is smiling at me. Admiringly. Gloriously. He is smiling, not just *at* me, but *for* me.

And his eye spacing doesn't matter. And his tooth gap is actually quite charming.

So I just do it—I give him the bold, daring Mariela smile. Forget about the rules of heartbreak, what about the rules of true love?

"Maybe I should call the police department," Sirina is saying as we walk home from school later that afternoon. She's been staying up late watching old *Law & Order* episodes.

"*Oooh.*" I suck in a breath. "I'm not sure that's ever a good idea."

"Why not? I just want to see the police report about the broken window." Then she looks at me and laughs. "Oh my god. You're thinking of Señora Trujillo again, aren't you? Wrongful imprisonment for the crime of pig stealing."

"And Luis!" I say. The most recent episode of *La Vida Rica* revealed that the police were in cahoots with the bad guys that kidnapped Cristina's love, Luis. "How could you possibly forget about him!?"

"Come on, Mabry. This is real life." We stop in front of her house. She's about to go to a dentist appointment. "Well, want to come watch them scrape my teeth? I hear there are some old copies of *Better Housekeeping* in the waiting room," she jokes.

"That sounds—uh—great, but, no."

She smiles. "Okay, I'll call you later, then."

I start the walk to my house. My phone buzzes and I fish it out of my jacket pocket, and almost immediately drop it.

Because it's *Nicolás*!

In the millisecond it takes for me to press the answer button, I have three miniature fantasies of what Nick could want, and where this could go. He could plead with me to forgive him. He could tell me how wretched life is without me, and how he's been unable to eat or sleep since his mom's fateful phone call. He could ask me what I'm doing—*dreamy sigh*—for the rest of my life.

"*Hel-loo?*" I say, my voice like satin.

But there's no voice in response. Just a few weird sounds—a crushy sound, a swishy sound, and that's it.

"Hello? *Hello?*" There's no more satin in my voice, just the breathlessness of desperation.

The call disconnects.

I stare at my phone and wonder what I should do.

Sirina's voice pops into my head: *Call him back! What if he has more information?*

And then there's Thad's: *Think nose picker, Collins. Public picker.*

I don't want to have to decide. Maybe I won't have to. Maybe he'll call me again. *Please, Nicolás, My Love, llámame!*

And then I put the phone back into my pocket and start walking again. Or, really, waiting in motion.

My phone stays still and silent, even hours later.

I call Sirina. The phone just goes to voice mail, but it makes that sound like she's on another call. So I call Thad.

"What's up, dorkus?"

"Nothing," I say. "Absolutely nothing. Can you call me right back?"

"Um, no."

"What do you mean? Why not?"

"Didn't you just call me?"

"Well, yeah, but I want to make sure my phone's working."

"*Uh.*" He pauses. "Look, I'm no genius, but I'm kind of sure that your phone's working. I mean, don't freak or anything, but we are actually speaking. On the phone. Right. *Now.*"

"No, I mean, *call* it. Sometimes, you know, ringers just stop working. And voice mail doesn't always kick in."

"Collins? Is this the stuff that goes on inside your head all day?"

"*Can you just please call me back? Okay?*"

I hear a beep. The call ends. Did he just hang up on me? Did he? *The nerve—*

But my phone rings. It's him. "Knucklehead," I say.

"Hangnail," he says back. "Anyway, did it ring, or are you just psychic?"

"It rang."

"So, it works."

"Yeah. I guess so."

"So what's the problem?"

"No problem," I say.

"Liar. You're waiting for Nick to call, aren't you?"

Sometimes this ruse is so hard to keep up! "*Only* because he called earlier and we got disconnected, that's all," I say.

There's a pause. It feels like Thad could be reading my thoughts. "I can't believe I have to say this. Don't even *think* about calling him back, Collins. Got it?"

Great. Am I really that predictable?

"Okay, fine, I get it," I say.

"Tell me you won't call him."

"I'm not going to call him. It's not like I wanted to in the first place," I tell him.

"Good. Also, I need a flaw. A new one. Go."

I sigh. "Fine, he needs braces."

"That's a stupid one," he says.

"Whatever," I say. "I'll try harder."

"Yeah, maybe you should actually *try*."

"I am! It's just that—well, the Cotillion's getting closer and I don't know"—*if he really likes me or not*—"if he's actually going to ask me. I'm never going to be able to break his heart if he doesn't ask me."

Thad sighs. "Collins, jeez. Chill, dude."

"I mean, what if he really doesn't like me after all? What if something's wrong with me?"

"Like, besides your ears?"

"You said you were joking about my ears!" I say.

"I was! I *am*!" He hyena-laughs, even though it's not funny.

"No, but what if—I'm not smart enough? Not pretty enough?"

I can hear some exasperation in his voice. "You're enough of those."

I feel myself blush, and I'm glad he can't see it. "Well, what, then?" I scan through all my possibly irritating habits. Chewing the insides of my cheeks; laughing too loud, sometimes accidentally snorting; talking a lot. I wonder which of these is the worst. I think about listing them out so he can rank them. I know it sounds painful, but the truth often hurts. I just have to know!

"Okay, Collins, *stop*."

"Stop what?"

"Doing this. Thinking you're not *whatever* enough. You've got to understand how a guy thinks."

"Okay, well, *tell* me."

"Okay. Here's the thing. A guy might like a girl—maybe he even likes her *a lot*. But he also likes Tex-Mex. And he likes cartoons or basketball or whatever. And he likes Xbox. Maybe he just wants to focus on a burrito in peace, and you know what? Maybe you should learn something from it. Find something else to do besides sitting around and wondering if your phone works."

I sigh.

"Think about it," he says. "What does Mariela do with her time?"

"She plots things," I say.

"Like what?"

"Schemes," I tell him. And then I realize that's kind of what I'm doing with Nick. Only I really do secretly love him.

"Well, whatever they are, I'm sure they don't involve waiting around for some *sack* to look at her or text her or whatever."

"O-*kay*," I say. I try to think of something else to do with my time, but feel a little stumped. My head keeps filling up with stupid things like bean dip and hot sauce. It's useless.

"And, Collins?"

"What?"

"The fact that sometimes calling you is going to be less important to a guy than, say, a Funyun?"

Ouch! "What about it?" I ask.

"Just don't take that personally. It's not you, it's just how our brains sometimes work."

But a *Funyun*? I'm stunned into silence.

"Hey," he finally says. I can hear him smiling. "You *asked*!"

Jeez. Yes, I did. I asked for it. And knowledge is power, right?

But *wow*. To be as significant as a Funyun. Sometimes I guess knowledge just doesn't feel that empowering after all.

Hot + Cold

When he comes back into the kitchen, Aunt Nora is giving him this weird smile. "Who was *that*?" she asks.

"No one," he says, embarrassed to have been overheard.

"Oh, it was definitely *someone*." She still has this strange smile on her face.

Oh god, he thinks. He doesn't need Aunt Nora grilling him. "It was nothing." He brushes past her, opens the refrigerator, and stares.

"There's some of that chicken in that Tupperware container. And mashed potatoes," Aunt Nora says. "Your mom ate half a plateful today."

"She did?" He looks over at Aunt Nora.

She nods, looking pleased.

"Why don't you just sit down, okay? I'll make you up a plate."

Thad takes a seat. It's not like he can't heat it up himself, but sometimes it's nice to be doted on.

"So," Aunt Nora says as she puts the chicken on a plate, "how is everything?"

"Oh," he says. "Okay, I guess."

"You know you can always talk to me, right? About anything?"

"I *know*," he says automatically. Since the accident, nearly every adult says that. It's like he'd be doing them some massive favor or something by spilling his guts. He finds it hard to believe, and even harder to take seriously. What good would it do anyway?

He watches her put the plate into the microwave, pour a glass of milk, and bring it to him at the table.

"About school," she starts. "We can't put it off much longer, you know."

"I know," he says.

Aunt Nora sighs. The microwave dings. She stirs the food inside and restarts it, leaning on the counter.

Thad feels her looking at him, but he finds a scratch in the surface of the table and traces it with his thumbnail.

"He'd want you to be in school by now," she says.

His throat starts to tighten, but thankfully, the timer dings again, popping the bubble of tension that always seems to be floating somewhere in the air around him.

She sighs again and takes the plate out, but it's too hot. She winces, plops the plate down on the counter, and shakes her hand.

"I'll get it." He stands up to get the plate while she runs her fingers under cold water, then goes to the table and starts in on the mashed potatoes.

Aunt Nora dries her hand and leans back on the counter. "It won't always be like this. She's getting better." And then she smiles again, but it's a whole different kind of smile than the one she gave him after his phone call. It's a better smile. Nicer, somehow.

And then—*Dude*, he thinks, *a better smile?* What's he doing? Turning into Mabry or something?

"What's funny?" Aunt Nora asks.

"Oh," he says, surprised, realizing that he'd just snort-laughed out loud. "Nothing, really."

She tilts her head, looking so left out.

So he says, "Did you know there are like a hundred and twenty-six kinds of smiles?"

"No, I did *not* know that." She laughs. It makes him feel that soft, melty feeling toward her again. "Is this what you're learning in online school?"

"No," he laughs. "Just from some girl."

Some girl. The words that fly out of his mouth feel wrong somehow. *Some girl* doesn't sound at all like Mabry. But, he reminds himself, that really *is* what she is. Some girl he knew in fourth grade. Some girl who has a stupid, pitiful belief in quote-unquote love.

"Just some girl, huh?" Aunt Nora says.

And he takes another bite of mashed potatoes and says, "Yep."

Just some ridiculous girl.

bailar *to dance*

That night, I get out of the shower to find that *Nicolás* has called twice in a row!

He must be deeply in love! *Desperate* with love!

The icon on my phone shows two voice mails! I check the first. I can barely hear him, it's like he's talking underwater. *GAH!* He could be professing his limitless love—little gems, little gifts of words and thoughts. How frustrating it is that I can't hear him!

The second message is no better. Maybe something about a "sandwich bag." Or could I have heard that wrong?

It's so upsetting. What am I supposed to do? Call him and ask him to repeat everything he said? What if he's also getting ready for bed—brushing his teeth, maybe? I can just imagine. It won't be the same.

He'll be like, *I don't remember, exactly. I was basically talking about how you were the most amazing, gorgeous person in the whole wide world and something about the cockles of my heart, and— Hey, can you hang on for a sec? I gotta spit.*

I try calling Sirina once again, and she finally picks up. But before I can really tell her about the voice mails, I have to cut her off.

"HE'SCALLING!!I'LLCALLYOUBACK!"

It's *him!* My *Nicolás!* I click over and try to subdue my excitement, for Thad's sake, if nothing else.

"Hel-*looo?*" I say. I try to make it both womanly and nonchalant.

"Oh, hi, Mabry," he says. Like a man in love. Humbly, sweetly, and slightly embarrassed at the depth of his poetic emotions, I'm sure.

"Hi," I greet him again.

He does one of those laughs that isn't really a laugh. It's like when you're supposed to laugh, but all you can do is make that awkward *huh-huh-huh* sound. And then he asks, "So, what, uh, are you up to?"

"Oh, I'm just . . ." I can't tell him what I'm really doing, which is listening again and again to his voice mails, trying to decipher the messages, with both purpose and passion. So I think, *What would Mariela be doing?* I picture her dancing. She is wearing a red sleeveless dress. She turns toward the camera, her gaze serious, a rose between her teeth. "Getting ready for salsa," I say.

And he says, "Oh, I like salsa."

I knew you were the Man of My Dreams, dear Nicolás. My Nicolás. It's a month into the future. We are at the Cotillion. He takes my hand and leads me to the dance floor. The song starts, our feet move, first forward then back, but our eyes stay connected in a passionate gaze—I can feel his love and devotion oozing through his pupils. The other dancers step back, in awe, just taking in the pleasure of our dance—which is more than just a dance, but an expression of our true, undying love.

I let the satisfaction seep into my voice. "So, what are *you* doing?" I ask, making my voice sound warm and succulent, like Mariela's—like a papaya that's ripened on the tree.

"Not much. I just wanted to say sorry about those calls. My phone was in my back pocket and those, uh, those were butt dials." Then a little panting chuckle.

"Oh!" I say. How disappointing is *that*? His butt called me. His *butt*!

"Yeah, sorry."

I think about saying something like, *So, is that it? It didn't need anything else, did it?* But I think about Mariela, who would never be engaging some potential suitor about his butt cheeks.

Anyway, none of that matters. He likes salsa dancing! He was made for me! "It's quite all right," I say in my new, ripe-fruit voice.

"Hey, Mabry?" His voice cracks a little. For a second he sounds too young. Too adolescent for my fruity richness. But then I blink and the thought goes away. It's just Thad getting into my head. He's like a virus. *Thaddeus vulgaris.*

"Yes?"

"I wanted to say—well, thanks for interviewing me for that article and everything."

"Oh. Sure."

"You're real—" *Huh huh-huh.* "I, uh—"

What, mi querido, *what???*

"Yes?"

"Just, nothing," he says. "Just that you're a cool girl."

My heart levitates. It soars. It's like a hot-air balloon destined for *forever*.

But I hear his mom's voice in the background—she's calling his name. "Well, I gotta go," he says, cooling down my hot, floating joy. "Guess I'll see you in school tomorrow."

He guesses. *He guesses?* Oh, he better bet his sweet phone-happy butt cheeks he will. But I just say, "I guess you will," in my best red-mango tone.

I call Sirina the second I hang up.

"Sorry about that! Turns out they were butt dials," I tell her.

"Yeah, you kind of freaked there a little bit."

"Guess what else?" I say.

"What?"

"He called me 'cool.' He said I was a 'cool girl.'"

"Okay, you zoid. But don't forget you still have a heart to break."

"Calm down. No one's forgetting anything. That's still the plan," I say, doing my best to sound convincing.

She just makes a skeptical *hmm* sound.

"Anyway," I continue. "I tried calling you earlier, but it rang like you were on the other line. Who were you talking to?"

"*La policía,*" she says casually. "To see what their report says about the window incident."

"What? You actually did that?"

"I told you I was going to." She sounds a tiny bit annoyed.

"So what did they say?"

"Pretty much? After calling around for an hour? Nothing. Nada. Squat. They said I have to call back tomorrow."

"Ugh," I say.

"Exactly," she says back.

A few minutes after we hang up, I get her text. *Good night, my three-toed scuba diver.*

Good night, my bassoon-lipped heartworm, I write back.

But I get one more text from her. *Remember what has to happen.*

I know! I write back. But I kind of feel like a kid whose mom has let her have ice cream before dinner based on the promise that she'll eat liver and onions afterward—every bite of it. But I'm still in the ice-cream phase of this deal, so any thought of liver and onions can wait.

THE VINDICATOR

The Official News Blog of Hubert C. Frost Middle School

Spiritleaders Place Second in Sideshow at County Goat Show

On Wednesday, the Frost Spiritleaders competed in the first "America's Goat Talent" Sideshow at the Annual County Goat Festival, ~~but didn't win.~~ *and came home with a second-place trophy.* They competed against four other middle-school cheerleading teams at the event, as well as a comedy duo from Briggville, and ~~an old guy~~ *a gentleman* playing ~~kazoo.~~ *mouth harp.*

   "We're all excited," said Mrs. Cassidy, English teacher and Spiritleader sponsor. "It's quite an honor."

   The team performed a dance-cheer routine to the song "Let It Go," from the soundtrack of the movie *Frozen.* ~~, which probably wasn't a good choice after all, because Paysley Cornwell did actually let go of Sophia Allen's foot during a move dubbed "the Spirograph." She said it was by accident, but there is talk about Sophia stealing Paysley's boyfriend, Chat Coddington.~~

   The A-List, a cheerleading team from Mary Anning Middle School in Fossilton, carried off the first-prize trophy.

[click for more]

172

Seventh-Grade Teacher Declares Class "the Smartest Ever"

Teen Life teacher Mr. Ricardo declared his current fourth-period class to be intellectually superior to any class he's ever taught. "You guys are the smartest ever," Ricardo boldly stated, after a successful class project involving macaroni and cheese. However, Truce Mayhew, who was a student of Mr. Ricardo just last year, alleges that Ricardo made the very same declaration to them, and an anonymous high-school senior, who had Mr. Ricardo five years ago, stated that [click for more]

tocar *to touch*

yo toco

tú tocas

ella toca

nosotros tocamos

ellos tocan

I'm sitting at Macho Nacho with Thad. He is staring at the wreckage of his burrito and is starting to eye my chimichanga, which I'm finishing up. I have only recently discovered the delight of the chimichanga—a fried, more compact version of the monstrous burrito, one that you actually *are* expected to eat with a fork and knife.

I'm telling Thad about the butt dials.

"Wow, it sounds pretty *serious*," Thad says with a straight face.

"Ha. *Ha*. Anyway, he called again. For real. Him, not his butt."

"And what did him-not-his-butt say?"

"Well, that I was a 'cool girl.'" I feel both defensive and a little embarrassed. "And he seemed interested. He asked what I was up to."

"Yeah, what did you tell him?"

I sigh. "I did the Mariela thing. I told him I was getting ready to go to salsa. And guess what? *For your information*, he likes salsa, too!"

Thad stops chewing. Then he breaks into a zoo-like laugh.

"What?" I ask.

"Dude." He looks amused. Strongly amused. "What exactly did you tell him?"

I feel like I've been holding on to a gift that is about to be taken away. "I told him I was getting ready for salsa lessons."

"No, exactly. What did you say? Did you actually say *lessons*?"

I think back. Maybe not. Okay, probably not. *I'm getting ready for salsa.*

Crap. Definitely not.

"He thought I was talking about this?" I ask, sweeping my hand toward the little cup of red sauce.

He just laughs in his wild way, and then eyes my plate and asks, "Hey, can I get a hit of that 'chong?"

It takes me a minute to realize he's talking about my chimichanga.

"Go ahead," I say, dispirited.

He takes it from my Styrofoam plate with his fingers, takes a bite RIGHT OFF OF IT, and places it back on the plate.

"Just finish it," I tell him, now that I don't want to touch the thing.

"Are you sure?"

I look down at the remains and see Thad's crescent-shape bite taken right out of it. "I'm sure."

Thad quickly takes another bite of my chimichanga. "Okay, look, Collins. Maybe the guy does finally like you. You're welcome, by the way. And maybe he *is* going to ask you out."

Do you really think? I feel myself inflate with hope. Then I remember that Thad's probably going to take my hope away, like he normally does.

But he says, "So, fine. Go out with him. Go discover another flaw. Or three."

"*Really?*" I ask.

"Yeah. Fine. Go. I think we have him where we want him at this point. I mean, that stupid dance is coming up soon, right?"

I nod. "It's not just a dance," I remind him. "It's the Cotillion."

"Well, if he doesn't ask you, he's going to ask someone else. So you might as well go out with him now, because if he ends up going with someone else, the whole plan is flushed down the toilet. You can't stand up someone else's date."

"Right. Good point." For a second, I'm impressed with myself. If I ever want to act in a telenovela, I'm certainly getting some practice. Because there's something else that happened today, something I'm not telling Thad.

Nick and I ended up walking down the same hall on the way to fifth period. It's not too unusual, because we have a similar commute at that time. But today, somehow, we ended up side by side. And his pinkie grazed mine. And he didn't yank his hand away. It was, I'm sure, a Deliberate Dangle, and our hands and fingers collided three more times before I got to Spanish. I felt a little like Dylan the worm—each time our hands grazed and collided, I felt the beating of many tiny little hearts in each finger.

So while Thad gobbles down the rest of my '*chong* down in his usual disgusting manner, I check my phone, hoping to hear from Nick, and not just his butt cheek.

"Put that thing away. That's your assignment for the day." Thad says. He wipes his hands off on a napkin, still chewing. His chair scrapes against the tile floor. "Come on, just forget about that chump for now. Let's do something fun."

I stick my phone back in my pocket. The suspicious eyebrow-threading lady tries to lure me over with promises of a pain-free experience. Thad starts to get distracted by the waft of Sbarro, unbelievably.

And me, I can't help myself. I pull my phone out again. Maybe I've lost service. I need to check.

"You're failing this assignment," Thad says. "Put it back in your pocket and *keep* it there."

As much as I hate to, I do. But I say, "For your information, I was checking to see if Sirina called."

He smiles. "I don't even care. Take a break from it. *All* of it." He puts his hands on my shoulders and steers me forward.

We stop in front of a Brookstone and he pushes me into the massage chair. The store clerk waits a minute, then walks over. "That's not a toy," he says to us.

"Yeah!" Thad says. "Not at thirteen hundred dollars it ain't."

"I'm going to have to ask you to leave," the clerk says. He points to a handwritten sign taped up near the chair that reads: *Please no unaccompanied minors.*

"That's okay," I say. "It feels like a robot is jabbing at me with sticks anyway."

We scurry out of the store and I follow Thad to the escalator. "Let's go upstairs," he says. Except that he's at the wrong escalator. The stairs are coming toward us. "You ever done this?" he asks. Based on the look on his face, we might as well be at Disneyland.

"No!" I say. "How do you do it?"

"Just run up really fast. Faster than it comes down. Come on!"

"What if someone gets on?"

"Yeah, no biggie. Then you just ride it down." He jumps three steps up and starts scrambling toward the top. "Come on, Collins!" he shouts. And it does look fun, so I hop a few steps up, but I'm not fast enough. I'm carried to the bottom, backward. Thad's nearly made it to the top.

I take a deep breath and try again, but I aim too high and my knees buckle, and I tumble onto my butt, and am delivered to the floor like a factory reject. Thad looks down at me, victorious, from the second floor. And then . . .

Whiiirrrrrrrr.

It's Captain Jerry.

He sighs. "Are you *hurt*." It sounds more like a general disappointment than a question.

If I was, it's clear that I wouldn't get any sympathy from him. "No," I say, pushing myself up. "I'm fine."

He takes his ticket tablet out of his pocket and scribbles something on it. Then he rips it off and hands it to me. "Now, first time is a warning. But the next time I catch you playing on the escalator—AND THIS CAN BE A DEATH TRAP—your parents get a call. Third time?" He whistles and points his thumb over his shoulder with a sweeping motion. "Kicked out. Barred from the mall. How do you like *them* apples?"

Then he spots Thad at the top of the escalator. "You!" he yells, and Thad runs off. Thankfully, he doesn't *skate* away. I don't think Captain Jerry could handle that right now. He gives me a threatening look and whirs off again.

I look around the mall. It's pretty quiet. There are only a few people walking around and most of them seem to be employees. The only sounds are a few shoes shuffling on the floor, the distant whir of Captain Jerry's Segway, and the hum of the escalator. And then Thad appears, lying lengthwise on the handrail of the down escalator. It looks dangerous. But it also looks fun. "This is actually much harder than it looks," he tells me.

"You're so stupid sometimes," I say, but I can't help smiling.

"You and me both," he says. Okay, I can't argue with that one.

And then my phone buzzes. I frantically grab it out of my back pocket. It's a text from Nick. FINALLY!

"Loserboy?" Thad asks.

"If that's what you want to call him," I say, hiding my excitement.

"What's he want?" Thad asks.

It's just one word. One lovely little word. *Hi.*

"He's saying 'Hi.'"

"Lame," Thad says. "Don't write back."

But I've already texted *hi* back. "Too late," I say.

Thad lunges forward and grabs the phone out of my hands. He lets out one of his feral laughs and rushes back to the down escalator, where he leaps up two stairs at a time.

I start to go after him, jumping onto the up escalator, but he yells, "Cheater!" So I jump off, and hop over to the bottom of the down escalator. The stairs are rolling toward me. I grab high up the handrail and take a giant leap, and then start running up the stairs as fast as I can. I manage to make it all the way up, even if I am huffing and puffing, and probably even starting to get some pit stains.

Thad is waiting patiently, with a smug look on his face.

"What?" I ask.

"So the question now is, do you want to go out Saturday?" His voice is all creamy and gooey, and he has this funny puppy-dog look on his face.

WHAT? Is Thad Bell asking me out? Oh no! Retract! Withdraw! Abort mission!

He seems to know what I'm thinking, and he laughs. He holds up my phone. "Those aren't *my* words, dorkface. That's from *Loserboy*."

I feel a jolt of annoyance. "You're *breaching* my privacy!"

"Congratulations, Collins. You're going to be a heartbreaker," he says. "Have him take you somewhere *romantic*." He rolls his eyes before tossing my phone to me, and luckily—but only luckily!—I catch it. *Is Nick really asking me out!?* It's like my eyes can't get to his text quickly enough. The text is exactly how Thad read it.

"It just makes me wonder," Thad says.

"Wonder what?"

"Is it really *him* who's asking you out?" He gives me a sideways look. "Or is it his left butt cheek? You just might want to make sure you know who's asking." Then he practically chokes on his jungle cry of laughter.

A laugh stirs in my own throat, but I say, "*Ha-ha*. You're so funny. I'm just *CRACK-ing* up."

"Good to know," he says. "*BUTT*..." He pauses and holds up a finger, as if making some incredible point. "BUTT on that note, I gotta go."

I smirk. "Ha!" I say it, rather than laugh. "Of course."

He looks at me for a second. And then another second. And just when it starts to get almost weird, he says, "So, I didn't really want to tell you this, but speaking of salsa, you've had like a gallon of it on your chin for the last hour."

And then he skates away, leaving me red with both salsa and shame.

preguntar *to ask*

yo pregunto
tú preguntas
ella pregunta
nosotros preguntamos
ellos preguntan

It's raining the next morning, so my mom drops me off in front of the school. I dash toward the front door and hear a car honk. I look back—it's Mrs. Wainwright, waving at me from an otherwise empty car. I wave stiffly back, surprised, and then, right as I get inside the door, I hear *Nicolás* call my name.

My name has never sounded so beautiful.

I turn around to see him trotting toward the open doors. "Hey," he says, pushing his wet hair back from his forehead.

"Hey," I say back, kind of shyly. I am, after all, wearing a bright yellow rain poncho. Oh, blasted rainy days! Mariela, where are you?

Officer Dirk interrupts us. "FIRE HAZARD! CLEAR THE ENTRANCE!"

We scoot over to the side of the lobby, and Nick looks at me in this little-bit-melty way and says, *"Sooo."*

"Sooo," I say. Also melty.

"So, about Saturday," he says.

"Yes?" I say, feeling tingly in the tips of things—my fingers, my toes, my nose. My uneven earlobes. I'd responded to his text asking me out the second that Thad skated off. Actually, I typed and deleted *WITH EVERY CELL OF MY BEING*, then typed and deleted *There are few things in this world that would make me as happy*, typed and deleted *I would love to!*, typed and deleted *That sounds like fun*. And then typed and sent the oh-so-brilliant *Sure*.

"Do you want to go to a movie or something?"

Wait. Not a movie. Somewhere romantic. And I'm stumped. There are no beaches nearby, no horse-drawn carriages, no cabanas.

"Well—"

"Or Starbucks? The one we used to go to?" he asks. He pants in his sort-of-laughing-nervously way.

Starbucks. Must it be? I'm about to agree, just to have a plan with him—any plan—but he suddenly says, "I know! The park. We can have a picnic or something."

I wonder if the whole school can hear my heart beating. It feels like it's on a PA system.

There is no other place I'd rather be, I think. But then he says, "Okay, great," and I realize I HAVE SAID THAT OUT LOUD.

But I don't have that much time to be mortified. Officer Dirk blasts, "MOVE! NOW!"

I'm blocked by a gaggle of seventh graders on the left, and a roost of pudgy teachers on the right, so Nick grabs my pinkie—GRABS MY PINKIE!—and leads me from the main hall through the science hall, and even though lights buzz above us, shoes squeak against the tile, and the aroma wafting from the cafetorium is the sour, tinny smell of canned spinach, I'm so happy I could faint.

I'm almost late for first period, so I don't get to see Sirina until lunch. I tell her the minute I see her. Well, actually, Amelia blurts it out the second Sirina sits down at the table with us. I guess I had trouble keeping my mouth shut while we waited for Sirina to buy her precious Chipwich.

"When is this supposed to happen?" Sirina asks all too calmly, her mouth full of ice cream.

"Saturday."

"*Oh my darling Clementine,*" Amelia says to me. "I think he's looking over here right now."

"Don't look!" Jordan says.

So I do my best not to, even though it feels like there's a magnet pulling my head in his direction. "Is he still looking?"

"No, but Axyl's looking at Jordan!" Amelia says.

Jordan goes rigid with excitement and squeals. "Really?"

"Act natural!" Amelia says. "Okay, he stopped."

Sirina turns back to me. "So I called the police again. About the official report?"

"You did?" I say.

"Of course. And guess what I found out?"

"What?"

"There *is* no police report."

"Huh? How is that possible?"

"Yeah," she says. "According to the police, there is no broken window. There is no crime." She narrows her eyes and shakes her head. "I know he's up to something."

"Nick?" I ask.

"No, dummy," she says. She looks at me like I've lost it. "Just FYI, Nick isn't the center of the universe. I meant Officer Dirk. *He's* up to something."

"Oh, right," I say. "Yeah, sounds like it."

Jordan starts calling our names. "Mabry! Sirina! Okay, so what if we don't get dates for the Cotillion?"

"We're getting dates! Come on!" Amelia argues.

"Well, I'm just saying, if we don't, why don't the four of us just go as a group?" Jordan suggests.

"Mabry will have a date," Sirina says. She doesn't sound too pleased about it, though. "Nick'll ask her."

My heart flutters, but I try to stay cool. "You think so?"

May I have this dance, he'll ask me, holding his left hand out. And I will curtsy—

"Probably. And then you'll have your chance to break his—"

"I *know!*" I say, slightly irritated. She can be such a buzzkill some-times. "I mean, *shhh.* Let's just see if he actually asks me, okay?"

"Fine," she says, sounding irritated, too.

That night, I lie awake thinking about Sirina. I've been feeling bad about things since lunch. I know how frustrated she is, and I don't blame her. It seems like we're getting nowhere with anything on the window incident.

Sorry about earlier, I text her.

I'm sorry, too.

I was a snit.

I was a snot.

Jajaja, I write back. Which is Spanish for *hahaha.*

Good night, my purple-hearted castle raptor, she writes back.

Good night, my levelheaded cuttlefish.

It's good to know that even when it's not a great day, there's always a good night.

compartir *to share*

yo comparto

tú compartes

ella comparte

nosotros compartimos

ellos comparten

It's Saturday afternoon.

    Nicolás is at my door. *Be still, my acrobatic heart.*

Nicolás is at my door with a picnic basket and a blanket. *Dreams really do come true.*

Nicolás is at my door and my mom calls to me from the kitchen, "Mabry, did Hunter already poop?"

And so do nightmares.

This is one of the ways I know the woman has never *truly* been in love.

"*Mother!*" I yell. "I have company!"

"Oh, sorry," she says, coming out of the kitchen. "Oh, hi, Nick."

"Hi, Ms. Collins."

"Mabry"—my mom looks right at my mouth—"is that my lipstick?"

"We better go," I announce.

"You're kind of dressed up for a picnic," she continues, looking my red sleeveless turtleneck and black skirt up and down. And maybe I am, but this is not just a picnic, this is a Junior Cotillion proposal. It just *has* to be. Her eyes land on my feet. I'm wearing a pair of strappy sequined heels that I found on the clearance rack at Forever 21. "You're wearing those?"

"*Mother,*" I say in a seething whisper.

"Why don't I drop you off at the park?"

"It's. Not. Far," I tell her, very quietly. "And. It's. A. Very. Nice. Day." I look at her with wide, pleading eyes, and a vise-tight smile.

She finally stops badgering us and we start on our walk. Well, for the first ten steps or so, I am walking. I am tall, elegant—the right girl for the shoes. Then it moves into teetering. For the next twenty steps, I feel like the force of gravity has changed. I am off-center, unbalanced, a little shaky. Then our walk becomes a wobble, where I am tossed from side to side, grasping for street signs, lampposts, stray shoulders.

Nick grabs my wrist—skin-to-skin contact!—to steady me. We stand there, gazing into each other's eyes, while my heels sink slowly into the soft ground. My shoes are stuck, and I don't even care. But then Stephen drives by and waves at us on his way to our house, which pretty much ruins the mood.

And then several things continue to do the same. I have to take off my shoes completely, just to stay ambulatory. And when we get to the park, we discover it's filled with screaming children. We find an open picnic table, but it happens to be right next to an arguing family—"You were supposed to bring the cheese!" "I *did*!" "NOT THAT KIND OF CHEESE!" "Mom, I want to go home!" "You smell awful! WHAT DID YOU STEP IN?"—so we have to move. And when we're moving, a little dog runs up to Nick and tries to latch on to his leg. This is hardly the romantic date I had envisioned, and we have to go deeper and deeper into the park, where there is less grass and more trees, and then—

I practically hear a chorus of angels. There, under a leafy canopy, is the perfect spot. Streaks of sun shoot between the branches of the trees above. I think I hear a babbling brook.

Nick unfolds the blanket and I help him shake it out and lay it on the soft ground. We sit down and I can't help wondering how many Glendas and Dylans are under us, their little worm hearts beating away. So *romantic.*

Nick looks at me shyly. "Are you thirsty?"

"Oh," I say. "Sure."

He reaches back into the basket and brings out a bottle of sparkling cider, which he twists open with finesse. He's brought salami and some fancy cheese, along with some wafery crackers. He's going to ask—he is! He's just trying to set the mood. We'll talk, we'll laugh, maybe we'll intertwine fingers and talk some more.

Except it hits me that I have no idea what to talk about. What do *lovers* talk about, when there are no kidnappings, or blackmailings, or secret babies to fight about? I try to summon a scene from *La Vida Rica.* I can picture a music-filled but otherwise silent montage—a candlelit dinner, a walk on the beach, an adorable moment of being caught, laughing wildly, in the rain—but it seems like if the lovers aren't embracing, trouble is brewing.

Nick takes a bite of salami and stares at me. Is he that nervous? *Ask me to the Cotillion, Nicolás. Oh, just ask me!*

He finally opens his mouth for words, not food, but it's to ask if I want some salami.

I say, "I'll be right back."

I scurry off toward the bathrooms, leaving him with a full mouth. I go behind the building and call Thad.

"Collins!" he says as a greeting.

"I need your help."

"Dude, what have you gotten yourself into?"

"This isn't funny. I'm at the park with Nick—"

"I hope it's a day of rainbows and unicorns and faeries—that's faeries with an *e*."

I don't have time to joke with him. "Listen—"

"How are his tiny ears?"

"What? Oh, they're fine, but—"

He laughs. "Do you have to talk really loud? Like Officer Dirk?"

"*You* know Officer Dirk?"

"Everybody knows Dirk. Anyway, so, did he ask you to that dance yet?"

"The Cotillion? No," I say, growing frustrated. "Not yet. It's like he wants to, but he's forgotten how to talk completely. And I have no idea what to say. So we're just staring at each other and it's weird. *That's* why I'm calling. "

"Oh, well, that's easy. Just ask him questions about himself. I'm sure it's his favorite subject."

It sounds easy enough.

"No-brainer," he adds.

"Okay, thanks."

We hang up and I go back to Nick, who is very close to polishing off the salami.

"Everything okay?" he asks.

"Yeah, everything fine—it's great."

"Good." Pant-laugh.

Oh no. That pant-laugh. Is that one of those flaws? No. I won't have it. No more flaws. No, thank you very much.

I sit down. "So, Nick—so." I look around. What to ask him—*what!?*

I grasp for something—*anything*. "What would you say your favorite color is?"

Ugh.

He looks a little surprised by my question, but then he smiles and says, "Green, I think. What's yours?"

I tell him, kind of throaty-like, "*Well, I love red.*" As it's, of course, the color of passion.

He nods. We look at each other, and then both look away quickly. I take a sip of my sparkling cider. And another.

"And, *so tell me*," I try again, "where were you born?"

"Louisiana," he tells me.

I picture a sleepy Southern town. For some reason, there are horse-drawn carriages. The women all wear puffy dresses, and their hair is swept into glamorous updos with cascading curls. They fan themselves while crying, *De-uh Lawd*. I imagine him in a suit with long tails, his hair slicked back. He is tipping his hat toward me, and he says, in a Southern accent, *May I request the* honah *of your presence?*

"*Why, yes,*" I say.

"Huh?" He is looking at me strangely, I notice, as my eyes flutter open.

"Oh, sorry." I swallow. "I thought— Well, what did you say?"

"I just said, 'What about you?' You know—where were *you* born?"

"Chicago," I say, and try to take another sip from my empty plastic cup.

"Chicago's nice," he says, refilling my cup.

"Yes," I say, although I don't really know. All I know about it really is that's where Flat Stanley lived. "The Windy City," I tell him.

The Windy City. What is the matter with me?

"So," Nick says, "do you like salami?" He takes a piece and holds it in front of my face, as if showing it off to me.

"Yes, it's beautiful," I say. "All the—uh, pepper pieces."

He still holds it there, smiling lazily at me.

"And—the—*delicious* lard dots?" I say-ask.

And then he says, "Don't you want a bite?"

And I realize very suddenly that he is trying to *feed me*. So, despite the fact that I feel like some awkward baby penguin, I say, "Yes," just so my mouth will have something to do, other than spurt out stupid things. I accidentally hit an incisor against his thumb. *Yeesh!* I'm not a baby penguin at all! I'm practically a Rottweiler!

"Oh, sorry!" I say too quickly. I try to chew daintily.

"It's okay," he says.

"Um, I'll be back," I say again, and once more scurry off to the bathroom building.

Thad answers the phone already laughing. "Dude, he's going to think you have the runs or something."

"Stop," I say, cringing. *Dear god, let's hope not.* "Listen, he tried to feed me!"

He says, in a maybe-British accent. *"Isn't that what* lovahs *do? Share their food?"* And then he laughs.

I sigh.

"Be careful what you wish for, Collins," he says.

"Okay, you're helpful. Bye!" I say, and hang up.

I walk back to our blanket, not feeling confident at all. But when I get there, he is leaning back on his elbows, smiling at me. He sweeps his sandy-blond hair off his forehead, and it hits me like a brick in the stomach how gorgeous he is, despite his tiny ears. He holds his hand out in my direction, and I feel myself sail toward him, swept by the wind closer and closer still. I am Rose on the deck of the *Titanic*, the wind rippling through my hair. *I am alive!*

And I am facedown on the blanket, my arms spread wide.

"You, uh, okay?"

I roll over, feeling like an idiot. "Yep."

But then a bird chirps nearby. He looks toward the tree. "You hear that?" he asks.

"Uh, yes." I sit up slightly and lean back on my elbows, like he's doing. I smile a little. "It's nice." And then, through a wide clearing in the trees, I see the sky. I think I even see a heart-shaped cloud in the making. For the first time since we've gotten here, I take a big breath in. Now *this* is romantic. Now *this* is what lovers do. Maybe we don't actually have to talk at all. Maybe we just have to *enjoy*. It's no less of a verb, is it?

I stare into his deep blue eyes, taking in the lighter blue flecks, watching the pupils respond to the shift in clouds, feeling like after all the worry about talk, words don't even matter anymore. And then he says my name.

He smiles at me. Then he looks down and clears his throat. "Mabry, I wanted to—"

Buzz. It's my phone. My stupid, stupid phone.

Sirina.

"Do you need to get that?" he asks.

"No," I say, but that doesn't feel right, so I hit the answer button anyway. "Hi," I say.

"Hey. Guess what?"

"What? 'Cause I'm actually out with Nick."

"Oh, right! Can you call me the minute you're done?"

"*Yesss,*" I hiss into the phone.

"Okay, hurry up," she says.

"*Okay,*" I say. I don't wait for the good-byes.

"Sorry. You were saying?"

"Yeah," he says. He smiles and picks at a thread in the blanket. He clears his throat. "I wanted to tell you something."

Tell. Not ask. Can you just *tell* someone you want them to go to the Cotillion with you? It's a bit rude. But maybe he just needs me that much. *Come with me, my dear Mabry, to the Cotillion. I will likely die if you don't.*

Okay, it makes sense now.

He sits up and takes a breath. He looks at me with a pained expression on his face.

"What?" I say with a new urgency.

He sighs and shakes his head, looking away again.

"Nick?"

"I wanted to say that I'm sorry."

"For what?"

"About the thing with my mom," he says. "Her calling you that day and, *well*, you know."

Oh. *Ooooh.*

"It's just that she kept telling all her friends I had a girlfriend, and it just got embarrassing. So I told her that I was going to break up with you, you know, just to get her off my back, and when I didn't, she thought she was doing me some sort of favor."

I can't help but feel thrilled. "So you *didn't* want to break up with me?"

"I mean, not, like, totally break up. But you were kind of intense, you know. You're different now," he says. He goes back to picking a thread in the blanket.

I am struck again with not knowing what to say, and somehow asking his middle name doesn't seem to be the thing to do.

He looks at me. I guess I have a weird look on my face, because his eyes go wide, and he says, "But I mean that in a good way! I *like* it. I like *you*. A lot."

An entirely different expression takes over his face. A soft one. Dare I say, a *loving* one? Well, definitely a *me too* one. And then he says, "The reason I said green? When you asked me my favorite color?"

"Uh-huh?"

"It was blue until today."

"It was?"

"Yeah. But green is the color of your eyes. So that's my favorite color now."

A sigh escapes me. My heart does a little leap, and slips—at last—soundlessly into the sweet, syrupy pool of love.

Nick looks up. "Great," he says. "Storm clouds."

My phone buzzes again.

"Four words," Sirina says when I grudgingly pick it up. "I have an idea. Bring Nick back to your house, and I'll meet you guys there."

She's gone over her quota, but I can't help but be intrigued. "You want me to bring Nick?" *Is it possible that she's somehow seen the light of our love? That she'll give us her blessing?*

"Yeah. I need him to do something for us. It's about the YoJo."

So no blessing after all.

"So can you guys hurry?" she asks. *The gall of her!*

Even though I'm not ready for this date to end, I think of our little snit-snot thing the other day and don't want a repeat of that. Plus, that heart-shaped cloud is starting to sprinkle rain, which is only good for worms. So I tell her, "Hold your horses, would you? We're heading back now."

Nick walks back to my house with me. Sirina's already there when we arrive, playing *Madden* with Aaron. There's a plate of nuked hot dogs sitting between them, bunless monstrosities that are bulging in weird spots. Hunter is resting his head on the couch, his big, begging eyes focused on the deformed hot dogs.

"Look at you, Martha 'A-Bag' Stewart," I say to my brother.

"Hey, loser"—my brother says this in an upbeat way that makes it sound almost like a compliment. His eyes shift briefly from the screen to Nick—"and friend. Want a dog?"

"No, thanks. We just ate," Nick says.

"I'm not talking about the *hot dogs*," he says. "I'm talking about Sirina here. *Woof, woof!*"

Sirina wallops A-Bag in the face with a decorative pillow at a crucial point for A-Bag. He loses the game and practically cries about it. Sirina gets up to meet us in the foyer, and Hunter, as usual, follows.

"You're not going to believe it," she says to me and Nick. "I found something that might help us crack this case. A sketch artist!"

"What? How?" I ask.

"My dad's friend used to work with the police department. He said he'll do a sketch if Nick will meet with him. What do you think, Nick. Will you?"

He looks a little nervous. "What do I have to do?"

"Just tell him what you saw," she says.

"But I already told Mabry what I saw. I didn't get a great look," he says. He turns to me. "You know that."

"Don't worry, Nick," Sirina says. "Some of it's like multiple choice."

He'll show you different features and you can tell him if it matches what you remember."

He shrugs. "Okay, I guess."

"It won't be perfect," Sirina says, "But it'll be something. Which is better than nada. Which is kind of what we have. A whole lotta nada." She smiles at him a little bit, and I find myself smiling pretty big. I'm happy to see *her* happy. It's like that seesaw is finally balanced.

Nick's mom pulls up in the driveway. "Thanks, Nick," I say. "I had fun."

And he meets my eyes, and holds my gaze. And then he says, without looking away, something that makes my heart get back on that hot-air balloon.

He says, "Me too."

29

Give + Get

Aurelio is still in the desert. It has been *treinta y un días*—thirty-one days. His skin is dark, his hair is long, and he can barely crawl. The credits roll over a still shot of him lying facedown in the sand.

Thad's phone buzzes. He turns off the TV and answers it. He hears the *La Vida Rica* theme song in the background. Mabry must have been watching, too.

"Hey, Salsa Breath," he says.

"Hey, Cheese Face," she answers.

"How was it?"

"How was what?"

"The show. I can hear the music."

"Oh," she says. "Stressful. I don't think Aurelio's going to make it."

"Seriously," Thad says. "I mean, can someone even survive thirty-one days with no water?"

"Well, I think he drinks from cactuses sometimes. I mean, he's got to if—" She stops herself. "Wait a second. You're still watching it?"

"I don't watch it—I just sometimes turn on the TV, and there Aurelio is. So sometimes we just coexist." It's not too much of a stretch. It's not like he watches it like she does. He sometimes needs a laugh. "Anyway, what do you need?"

"I'm calling to tell you I think we're getting close," Mabry says. "Nick just texted to ask me what my favorite flower is."

That's easy. "Roses!" Thad says. "Red, of course."

She huffs into the phone, and then says, "No, you're wrong. *Yellow.*"

"You're lying," Thad says.

"Okay, whatever. So red roses *are* my favorite. *Sor*-ry!"

"Dude." He feels a laugh bubble up. "You can't tell him that. Just cross off any flower you can get at 7-Eleven. You gotta make him work a little harder than that."

"So what should I say?" she asks.

"I don't know. I'm not a girl. I don't do flowers."

"Orchids?"

"I don't know. Can you get them at the same place you can buy a Ding Dong?" Thad asks.

"Probably not?" It's a statement, but she sounds unsure.

"How about this?" he says. "If I've heard of it, it's too easy. Scratch it off your list. And I've heard of orchids."

He listens to her breathing, thinking. Finally, she asks, "How about oleander?"

He makes a buzzing sound like *eeeeeeh* and says, "My great-aunt was named Oleander. I just didn't know it was a flower. But that would still be a no."

"Mums?"

"Uh, definitely no." He remembers mums. Mums are a hospital flower. "No mums. Trust me. Bad choice."

"What about gladiola?"

"Everyone's heard of that. Too easy," Thad tells her.

"Everyone *hasn't* heard of that," Mabry argues.

"Okay, well, *I* have."

"How have *you* heard of a gladiola?"

"I don't know. There's like a Febreze spray of it or something." Thad bites his lip to keep from laughing. He's glad she can't see him.

There's another pause. For a second, he wonders if they've been disconnected. Then she asks, "Jerothium?"

Even though he's never heard of it, he says, "Would you like a Slurpee with that?"

"Are you *kidding* me?" Now she's laughing. "Jerothium's not even *real*! I made it up!"

"Oh," he says quietly. Then he rips into a laugh. "Okay, sorry."

"What is your *deal*?" Mabry asks. "Why do you want me to make it so hard for him?"

"I just don't want you to be so predictable," he tells her. It's an excuse, but it's still true.

"You're the predictable one," she says. "I bet you're going to sit around all night eating Cheetos in your underwear. No, wait— *Funyuns*!"

"Yeah, I wish, okay?"

"Well," she says with a curious tone in her voice, "what *are* you going to be doing?"

"Ha! Having to go. See you tomorrow," he says.

"Thad? About tomorrow, want to meet over here? My house or something?"

"Nope. I gotta go."

But she keeps at it. "Don't you ever get tired of the mall?"

What's there to get tired of? The easiness of it? The frivolousness? Come on. Everything about it is optional. It's hard to think much about life and death when you're deciding between bean dip and guacamole. Peppermint gum or spearmint. Black shoelaces or red. But she won't understand that, and he doesn't want to explain it anyway, so he pretends not to have heard her, and hangs up.

encontrar *to find*

yo encuentro

tú encuentras

ella encuentra

nosotros encontramos

ellos encuentran

That night, I'm having dinner with the family. By that, I mean my mom, A-Bag, and Stephen. Stephen's made chicken Divan. It's chicken with broccoli sauce, and A-Bag is busy picking all the teeny, tiny green buds out of his. My mom's irritated.

"You can't even taste it!" she says to A-Bag.

But I guess by saying that, she accidentally offends Stephen, who looks a little hurt, and says, "Well, it just requires a smart palate."

"I hurl if I eat broccoli," A-Bag says.

"That was once," my mom says, "when you were four."

"I'm serious," A-Bag says. "I'll yack."

"Why don't you and your dumb palate just go and rinse the sauce off?" I suggest.

He looks at me. "Good idea!" And he gets up to go into the kitchen. We hear the faucet turn on.

"Mabry," my mom says, "don't encourage your brother when he's like this."

"It's fine, Ellen," Stephen says.

A-Bag comes back, sits down with his naked piece of chicken, holds it above his mouth, and eats it like a fish going for bait.

"You're disgusting!" I say.

My mom just closes her eyes and shakes her head.

"What? You said not to encourage him! That's what I'm doing!" I say.

"Aaron, don't forget about your squash," my mom says.

"I already forgot about it," he says, and starts practically choking on his laughter.

I try not to laugh. I mean, I think it's funny, but there's no way I want to give him that satisfaction.

My mom turns to Stephen. "I'm sorry."

Stephen just pats her hand. "One day he'll appreciate a nice Divan."

"One day he'll act like he has manners," my mom says.

"*I* quite like the chicken Divan," I add.

My mom smiles at me.

Stephen does, too. "Well, that's very good to hear!" And then he goes into the history of chicken Divan, and how the word *divan* meant some kind of fancy sofa, and that the restaurant that came up with it was trying to make it sound like something rich people would eat. Which is okay-enough interesting, but then he starts going into the history of *all* poultry dishes, which is more than anyone should have to bear. My eyes start to feel glassy and my ears stop recognizing words.

I have to interrupt. It becomes a matter of survival, as it's starting to feel very possible to be bored to death. "Can we possibly talk about flowers?" I ask, very politely.

"Can I *possibly* leave this table and never return, ever?" A-Bag asks, very impolitely.

My mom excuses him. She actually says, "You know what, Aaron? Just go. You'd be doing the rest of us a favor." So I know she's fed up.

When the attention is back on me, I ask, "What do you think is the prettiest flower in the universe?"

"Oh!" my mom says, looking pleased. "Are you doing a project on spring flowers?"

"Sort of," I say.

"I like sunflowers," my mom says.

"Yes, the sunflower is nice because it's a good mix of form *and* function. They're pretty, *and* you can eat the seeds." That's Stephen, of course.

"I don't know," I say. "I mean, the sunflower's cute, but I mean truly beautiful."

"Practicality *is* true beauty," Stephen says.

Which explains why he bought my mom a heating pad for her last birthday.

"Orchids are nice," my mom says.

"Well, Ellen, sure, orchids are lovely, but you have to be more specific than that," Stephen says, snickering. "There are twenty thousand species of orchids."

She looks at him like she's impressed. "Really? How'd you know that?" She gives him this stupid look of admiration.

"No orchids," I say. "What else?"

"How about lily of the valley?" my mom suggests.

"Yeah." I give a sarcastic snort. I mean, I may not know a ton about flowers, but I *do* know Hilda tried to get rid of Cristina by garnishing her drink with a lily of the valley. "If you want to kill someone! They're poisonous!"

"That's true," Stephen says. Then he sits back. "You know, now that you mention it, I'd have to say the most beautiful flower in the world is the king protea. It's a South African flower—when it opens up, it looks like a king's crown!" He shakes his head and lets out a low whistle. "It's *stunning*."

"Sounds *wonderful*," my mom says.

"I've never heard of it," I say.

"Well, go look it up in the encyclopedia. Or is that *so 2014*?"

I don't even know where to start with him. I just look at him, and he winks. "I'm kidding, Mabry. Just go put it in the Googler."

And even though he's said it that way, I think I will. I get up and start clearing the plates, enjoying my role as the Favorite Child.

As I go into the kitchen, I hear my mom say, in kind of a buttery way, "How do you know so much?"

And Stephen explains how it's the name of the South African cricket team, and how the name changed from something else, and then starts yammering on about some near shakeup with the South African flag. *Blah, blah, blah.*

I go up to my room and Google it, and sure enough, Stephen's right. The king protea is a gorgeous flower. I finally have my answer for Nick.

I've got to hand it to Stephen. It's elegant, and colorful, and unique. And it's definitely not something you could get on a Slim Jim run, so take that, Thaddeus Bell.

Take that.

Good night, my strawberry-scented cantaloupe, Sirina texts me that night.

Good night, my sand-filled melon head, I text her back.

And then I put my phone down and try my very best to sleep, despite all my excitement. Despite the fact that The Love of My Life is nearly mine again. But it's about as easy as crossing the Atacama Desert. No offense to Aurelio.

confiar *to entrust*

yo confío

tú confías

ella confía

nosotros confiamos

ellos confían

"King protea," I announce when I join Thad at our food-court table.

"Queen Victoria," he says back. "Um, what are we talking about, Collins?"

"My favorite flower. You're right. I'm over roses."

"Glad to hear it. Such a cliché. Hey, want to thumb-wrestle for a burrito? Loser buys."

"Fine. Lefties?"

"No," he says. "Right." He removes his glove. It's the first time I've seen his hand *fully* naked like this since, well, fourth grade. It's pale, and still Frankenstein-y from his skating accident, with crisscrossing pink lines.

"Are you sure? Because it's still kind of ugly," I joke.

He just does his little half smile and cups his fingers around mine. "Ready, set," he calls out, as our thumbs dance right, then left. "Go." Our thumbs wiggle around in a standoff. He presses mine down, but the lotion I recently applied helps my thumb squirm free. But then he traps it once again and starts counting, "One, two, three." And then he declares victory over our thumb match.

And I stomp on his foot under the table and declare victory over our toe match. Which leads to his foot landing on mine, and mine on his, and me using both feet, and—

"Mabry?"

I draw in an involuntary breath at the sound of the voice. I look up. It's Nick.

"Hi-*ii*," I say, my breath catching in my throat.

"Hi," he says.

I glance over at Thad, but he's looking in the other direction. I feel like I've been caught cheating, but I don't know on what, or even on who.

"Do you remember—?" I start to introduce them, but Thad is getting up, putting his gloves back on. "Hey, where are you going?" I ask him.

He murmurs something about salsa.

"Thad!" I say.

"*Thad?*" Nick says. "Thad Bell?"

Thad drops his head a little and turns around slowly. He crosses his arms in front of his chest.

Nick is staring at him. Intensely. It's all sorts of weird.

"You guys remember each other, don't you?" I pretend I don't know what Thad thinks of Nick.

Nick nods. "Yeah, of course. We were friends."

"Yep," Thad says. "We *were*." There's an emphasis on the past tense.

"I thought you moved away," Nick says.

"I did," Thad says.

Nick takes a breath and shakes his head. "This is weird," he says. "I feel like I've seen you recently, but I don't know—"

"I doubt it," Thad says.

"Nick, sweetie," we hear. It's his mom. She's calling him from out in front of the Levi's store. "I've got four pairs waiting for you in the fitting room!"

I shrink in my seat.

"Oh, is that Mabry? *Hiiii*, Mabry," she calls out, embarrassing me. She waves wildly, like we're old friends. I wonder how she can act so nice when she's the one who actually dumped me, but I am reminded of Hilda, who can steal your boyfriend and trash-talk you in the *mercado*, but then smile and wave *hola* to you the next day. And also steal your baby.

I smile and wave tamely back.

His mom hurries over, "Mabry, how are you, sugar? And who's this?"

"It's Thad Bell, Mom," Nick says. "Remember him?"

"Well, my goodness! *Thad!* You're becoming so handsome, dear. How are you? I haven't seen your mom in forever. How's she doing?"

"She's, uh, you know, okay, I guess."

"Probably busy as ever. Is she here with you?" Mrs. Wainwright looks around hopefully.

Thad stares at the tile floor. "No."

"Well, tell her to come see me when she can! I'm working at the Hairport now. Let her know, okay, dear?" She doesn't wait for an answer. "Nicky, honey, come on. Four pairs to try on."

"When did you say you moved back?" Nick asks Thad.

Thad stays quiet, so I answer. "About six months ago."

"Nicky, come on, you can text him later," his mom says, turning around.

They go off, and I look at Thad. He looks like a different version of himself. His eyes are wide, but shadowed. His jaw looks tense. He looks like he needs to be given soup and a warm blanket, like an earthquake survivor.

"Will you please sit back down?" I ask him.

He does.

"So. *That* was awkward," I say.

He doesn't say anything.

"Okay, you're acting way too weird. I don't know why you hate him so much but clearly, this isn't about a Star Wars figurine."

I expect at least a smirk, but he just starts bobbing up and down.

"Are you ever going to tell me what really happened between you two?"

Nothing.

I take a deep breath and exhale through my mouth. I don't like how things feel right now. I just want to go back to thumb wars, or foot wars, or one of our normal battles.

"Rematch?" I ask, placing my hand on my table.

He doesn't even look at me.

"Okay, fine, I lost fair and square. I guess you want your loser burrito now."

"I don't want a burrito."

"A 'chong?" I joke.

He just shakes his head.

I feel like the world has come to a sudden stop. "Jeez, I wish I knew what the problem is right now."

"I hate. *Questions like that!*" he says.

"Fine," I say, offended by his sharp tone. "That's the last chimichanga *I'll* offer you."

"No, I mean . . ." He takes a breath and says in a mocking tone,

"'How's your family? How's your mom?'"

I can understand why it would be hard to answer questions about how his dad is, but— "Why do you hate when people ask about your mom?"

He shakes his head again, still bobbing up and down.

"What?"

"You know what, Collins?" There are no zoo animals in his sarcastic laugh. "If your *La Vida Rica* people could come and rewrite my whole life, I would totally be on board, okay?"

"Is your mom—?" I don't want to ask this, and thankfully he cuts me off.

"She's alive, yeah," he says.

"Sorry, I didn't mean—"

He looks down at the table. I hear him exhale. His shoulders drop away from his ears. "She was in the accident with my dad. Part of her spine got injured. She's alive, but she—she still can't walk. Which is one of the reasons I'm not back in school yet. We live with my aunt now, but sometimes they need me around, you know?"

"Oh," I say, feeling like the biggest idiot who ever breathed. "Thad, I'm—"

"I know, I know, you're sorry. Everyone's sorry. It sucks." He finally looks at me. "I'm sorry, too, okay?"

I nod.

"No, for, like, snapping like that. At you, all right?"

"All right," I say.

He picks at his cuticle. I press the tips of my fingers in the metal mesh of the table.

"My mom's only been able to leave the house twice since we moved into my aunt's house."

"Twice?" I say, shocked. "Does she have a wheelchair?"

"Well, yeah, but it's hard to get her in and out of it. And then there's like seven steps up from the sidewalk to the front door. Have you ever carried someone up and down seven steps?"

Of course not, I want to say, but I just shake my head.

"Well, it's not easy," he says. "It takes two people, and my aunt has a bad back."

"So your mom's, like, *trapped*?" I think of Graciela, when she was living in the cave and a boulder fell down the hill and trapped her inside. She lived off cave water, moss, and the memories of her love for Marcos for six episodes. It was harrowing.

"I guess, sort of, in a way," he says. "We're hoping to get one of those ramps soon, or move somewhere that's easier for her—"

"Wait. Move?" I ask.

"I don't know." He shrugs. "Not anytime really soon, though."

Don't move.

He looks up at the skylight. "But even with a ramp, that's only half the story. You don't think about it much if you don't need them, but it's hard to get around on wheels."

And then it hits me. "That's why you started skating? To see what it's like on wheels?"

"Yeah." He looks at me. "You don't realize where you can go—or not go—until you're on them."

Wow. So all this skating around. He's not trying to be cool. He's trying to be—*helpful*. To map out the world for his mom. To give her a sense of freedom.

"Okay, Collins, stop looking at me like that," he says. "It doesn't make me a saint or anything. *Don't* feel sorry for me, or for her, okay? Just *don't*."

I nod. I breathe a little, just enough to say, "Okay." Although I'm not even sure what I do feel. I'm aware that if I were on *La Vida Rica*,

I'd start making out with him. But that's not what I feel like doing. My arms want to wrap around him, and yet they also want to stay glued protectively at my sides. I feel like I'm a marshmallow burnt a little on the inside, if that's even somehow possible.

"Anyway," he says. "Can you see now why I don't like questions?"

"Oh," I say. "Yeah."

I wish all those things hadn't happened to you, I think, but saying such a thing out loud makes it seem ridiculously obvious. Like when people say *I'm against crime,* or *Drugs are bad.*

He shrugs. "It's kind of a strange situation, you know?"

"Yeah," I say.

After a few minutes of wordlessness, I say, "I guess I have a strange situation, too."

"Regale me," he says, smirking. Finally.

I laugh, kind of. "Well, my mom's pretty normal. Boringly normal, actually. But my dad? I have no idea. I never even met him. My *mom* never even met him."

"So, what—?" He seems confused. "You were hatched from an egg?" Then his eyes get wide, and he starts to grin. "That would actually explain *a lot.*"

I grin back, but I also punch him in the bicep—or what passes as a bicep. "No, dummy, one of those fertility clinics. My mom only knows my dad from a piece of paper—his resume or something. We call him Flat Stanley. Well, Aaron and I do. Secretly, sort of. "

He tries to keep a serious look on his face, but he can't. He breaks into a laugh. "Flat *Stanley?*"

"I'm *serious,*" I say, but I'm sort of laughing, too.

He leans back on the bench and takes a breath. "Wow. Aren't you worried?"

I stop laughing. "About what?"

He shakes his head.

"*What?*"

"Well, it means that your dad could be anyone! I mean, what if he's—I don't know—what if you and Nick are actually brother and sister?"

Oh. My. God. He's right! What if? *What if??* I start to feel a panic surge. I could be in love with my brother! *Gag! Retch! Puke!*

But Thad breaks into a big laugh. "I'm joking, doofus. You're not related to him."

"How do you know?"

"I mean, you definitely have your flaws, but you're not a *total* wad."

"Oh," I say, exhaling, coming back to reality. "*Ha-ha.*"

He lets out one of his trademark safari guffaws.

"Come on, I'll buy you a taco," I say.

"You said burrito earlier," he tells me.

"And you said no."

He smiles. "And you and I both know that tacos are two-for-one right now," he says.

I shrug. "So let me buy you a free taco."

"Be my guest," he says.

And then I open up my wallet and find that I have no cash. *Drat.*

He sees me rummaging through my bag. "Relax, Collins. I'll spot you the cash to buy me the free taco, and we'll call it even."

Thank god. Because oddly enough, I'm craving one bad enough to pull a Rafael. When he was homeless, he would earn meals by dancing in the street. That's where he met Elia, who turned out to be a fugitive princess from the island country of Isla Mola. But I also remember that my dancing couldn't so much as earn me a package of ketchup.

He smirks. "One condition." Thad and his *conditions*. "You have some hot sauce."

I grimace. But I am hungry. And it's free. So I agree. And you know what? Hot sauce isn't that bad, now that I respect my limits. In fact, it's not bad at all. Especially now that I know the chip trick.

Nick calls me that night.

"Hi," I say. I think he's calling about the sketch artist, who he's meeting with tomorrow, but instead he wants to talk about Thad.

"So," he says. "That was weird. Thad Bell."

"Yeah," I say.

"Are you seeing him or anything?"

"Thad? *Nooo.* Way," I say, maybe too quickly. Perhaps he was going to challenge him to a duel or something equally as romantic. "Why?"

"Just wondering," Nick says. "He seems different."

"Maybe. A little," I say. "Well, for one, he's not nine anymore. And his father died, so that's kind of an issue."

"What? He *died*?" Nick asks.

"Yeah, in a car accident. And his mom was hurt in it, too. A spinal injury, I think. She has to use a wheelchair. That's why they moved back."

"Oh. Wow," Nick says.

And then he gets quiet.

"Nick?"

"Sorry, I'm just— *Wow.* That's— I didn't know—that's rough."

"Yeah. I would think."

He's quiet again. I'm about to ask him about the jeans that he tried on today at the mall, just because I don't know what else to ask about, but he says he needs to go, so we just say good-bye.

Secrets + Lies

"Do you have any nines?"

"*Maay-bee,*" Thad says.

"Hand 'em over," his mom says, putting her palm out.

He gives her two of his remaining cards. She puts down another set, leaving three cards in her "hand," which is technically on her lap, covered with a dish towel, since her actual hand still gets tired sometimes.

He crunches up his face. "Any threes?"

A funky Jamaican tune starts playing suddenly in the other room. Thad's mom looks around. "What's that?"

"Oh, Aunt Nora changed her ringtone again," he says, grinning.

She laughs. "Okay, go fish," she says.

He picks up a queen from the top of the pile and tucks it into his hand. And then it's her turn again.

"Do you have any queens?" she asks.

"What? Seriously?" He gives her a disbelieving smile.

She just smiles at him and holds her hand out again. He hands it over. "When did you start reading my mind?" he jokes. He's glad she can't really.

She puts her cards down, a set of queens.

"Sorry, sweetheart," she says to him.

He makes a sound like *agh.* "Next time, we play blackjack or something."

"Blackjack? No thanks. You're brutal," she says. She reaches toward him and he holds on to her hands, pulling her slightly forward. Then he restacks the pillows so she can lie down in a more reclined position. "But you know what I was thinking? Origami or something. The therapist today suggested it, to keep my fingers exercised, and it sounded kind of fun."

But origami doesn't sound all that fun to him. He pictures himself making angels and butterflies. *Ugh. Sounds like Mabry's in charge or something.*

She rolls to her side, and he pulls the blanket up to her chin.

She yawns. "Wake me up in an hour or so, okay? I don't want to sleep too long."

"Okay. Good night," he says—even though it's *not* night, and *good* seems like a stretch—and he walks quietly out of her room, shutting the door behind him.

Aunt Nora is sitting at the kitchen table in front of her open laptop. "Hey, hon?" she calls to him without looking up.

"Yeah?" he says on his way to the pantry. He's craving a Little Debbie.

"That was Mrs. Vander-Pecker. The principal from the school."

Thad pauses mid-step. He feels like he's had a sudden injection of ice water into his veins. It's the worried look in her eyes that makes him think, *this*. *This* is the moment that he's been dreading. Those visits by Officer Dirk? *Recon*. And Nick must have had that moment of recognition, and ran and told his mommy. Who told the school. Of course. He'd do that. *She'd do that*.

"Okay." He sits down and takes a big breath. He studies the corner of the table. He'll start with an apology, that's always the best thing to do, and then he'll explain how upset he was that day—what he overheard Nick say. At least Aunt Nora would understand why it upset him so much.

"Well, she's really concerned. She said you haven't been keeping up too well with your online classes."

It takes Thad a second to realize that the worst thing—okay, the second or *third* worst thing—hasn't happened. Yet.

"Oh," he says, finally relaxing a little. He gets up and walks over to the pantry, because yes, he wanted that Little Debbie all along.

"Well, is that right?"

"It's pretty right, I guess." He opens the Swiss Roll and starts peeling the outer chocolate part off. He likes the cake and filling, not the fake waxy coating.

She's staring at him like she's disappointed—like he's done something wrong. Which he has, but she actually doesn't know that. *Does she?*

"I'll do better."

But Aunt Nora doesn't look all that reassured. "I really think it's time for you to enroll. I think you'll do better with a regular routine."

He doesn't say anything for a few moments. He'd rather just enjoy this Little Naked Debbie.

But she's waiting for some sort of reply.

"What about Mom?"

"She's doing so much better," Aunt Nora says. "We still need your help, but not like before. I really need you to seriously think about it."

The truth is, he thinks about going back to school a lot. What it would be like to slip back into a sort-of-regular life. To go to classes and have a locker combination and wear a stupid P.E. uniform and eat the school's version of orange-cheese nachos. To see familiar faces, and not just Mabry's.

He pictures her face. He snorts a little, thinking of the ridiculously intense look she got when she ran up the down escalator for the first time—eyebrows low, nostrils flaring, feet flailing. Hilarious. That "meaningful gaze" she tried to re-create for him, the one that made her look like a pained clown. He only told her she looked like a dragon that time because it seemed, somehow, kinder.

"It's not funny, Thad," Aunt Nora says now.

He looks over at her. "Sorry, I know."

"I really think school would be a good thing for you," Aunt Nora says.

Yeah, if the coast ever *truly* clears and the window incident becomes just another unsolved and forgotten mystery, maybe going back to school wouldn't be so bad at all.

descubrir *to discover*

It's Saturday, late afternoon, and I was due at Sirina's fifteen minutes ago. The drawing from Nick's meeting with the sketch artist should be ready, and we need to get started right away on the article that will run with it. But after a two-hour nap, I'm having trouble moving at all.

I finally roll, literally, out of bed and go downstairs for a glass of water. My mom and Stephen are on the couch in the living room watching something newsy, with Hunter at their feet. Stephen's in his science-teacher clothes—khakis and a button-down shirt with a loosened bow tie—and my mom's in her fleece sweatpants. His arm's extended along the top of the couch, and her shoulder is practically in his armpit. I know they claim they love each other, but I guess I'm glad they're not *really* in love—like, if they had romantic dinners, and

I had to worry about barging in on them. Or if I caught them outside on the patio, making out in the breeze. Now *that* would be uncomfortable. Still, I feel a little sorry for them.

"Howdy-doo," Stephen says when he sees me. He bends his arm up from the elbow, like he's about to take his arm away from the couch rim, but doesn't.

"Oh, hi, honey," my mom adds.

"I'm just getting some water," I tell them.

"Good ol' H-two-O," Stephen adds, unnecessarily.

I force a pleasant-enough smile and keep moving toward the kitchen. The doorbell rings and Hunter springs up, like all the predatory instincts that have been lazing around inside of him suddenly have some purpose. In three seconds, he's run to the door and back twice, barking so loud that my mom has to resort to gesturing to me to answer the door.

And I do. And immediately want to retreat. Because while Hunter stops barking, I am feeling my own wild panic.

It is *Nicolás.*

My Love. Holding a pink rose. In a plastic tube.

And I look like I've been stowing away in someone's attic for three weeks, like Elisabet. I am sleep-crusty and unbrushed, in penguin-patterned pajamas. *Please don't let this be The Proposal,* I think. *Not here. Not now. Not like this.* But why else would he be here?

"Mabry?" he says my name like a question, and I'm tempted to announce that I'm just her twin, who actually *has* been stowed in the attic. For thirteen years. But that I'd be happy to get the real Mabry if he can wait twenty minutes, thirty minutes tops.

But he doesn't wait for me to answer. "Sorry I didn't call or text, I just wanted to talk to you in person."

Oh, no! He is *so* going to ask me to the Cotillion, and I feel nothing but panic. This isn't the moment I've been waiting for. *"Now?"* I ask. My voice sounds harsh—stripped of its fruity richness.

"Yeah." He shifts his weight from one foot to the other. "It probably can't wait."

My mom finally comes to find out who's at the door. "Oh, hi, Nick," she says. "Oh, a flower! Let's put it in some water, Mabry."

She invites him in. I try to sneak some of the sleep out of my eye. She leads us both into the kitchen. After she finds a narrow vase, she fills it up, puts the rose in, and leaves us there.

"Thanks for the rose," I say.

"I would have gotten you that flower you said—"

"The king protea?"

"Yeah, that, but I couldn't find it anywhere."

"It's—pretty," I say. I lean over to the flower and sniff it. It *does* smell like a Ding Dong. *Darn you, Thad.*

I feel Nick's eyes bearing into me. *Oh no. He really is going to do this while I stand here looking like a bedbug.* My eyes dart all around, from the counter to his non-Frankenstein hands, from the tile floor to his feet flat on the ground, from the oven to his minuscule ears.

My phone dings from the counter. It's Sirina. *Where are you?*

I feel a flutter of relief. "Nick, I'm sorry. I've really got to go." And then I remember *why* I have to go. "Oh, how did it go with the sketch artist?"

I text her back. *On my way!*

But Sirina's text comes quickly. *Hurry up. Urgent.*

I look back up at him.

"Well, you'll see. You better go."

"Yeah, Sirina's nagging me like crazy," I say.

I walk him to the door and we say good-bye. He still looks at me in this strange, almost sad way. I feel bad that I've rushed him off, but

I don't want the memory of my Cotillion proposal to be ruined by nap breath and sleep boogers. I really don't.

I text her. *Sorry! Be there ASAP.*

I expect her to text me something like, *You're a pain in the toe knuckle sometimes, you know that?* But instead I get one that says, *Just get here now.*

Sirina's mom lets me inside and tells me Sirina's waiting in her room upstairs. When I open the door, she looks up from the computer. "You're finally here."

"Yeah, sorry," I say. "Nick stopped by out of the blue."

Her eyes narrow. "*Did* he now?"

"Yeah." I flop down on her bed. "He was acting a little bizarre, though. I think he was going to ask me to the Cotillion, but I kind of panicked."

"He came over *today*? To ask you to *the Cotillion*?" She's acting like it's the most absurd thing she's ever heard.

I tuck my chin back. "I think so. But I kind of freaked. I mean, I was still in my pajamas!"

"And let me get this straight. He didn't mention *this*?"

She angles the computer toward me. On the screen is a drawing of a brawny, bald man with a gold hoop earring.

"That looks like Mr. Clean," I say.

"Exactly!" Sirina says, her nostrils flaring. "So apparently Mr. Clean is the culprit who broke the window. Imagine that!"

"What are you talking about?" I say, shifting to the edge of her bed and sitting up. "Nick said the guy was kind of thin, and had brown hair, brown eyes—"

She's just staring at me.

"What?" I ask. "You mean he changed his story?"

"Well, that's what it looks like, doesn't it? This is the description he gave to the sketch artist!"

"Who is this sketch artist, anyway?"

She shakes her head. "Listen to you—you're doubting a professional when you should be doubting your boyfriend!"

"He's *not* my boyfriend!"

"Oh, right, Mabry. Let's just stop pretending that's not what you really want. *I* know it, *you* know it, and if *Thad* doesn't know it, then he's dumber than I ever could have thought."

I'm stunned. I think the last time she talked so harshly to me was in sixth grade, when, for like three and a half hours, I believed Hannah Coates when she told me that Sirina said Emily Wong was her best friend.

She breathes in sharply through her nose and lets it out of her mouth with a throaty hissing sound. "I'm sorry," she says, looking at me with eyes that have lost their usual spark. "I'm just so stressed. I'm sorry, Mabry."

Even though there are little pings of pain still darting around in my body, I know she means it.

"It's okay."

"I mean, this makes no sense. He didn't say anything to you about this?"

"No—" I say, but now I wonder. Is this what he wanted to talk about? Not the Cotillion at all? Was the rose just some sort of apology?

She shakes her head. "This *really* makes no sense."

"Is this"—I know the answer before I even get the question out of my mouth—"going to affect the YoJo?"

"Yeah, you think? I mean, he changed his story! That means

something's not true. This series is dead. And what else do we really have to write about? Goat shows and bake sales?" She laughs in a not-funny way.

"Maybe something else will happen."

"As big as this? By the deadline?"

"We have a month."

"And we've waited almost *two years* for something of this magnitude." She shakes her head. "No way. I have to figure out what's going on. I've got to talk to him about this."

"I'll talk to him," I offer.

"No. I think it should be me," she says, giving me a look that says *You've had your turn.* "Sorry, Mabry, but I know where your heart is. I know you'd want to believe anything he says."

Where my heart is? What's she talking about? *I* don't even know where it is anymore. Sometimes it feels lost somewhere in my body—hiding in all the thoughts in my head—and sometimes it feels like it's taken over every cell I have. I feel it beating in my toes and fingers. I feel it swelling up into my throat. Sometimes it overwhelms me, and I feel like I could have five hearts, like Glenda or Dylan. And sometimes I wonder if I have a real heart at all, or if it's just some kind of fancy pump system fueled by gorgeous boys and made-up stuff on TV.

And right now, it feels like it's shriveling up a little, like a worm on the sidewalk that forgot to wiggle home after the rain.

Her mom asks me to stay for dinner, but I just want to go home. Sirina's been huffing about the article, and has even tried to call Nick. When he didn't pick up the phone, she said to me, "Great. Now he's going to be running down the halls to avoid *me*."

Instead of writing the article, we end up writing a totally *blah* story that Mrs. Neidelman hounded us about—one that neither one of us could care less about.

Before I leave, she apologizes again for being so snippy with me. Again, I tell her it's okay. But I wonder if it is. I mean, if we can't enter the article, is it kind of my fault in some way? Was I blinded by my own agenda? And is it all backfiring now?

I try to ignore the yesses that keep bubbling up to answer the questions in my mind.

That night, when I get into bed, I text her. *Good night, my blue-belly shark tooth.*

I put my phone down and wait. And wait some more. And then her text *finally* comes through, so I can go to sleep. *Good night, my mountain-bike lip fuzz.*

THE VINDICATOR

The Official News Blog of Hubert C. Frost Middle School

~~Bored~~ *Board* Game Club Invited to Regional Convention

The Hubert C. Frost ~~Bored~~ *Board* Game Club was invited to the Connect Four Hundred Convention, a regional convention for nonelectronic gamers and fans.

While chess clubs have an established following, traditional, new, and evolving board games have had little fanfare in the convention scene. The team of twenty-one students will be traveling by bus to Hillsdale, where they will [click for more}

IN OTHER NEWS . . .

Ventriloquist and Puppet Pack It In After Eraser Assault

After being pelted by rubber erasers during a presentation on self-esteem, ventriloquist Paul Wiseman packed up his puppet, Brent, and left school grounds. Before his hurried departure, he stated, "These kids are just horrible." When reached at his home later, he released a statement by e-mail, declaring: "After today's incident, I'm reconsidering the belief that everyone [click for more]

dudar *to doubt*

We're sitting on a bench in the food court. Thad offers me some of his bean dip, but I shake my head.

"What's the problem, Collins? All beaned out these days?"

"No," I say, although there's probably some truth to that. "Just, nothing seems right."

He takes another bean-coated chip. "Okay, what's wrong?"

I start to say *everything*. Because that's how it feels right now. Things between me and Sirina feel a little off. The YoJo is out of our grasp after all. And I still have to either break a heart, or convince Thad and Sirina that they're doing a disservice to humanity by interfering with true love. Both options fill me with a sense of dread. But how do you tell your friend with a dead father and a trapped mother that *everything's wrong*?

"Come on, Collins. Spill it."

I shake my head.

"Oh, right. You already have Sirina to tell all your woes to."

"Actually, things are a little weird between us at the moment."

"Oh. Why?"

But if I tell him, I have to tell him *why* things are weird, and he always starts acting so annoyed whenever I talk about the article or the YoJo. So I just sit there crumpling and uncrumpling my burrito foil.

"That's okay—you don't want to talk about it. I get that," he says. "Anyway, she'll get over whatever it is. No one can stay mad at you for too long. Come on."

I stay stuck to the bench.

He grabs the crumpled foil out of my hands and launches it artfully into the trash can, landing it in the basket. And then he bows. Seriously.

"Well, come *on*," he says again. He looks at me like he might grab my hand, but then takes my phone from the bench next to me and runs off.

"Hey!" I say, scurrying off behind him. *What if Sirina calls? Will she leave a message?*

Thad runs a few circles around me, laughing in his Animal Planet way. And then he disappears around the corner of the sunglass kiosk. When I get to the other side, he's wearing a pair with little round lenses.

"You look like a dweeb," I say, feeling my mood lighten a little. "Like someone who works in a cubicle and clips his toenails at his desk when he thinks no one's looking."

I put on a pair with big lenses, and he tells me, "You look like a fly. About to give birth to a thousand maggots."

"You really are disgusting," I remind him. I don't smile, even though I sort of want to.

He tries on another pair—one that wraps around his head.

"You look like a total tool bag," I say. "With all the sharp tools missing."

"Ouch," he says. "I actually thought those were pretty cool."

"Nope, not even a little bit." I slide a nice purple pair on.

"Dude. You look like an alien."

"Really? Is that all you can come up with? Mars is actually kind of cool."

"Not from Mars," he says. "From *Uranus!*"

And then we both crack up, and the sunglass lady shoots us a dirty look and starts wiping down everything we touched.

My phone buzzes with a text. It's not Sirina. It's Nick. *I'm sorry*, it says. I look at it and put it away.

"You're learning, my little cricket," Thad says.

"I think you mean grasshopper."

"I think I mean cricket. So let's talk about D-Day," he says, and starts clutching at his heart and gasping, buckling at the knees.

He means Dump Day. The day I dump Nick. The day I break my very first heart. The very idea of it fills me with such angst that I suddenly feel sick to my stomach.

"What about it?"

He drops his dramatic interpretation of heartbreak. "Well, you're going to do it, right?"

"I told you I would," I say. Which isn't a lie. Which may *not* be a lie. I don't even know anymore. "But he still has to ask me."

He studies me, with one eye squinting, like he's skeptical.

"Okay, you want to know something? All my life I've been

looking forward to the Cotillion. I mean, it's a huge deal for me. And now, the whole memory of it is going to be shot by this heartbreaking thing. I mean, if I stand him up, what then? I sit home while everyone else goes and has fun?"

Thad is still eyeing me suspiciously.

"Stop giving me that look," I tell him. "This isn't about Nick. This is about me not missing one of the most important events of my life."

"Okay, then, I have an idea," Thad says.

"What?"

"You dump him when he asks you to that dance. *Boom*. His heart is broken. Your job is done."

"And miss the Cotillion completely? I can't do *that*!" I start to feel panicky.

He shrugs. "Yeah, so, how about this? I'll go with you."

He's got to be kidding. "*What!?*"

"Well, why not?"

"Why *not*? Because, dum-dum, you hate those kinds of things!" I tell him. "You've probably never been to a dance in your life!"

"So, *what*? That means I should never go?"

"I didn't mean that," I say, a little apologetically. I picture us at the Cotillion. Or at least I try to. I can't see us spinning around on the dance floor, but I can see us huddled over in the corner. Laughing about something. It could be fun. It could be— Well, it won't be boring, that's for sure. "I mean, do you even *want* to go?"

"I don't *not* want to go."

"What's that supposed to mean?"

"Two negatives make a positive, right? Can you tell I've been doing my algebra?"

I roll my eyes, but I laugh. Maybe it wouldn't be so bad. "Okay, fine, but for the record, never, *ever* ask a girl to a dance like you just asked me."

"Collins," he says, giving me a fake-shy look, "I believe *you* just asked *me*."

And then he yanks my hood over my head and I chase him from the eyebrow kiosk to the second jewelry store, until I almost run into a housewifey-looking lady who yells at me, "What are you? Nine?" and both Thad and I are out of breath from laughing.

Bow + Arrow

Thad passes by Ron's Formal—the shop he always skates by on his way out of the mall. This time, he practically skids to a stop. A banner in the front window reads *Prom Season!* He studies the mannequins, headless, posed stiffly, arms toward each other. He feels a cloud set in—can he even do this thing? What was he thinking? *Was* he even thinking? He doesn't even know how to dance—especially not in some stupid Cotillion. Maybe Mabry will be happy just to drink punch and ride up and down the fancy glass elevators in the hotel.

He wonders what he would even wear, just before it hits him that he's thinking like a girl.

Whatever. Maybe this will be even better. Maybe it'll be worth it to see the look on Nick's face. He hopes Nick'll go to the Cotillion after Mabry dumps him—hopes Nick can still cobble together some sort of date, for Thad's sake.

He skates down the hall to the mall exit, but before he pushes open the glass doors, he sees a police car passing by slowly in the parking lot. It takes a second for his nerves to catch up, but it's just mall security. A guy driving around, eating a giant pretzel and chasing it down with a Starbucks shake. And anyway, if Nick hasn't turned him in by now, maybe he didn't have that moment of recognition Thad was sure he had. And if the school hasn't found him by this point, what does he really have to worry about? The Case of the Broken Window. Even Scooby-Doo could have sniffed him out by now. It's been well over a month—even the evidence is disappearing. His hand's almost fully healed.

He's about to leave and start his skate home when he notices a little shop tucked away by the door. He's passed it a million times, but he's never given it a second glance. It's a little craft store. There are art kits and colored pencils and a sign—*All Your Paper Needs!*—in the window.

Origami. That involves paper, right?

He would never have predicted he'd one day be the kind of person who has "paper needs"—you know, besides toilet paper and paper towels and the occasional Kleenex—but today, he picks his skateboard back up and walks into the shop.

equivocarse *to make a mistake*

me equivoco

te equivocas

se equivoca

nos equivocamos

se equivocan

I go to Sirina's house early the next morning so that she has no choice but to walk to school with me. She's in a foul mood, still seething about the YoJo, and the fact that the articles that *did* run are now no more than unverified gossip.

"Maybe there's still something we can do—a totally different topic," I say. I don't even buy it myself, but I really want the old determined, hopeful, stubborn Sirina back.

"Like what?" Her tone is flat. "That the school is donating all unclaimed lost-and-found items to charity? That some poor person is supposed to be thrilled to get an unmatched sock? No thank you, Mrs. Neidelman."

"I don't know," I say.

"Just give it up, Mabry. We're no longer in the running for the YoJo."

"I'm sorry, Sirina. Did you talk to Nick?" I ask.

"Well, when I finally got him on the phone, which was no small feat—I just kept calling until he finally gave in and answered it—he told me that he'd been stressed out, and just made a mistake with his original description. He says he realized it when he was with the sketch artist. Like, who makes a mistake like that?"

"I don't think it's so weird, Sirina. When something traumatic happens, sometimes the mind can't really process anything until later."

"Yeah, Mabry," she says. "Where are you getting this astute research? Let me guess. *La Vida Rica*."

I redden. I guess there's no reason to bring up Paolo and the road-bandit revelation, then. Sirina's not going to care that it took four episodes for him to realize that his attacker was his own half brother. We walk the rest of the way to school in near silence.

When we get to school and open our locker, a folded piece of notebook paper falls out.

Mabry and Sirina, the note says. *I'm sorry. Please believe me. Your friend, Nick.*

Sirina crumples it up.

"Maybe he *was* stressed out, Sirina," I try. "People make tons of mistakes under stress."

"Maybe he's just an idiot."

"Maybe it's my fault a little," I say.

"How would it be your fault?"

"Maybe I just wanted a story. Maybe I pushed him a bit."

She looks at me tentatively. "Yeah, you know what? It *is* a little ridiculous that you tried to make him some sort of crime fighter. He was basically a bystander, Mabry. That's all he ever was. A glorified one, thanks to you. And not even a reliable one, as it turns out. And you need to stop making him some sort of hero, okay? It's *sickening*!"

Ouch.

Jordan walks up and sees us staring at each other. "What's up with you guys?" Jordan asks, looking from me to Sirina.

Sirina turns back to the locker. "Nothing," she says.

"Well, are you guys okay?"

"I don't really know. Are we?" I ask Sirina.

She sighs. "We'll be okay," she says. "I'm just— I just needed to vent."

"Okay," Jordan says as she starts to walk away. "See you at lunch. *Oh!* Amelia says she has news."

I look at Sirina and she looks at me, and then her face softens a bit, and she says quietly to me, *"Oh my darling Clementine."* And we start to laugh. A little because it's funny, and a lot just because we're relieved we still can.

At lunch, everyone's talking about the Cotillion. It's less than two weeks from now, but it feels far away, more in distance than time.

"So," Amelia says, "Ray Shaw asked me over the weekend. We were working on our PowerPoint presentation for French with our study group, and he put this great slide in. It was like, *Will you go to the Cotillion with me?* Except for, in French. And I was like, *oui, oui!*"

"That is *so* romantic," Jordan says, but she seems a little distracted.

"Oh, don't worry," Amelia tells her. "You'll get asked. I'm sure you will." She turns to us. "What about you guys?"

I don't really want to tell them about Thad asking me to the dance. Or, rather, *me* asking *him*. Sirina's the only one who knows. I texted her about it last night after I met up with him, but it feels sort of like a baby-bird secret. That if I let anyone else touch it, it could easily die.

Sirina looks at me. I must look uncomfortable, so she saves me. "Mabry and I might go together," she says, joking, only Amelia and Jordan don't know it. "You know, girls night out."

"*O.M.D.C.!* That would be so much fun," Amelia says, though we both know she doesn't mean it.

And then Ray stops by our table, so we all stop talking and listen to the two of them butcher French.

Sirina turns to me. Quietly, she says, "I'm glad you're not going with Nick."

"What?"

"With Nick. To the dance."

I glance up and see Nick looking at me from his table five rows down. It's like he's pleading for forgiveness with only a stare.

"Oh," I say. "Right."

And though my heart may no longer be broken, it definitely is torn.

Paper + Scissors

Aunt Nora's got one of Thad's textbooks on her lap—she's using it as makeshift desk, and she's folded her origami into some unrecognizable shape.

Thad's mom laughs. "What *is* that?" she asks Aunt Nora, as she folds her own paper into what looks like a mangled cootie catcher.

"Let me try again," Aunt Nora says. "I was going for a swan."

"Well, I guess it sort of looks like a swan," Thad's mom says. "Or maybe a duck."

Aunt Nora smiles, and sighs. "This is a lot harder than I remember."

"It is. My eagle looks like a vulture." Thad's mom puts her origami paper down on the bed tray and looks across the room to where Thad sits, hunched over his own project. "Have you already given up on origami, Thad?"

"No, I haven't 'already given up.' I got it for you."

"Well, what are you working on over there? That looks easier."

He is coloring coffee filters with a red Sharpie. He looks up. "Want to help?"

"Yes!" she says.

"You're coloring?" Aunt Nora asks. She looks down at her botched swan. "I think I'd rather color, too."

"Great," he says. He hands them both some coffee filters. He gives his mom a pink Sharpie and Aunt Nora an orange one.

"What do we do?" Aunt Nora asks.

"Just color the whole thing for now," he says. "I'll be right back."

He goes into the kitchen and opens the cupboard where Aunt Nora keeps her Tupperware, and starts rummaging through it.

"What are you looking for in there, hon?" Aunt Nora calls to him.

"A plastic lid?" he calls back.

"I should have a couple old containers under the sink," she tells him.

Thad hears a siren in the distance. It fills him with a new kind of dread; there's more to lose now than there was yesterday. The siren gets louder, closer, and he eyes the back door. *If I were stupid . . .* he thinks. But then the sound passes, getting softer in the distance, and he realizes everything's okay. He's home. He's safe. He's looking for a plastic lid. So everything's *got to be* okay.

He opens the cabinet under the sink and grabs an old yogurt container. Back in his room, there are cotton balls and glue. He goes upstairs, grabs them, and runs back down the stairs to his mom's room.

"Sounded like an elephant stampede," his mom says.

"Sorry." He laughs.

"What is it that we're making anyway?" she asks now.

"Just a flower," he says. "I saw it online."

They both smile and make little *ahh* noises. They don't even need to know that it's a king protea. Or that, okay, maybe with a little more practice it will be. They're already impressed.

rasgar *to tear, to rip*

yo rasgo

tú rasgas

ella rasga

nosotros rasgamos

ellos rasgan

It's after seventh period, and Sirina and I are at our locker getting our things together to go home. I've sort of been avoiding Nick all day, hoping that the tear in my heart won't get any bigger. I don't want to see Sirina upset. I feel like I'm on a tightrope, about to fall in one direction or the other.

I'm so absorbed in my thoughts that I barely notice Sirina staring at me, biting her lips shut.

"What's up?" I ask, closing the locker.

She shakes her head.

"Come on, *what?*"

"Okay," she finally says, smiling a little as we start walking. "There's something I've been dying to tell you."

"Well, *tell* me!"

She gets sort of red. "Well, so, I think—"

But then we hear, from behind us, "Mabry?"

It's Nick.

We turn around. "*Hey,*" he says, his tone low and humble.

"Hey," I say.

"Seriously?" Sirina says to me, loud enough for Nick to hear. "You're still *talking* to him?"

I cringe a little and look over at Nick. He looks as uncomfortable as I feel. He asks, "Did you guys get my note?"

Sirina groans.

"Yeah, we did," I tell him.

"Apologies are great and all, but they don't do us any good, you know," Sirina tells him. "The YoJo's shot, thanks to you. We've got nothing to submit now."

He shrinks a little. "I really am sorry—I didn't realize any of that. The whole journalism award and everything. I didn't know what a big deal all of this was."

"Well," Sirina says, "now you *do*. So what do you want?"

"I want— Well, Mabry, can I—? I mean, will you just come with me? I have something to show you."

He looks so hopeful, so sincere, so desperate to talk to me. It hurts to even think about not giving him this chance. "Can I—?" I start to ask her.

Her face drops. "Hey, I'm not your keeper," she says to me, and walks off.

I shout out her name, but she keeps walking away. "I'll call you as soon as I get home!" She still doesn't answer.

I turn back to Nick, and he motions for me to come down the hall, so I do. I can almost smell the cinnamony red-hot love coming off of him, and it hits me with a sense of both thrill and dread. I *so* want him to ask me to the Cotillion, but I *so* don't want to break his poor, beautiful heart.

I picture my words going into his fragile, tiny ears.

Stop!

When I get to him, he takes my hand, leading me farther down the hall, around the corner, and down the stairs into the basement of the building. Where everything looks gray and smells musty.

And then we get to a classroom. One I've never been in, but have heard about. The mechanical arts room—"the shop." He opens the door of the room and I see all sorts of little machines and tools. "I made you something," he says.

He motions to a table where tools are splayed out. I follow him there. He picks up a necklace. Dangling off the chain is a pendant of the letter *M*.

"I made it with a soldering iron," he says.

"Wow! It's so—crafty!" I hear myself say.

"Crafty?"

Okay, so maybe it's not given to me in an elegant case over dinner, while a violinist hovers and plays above us, but it's still . . . pretty much everything I had hoped for. Wait. *Have* hoped for. "I mean, *gorgeous.*"

"Try it on," he tells me. He walks behind me and puts it around my neck. I hold my hair up and out of the way. His breath feels warm on the back of my head as he latches it. When it's clasped, I turn to face him. All sorts of checks are going into all sorts of boxes, and for a second I wonder how I ever got distracted by his ears or teeth or anything. For no physical flaw should ever get in the way of quote-unquote love.

Wait. Quote-unquote? *What's happening to me?*

"It looks nice on you," he says, his eyes wide.

Never mind. This is it. This is the moment. He is staring into my eyes—those emerald-green ones. He sweeps a piece of my hair back. My heart has migrated into my throat, and I find it hard to breathe or swallow. This is it. He's going to ask me to the Cotillion, and I'm going to say—

"Exactly *WHAT* is going on here!?"

The booming voice belongs to Mr. Thomas, the mechanical arts teacher. He flips a switch and the fluorescent lights above us buzz and flicker on. And Nick and I move away from each other as if some sort of unseen force is tearing us violently apart, and our words crash and collide as we both mumble things like *Nothing! We were just. Nothing! Got a necklace. Didn't mean. I mean. Nothing!*

"Well," Mr. Thomas says, rubbing the top of his bald head, calming down. "The school day's over. You're officially trespassing at this point." And then he invites us to leave. Now.

And so we do. The mood is not just ruined, it's bludgeoned. And even though we trod upstairs like two battle-worn soldiers and say a very unromantic good-bye, I'm feeling a sweep of relief. It was a narrow escape. All hearts are still intact. Everything is still possible at this moment. *Everything.*

The buses have gone, so Nick goes into the office to call his mother, and I start my journey home, alone and on foot. Try having a shred of dignity in middle school. I dare you. Just try.

I pull out my phone and dial Sirina. But it rings and rings and goes to voice mail. Instead of leaving her a message, I text her: *Sorry about that! Call me.*

But my phone remains quiet on the walk home.

When I arrive at my house, I call her. I get her voice mail again. "I'm really sorry. Please call me," I say after the beep.

But still, I get nothing back.

My phone hasn't rung or buzzed or lit up all night, so I pick it back up and try calling Sirina again.

This time she answers!

But her voice is pancake-flat when she picks up. *"Hello,"* she says.

"Hi!" I say, with enough enthusiasm for both of us. "I'm really sorry about earlier."

"Yeah, I hear those words a lot lately."

"I mean it, Sirina!"

"Doesn't really feel like it."

"I'm *sor*—"

"Mabry, please. What do you want? Just to say you're sorry, sorry, sorry, *sorry*?"

"Well, I am, but *no*. That's not it. I wanted to *talk* to you." I try to ignore her tone. She can be *so* difficult sometimes. "What were you going to tell me today? You know, before we got interrupted?"

"Nothing."

"Come on, Sirina. *What?*"

"I don't feel like talking about it."

I sigh. Difficult, see? "Well, guess what?"

"What." She doesn't sound that interested.

I continue. This is how she usually is when she gets mad—it's like pulling teeth to get her to talk. But usually once I make her laugh, she gets over it. So I try. "So Nick took me down to the dungeon of the school."

Nothing.

I try again. "Like, the bowels of the building."

Nothing but a sort-of sigh.

I try harder. "Like, if the school were a person, we would have been in the *large intestine*." I laugh at my own joke.

"That's seriously gross," she says, and not in the fun way.

And, *ew*, I realize it kind of is. I also realize she doesn't seem the least bit curious about why I was in the building bowels with him. I try not to let it bother me—it'll just take a little more work. She's still upset about the YoJo, understandably. So I laugh a little. "Well, it was really the mechanical arts room. He brought me down there so he could give me this necklace he made."

"Oh. *Woo-hoo*." Again, her voice is sarcastically flat.

"Well." I chuckle. "Yeah, *woo-hoo*." I fling my finger around in a circular motion even though she's not there to see it. Whatever sense of ridiculous hope I had simmering inside of me has been doused with cold water.

"Sirina?"

"*What?*"

This is hard work. But I just need to be honest with her. I can tell her how I don't think I want to be a heartbreaker after all. Maybe she'll have a solution. Hey, maybe I can go to the Cotillion with both of them—Nick *and* Thad! Instead of a heartbreaker like Mariela, I can be the Belle of the Ball! But wait. That's like two worlds colliding. My picnics-in-the-park world with Nick. My bean-dip-in-the-food-court world with Thad. *Yikes*. I need her help.

Even over the phone, I can feel her impatience mounting. So I take a breath in and say, "So, I feel like he's going to ask me to the Cotillion any minute, and—"

"You know what I was going to tell you?" she says suddenly, interrupting me.

I take a breath. "What?"

"You *are* getting boring."

I take another breath, but this is more like a gasp. "What do you mean?"

"You always said I should tell you if you're getting boring. Well, here you go. All you do is talk about Nick, and you're *boring*."

I feel *crushed*. "Well, I'm sorry you feel that way." My voice is like an out-of-tune ukulele.

"Yeah, well, me too."

"Sirina? Come on, can we just—?"

"You know what? I gotta go," she says. And then she hangs up.

I sit there, frozen with shock. I wait for the phone to ring again, for her to call and say, *Wow, I sure had a bug up my butt*. It's happened before. But no such call comes. And I think about calling her back and saying something like, *Okay, let's start over*. But it's like the idea of moving anything at all is a completely impossible concept. I might as well be gagged and tied to my desk chair, like Andres was when the cartel made off with his secret gold trunk.

Before bed, I give in. I text Sirina, *Can we please talk tomorrow?*

I wait fifteen minutes, and hear nothing.

I try again. *You're my best friend ever!*

And nothing.

Okay, she's still mad. I take a deep breath. Then I text: *Good night, my lemon-chiffon griddle cake.*

Then, minutes later, as I am still staring intently at my phone, willing it to light up, I get a response. From *her*!

Good night, Mabry.

Which is the absolute *worst* thing she could have ever said. No *dry-roasted yogurt butter*? No *carbon-dated ant trap*? No *snot-soaked nail polish*? I feel the sharpness of tears forming at the back of my eyes, and then pushing forward, like those lemmings you read about. Once one starts off the cliff, the rest mindlessly follow.

I mean, *Good night, Mabry*!? I would have rather heard back nothing at all.

I guess sometimes even the people you're not in love with can break your heart.

caer *to fall*

yo caigo

tú caes

ella cae

nosotros caemos

ellos caen

When I get to my locker the next morning, Jordan smiles and waves frantically. Then she slams her own locker shut and practically skips over to mine.

"Oh my god. I'm so happy to see you!" she says, and for a moment—just a moment—it feels possible that my world might not be falling apart. That everything might still be okay. "Axyl just asked me to the Cotillion!"

Oh. That. I try to muster some excitement, but all I can bring forward is a weak smile. "Great," I say. "That's great."

She looks a little disappointed for a second, but glances over my shoulder and suddenly brightens back up. "Sirina!"

I whip my head around. *Is she coming to talk to me?* I feel a quick flutter of nerves. Jordan rushes toward her. "Guess what? Axyl just asked me to the Cotillion!"

"Oh, congratulations! I'm so happy for you!" Sirina says, a lot more appropriately, and appears to mean it. She gives Jordan a hug, and I feel even more stupid about my lackluster response.

"Yeah, that's awesome news!" I say now, trying to put genuine feeling behind my smile.

"Aw, thanks!" Jordan says. She is beaming.

"Maybe we can double," Sirina says.

Double? My mouth drops. *Sirina is going to the Cotillion? With* who?

But Jordan doesn't seem to have the same questions. "Oh my god. You did it! *You asked him!*"

Sirina smiles and blushes. "Yup."

There's a 'him'? And I didn't know this? I feel as empty as an Oreo without its center. As discontinued as a Screaming Yellow Zonker.

But Jordan squeals and bounces on her toes. "You are the *woman!*"

"What did you do? You asked someone to the dance?" I ask her now, although I feel like I barely have the air in my lungs to talk. "*Who?*"

Jordan looks at me with a severely wrinkled forehead. "You don't know?"

"She's been *busy,*" Sirina says without looking at me.

"*Ooh,*" Jordan says. She starts looking around the hallway uncomfortably. "Well, I better get to class. See you at lunch," she says to Sirina, and takes off.

My mouth is still hanging open, but I manage to make it say, "So *that's* what you wanted to tell me. I guess I've been so, you know, into my own *stuff.*"

"I know," she says. Not like it's okay, but just an acknowledgment that I've been a letdown.

"I see that, okay? I haven't been paying attention. I'm really sorry."

Her eyes meet mine for a brief second and then she turns her head away, crossing her arms in front of her chest. But she's still standing there, so I feel like there's some hope.

"So will you tell me now? *Who* did you ask? And *when*?"

She shakes her head. "I'm really not here to talk. I'm just here to get my stuff out of your locker." She brushes past me, toward the open locker.

"You're—" I feel my breath leave me. "You're moving out?"

But she doesn't answer. She pulls a CD sleeve off the top shelf. Inside of it is a music mix she made me a couple weeks ago. "Are you ever actually going to listen to this?"

I nod. "I loaded it onto my iPod." I don't tell her that I haven't listened to it yet.

But she seems to know. "Whatever," she says, and puts it back on the shelf. Then she holds up a Mad Libs book. "Yours or mine?" she asks.

I'm a little surprised at the question, since we've done all of the Mad Libs together. I don't even remember who the book belonged to originally. "Um, *ours*," I say.

She just looks straight at me and says, "There's no such thing anymore."

I bite my bottom lip and try to hold the tears back, but I have to turn and walk away.

For the first three classes of the day, the only thing I learn is physics. Specifically, that water is one of the most powerful forces on earth. I learn that looking up toward the ceiling only delays—but doesn't prevent—the flow of tears. I learn that trying to chew gum, or fake a smile, or talk about *The Red Badge of Courage* are useless defenses against the force of tears. I learn that waterproof mascara—at least the kind that I can afford to buy—isn't necessarily tear-proof, and that even one odd look from someone you hardly know can undam the tears all over again.

When I get to our normal lunch table, Amelia's the only one there. Still, she gives me a look that doesn't make me feel welcome. "Someone's sitting there," she tells me when I set my lunch down at my usual spot.

"*Who?*" I say.

But she just glares at me until I finally retreat. I find a secluded spot at a table near the teachers and watch from a distance while Jordan bops over, and then Sirina, and then—Kipper.

Kipper!

How did I miss this? I'm a self-absorbed idiot. All this time I've been thinking Sirina Fein's immune to love—and she is not. She is *not*! It's so disorienting. How long has she had a crush on him? How did she ask him? Was she nervous? Excited? Scared? All of the above?

I feel like I'm just an extra on the set of my own un–*La Vida Rica* life—just a nameless character filling in the background, barely making the credits. *Niña en la Cafetería.*

Nick is walking with Abe and Patrick. They carry their trays past me, but then Nick notices me and does a double take. "Hey," he says to me. "Why are you over here?" He glances toward my usual table and then back at me.

I try to answer, but I know it'll be a wet explanation, so I just try to shake my head and wave him off.

He looks concerned. "Want to sit with us?"

"No, no," I say. "I'm going to listen to some music. I'm fine."

He looks unsure, but says, "Okay. I'll talk to you later, then?"

"Sure, yeah," I say.

I exhale with relief as he walks away. Maybe now would be a good time to finally listen to Sirina's music—no one will bother you if you've got earbuds in. I rummage through my backpack, but I can't find my iPod anywhere.

Crap. My mom will kill me. I dump my backpack out on the vast table in front of me. Still nothing. Even though I'm frustrated, I'm partly relieved. Now I have an excuse to get out of the cafetorium.

I throw my uneaten lunch into my backpack and head toward the door.

"Lunch isn't over. Where are you going?" Mrs. Hurst asks as I try to walk past her.

"Can I please just go to the lost and found?"

"You'll have to wait till the bell rings."

Typical middle school. I start to tear up again. "You're way too old to be carrying on like this," she says.

I feel a shudder of humiliation. After all this pretending to be Mariela, all I can think about now is Cristina, and her elusive, graceful cry. It's just another thing I've failed at. I start back to the empty table, but then stop.

I'm not going back there. I'm not.

I turn around. Mrs. Hurst is busy chatting with another teacher. Good. I move toward the edge of the room. There's a door in the corner. I'd rather be a refugee like Rafael than a prisoner like Luis.

I take another glance over. No one's watching me. It's like I'm a ghost. And not the beautiful, haunting kind, like the ghost of Arabela, who lives in Señora Lomas's mansion. Just the totally invisible, garden-variety kind that no one seems to notice. So I push through the door. I am free.

Except that I'm not. Mrs. Hurst bursts through the middle door. "Miss *Collins*!" she says, in a how-dare-you voice. "You can have a seat in Officer Dirk's office! I'm calling him right *now*."

Mrs. Forester, the school secretary, is already on the walkie-talkie with Mrs. Hurst when I arrive. "She's *here*," she says, in a tone that would make me tuck my tail if I had one. She waves me down the hall like I'm an annoying mosquito she can't get far enough away from.

I sit in the chair in front of his desk. It's a tan metal folding chair, cold and unyielding, like Officer Dirk himself. I fold my legs up in front of me and hug them in for warmth and protection, resting my chin on my knee. Everything in the room seems stripped down to its basicness. There's an artless, full-year calendar pinned on the wall. A bulletin board of neatly arranged memos, each with clear pushpins on all four corners. On his desk, which is nearly bare, sits a black frame. I can't tell what's in the frame from where I'm sitting—his mother? A girlfriend? A child? What would mean enough to him to put in a frame and place on his desk? What looks like *love* to someone like Officer Dirk? After a few moments of guessing, my curiosity growing, I get up from my chair and go around to the other side of his desk.

It's a watercolor painting of a tree over a lake, some mountains in the background. I step a little closer to get a better look and my foot hits something under the desk. I look down and see a skateboard.

It looks old. It's wooden, painted red, but most of the color has worn off and faded. I pull the skateboard out from under the desk and put my foot on it. I wonder what it would be like to be able to get from one place to another on a rolling board, like Thad does. I push it a few inches forward and back and feel the hum of motion in my foot.

The phone rings down the hall. I hear Mrs. Forester pick it up.

"For a delivery of *what*?" I overhear her say. It's good to know that her annoyance is directed at pretty much everyone, not just me.

I step my other foot on the board, so that I'm standing on the thing and holding on to the desk for balance. The skateboard slips backward a bit and I gasp in some air. Is that what it feels like to be Thad?

"*Pond scum?* Is that what you said?"

I try to shift my weight forward a little, and when I feel like I'm balanced, I remove one hand from the desk. And then the other.

"Okay, listen, I'm going to have to put you on hold for a minute."

Oh no! Is she going to check on me? I scramble to dismount the skateboard quickly, which is harder than I'd have thought. I can't just step off, because it'll become unbalanced, so I do a little hop. I land on the side of my left foot and crumple awkwardly to the ground, with the expected thuds and clangs. I'm on my back—and so is the skateboard, wheels spinning.

And there I see a name written in black marker on the underbelly of the board: *Bell.*

Bell. Like Thad Bell. I have a flashback to the day Sirina and I first saw him in the mall. He'd just lost his dad's skateboard. Could this be *that* skateboard? Could this have been Thad's father's? Thad's *dead* father's? *Could it be?*

I hear Mrs. Forester's voice from down the hall, "Barbara, do you know anything about a delivery of *pond scum*?" She is talking to our principal, Mrs. Vander-Pecker.

I make my way back to my feet. If it *is* Thad's father's skateboard, I wonder how it wound up in Officer Dirk's office, when Thad doesn't even go to school here. Did someone steal it from him? I feel a rush of justice. *I can make things right!*

"Oh, is that it? I just wanted to make sure it wasn't a prank call. You know how *these kids* can be," I hear Mrs. Forester say. "I'll tell them they can deliver, then," she says, going back to her desk.

I hear the door to the front office open. "IS SHE IN THERE," Officer Dirk asks Mrs. Forester.

I scramble back to the Seat of Shame.

"I believe so."

I hear his big, rubbery footsteps in the hall, getting louder and louder until they stop. I look up. "WHAT SEEMS TO BE THE PROBLEM."

"I don't know."

He just looks at me until I blurt out that I broke out of the cafetorium. I try to tell him how unfair and unjust it is to confine students with *no* friends to a room where *having* friends is the only path to survival.

He stares at me wordlessly. His face doesn't change.

"Am I in trouble?" I finally ask.

"YES. YOU HAVE TO STAY HERE UNTIL THE CONCLUSION OF LUNCH."

"Really?" I'm actually relieved. Anything's better than going back in there.

"DOES IT LOOK LIKE I'M JOKING."

"No, no, not at all," I say. Quietly, I say, "Thanks."

He doesn't acknowledge my gratitude but goes to his side of the desk, sits down, and logs on to his computer. His typing is methodic, steady, even soothing. After this crapstorm of a day, I'm finding myself starting to relax.

"Can I ask you a question?"

"YOU JUST DID."

"That skateboard?"

He stops typing.

"I think my friend lost it. Thad Bell. I think it was his dad's. "

He stares at his computer screen. "THIS IS NOT YOUR CONCERN."

"The only thing is, his dad died, so it might mean something to him."

"I REPEAT. THIS IS NOT YOUR CONCERN."

"But—"

Once again, he shuts me down. His hand whips toward the door, and he points down the hall.

"REPORT BACK TO THE CAFETORIUM."

"What? *Why?*"

"IF YOU'RE STILL HERE BY THE TIME I COUNT TO THREE, I WILL SEE YOU IN DETENTION."

I want to throw myself at his mercy. I try to remember what that actually entails.

"ONE."

I press my palms together like a prayer. "Officer—"

"TWO."

I shut my eyes. *"Please don't make me, please don't make me."*

"TWO AND A HALF."

I jerk myself into a run, but trip on the leg of the chair, pulling it down with me as I topple to my palms.

"TWO AND THREE-QUARTERS."

I press my hands into the ground and push myself up as quickly as I can, leaving the chair mangled in a half-folded position behind me.

"TWO AND SEVEN-EIGHTHS," I hear as I hurry past Mrs. Forester's desk and out the door, like Cristof running from the secret attic dweller, Elisabet.

I'm on my lonely, despondent way to seventh period when I look up and see Nick standing in the hallway, against the opposite wall, staring at me.

I stop in my tracks. Some guy bumps into me from behind; the corner of a textbook jabs me in the back. "Watch it," he says to me.

Nick makes his way across the crowded hall.

"Hi," I say. "What are you doing here?"

"Just looking for you. I heard about you and Sirina. Now I get why you were alone at lunch. I'm sorry if I had anything to do with it."

"Oh. Thanks."

The look in his eyes is a little pleading. "The description—I really didn't mean to screw everything up."

"I know. I get it," I say.

He grabs my hand. "Hey, Mabry? Can you meet me at Schatzi's Saturday night?" he asks. "There's something I've been wanting—trying—to ask you."

My heart jumps. And then lands with a splat.

Crap. So on Saturday night I'm supposed to break his heart. His poor, dear, sweet, increasingly fragile heart. Or piss Thad off. Either way, I'll manage to upset *yet another* person.

"Well, Saturday's—" I'm not ready for this. Not at all. "Okay, Saturday's fine."

I should feel elated, but instead I feel like disappointment, in human form.

I know this sounds strange, but here's what the whole situation makes me think about: pâté. Duck liver pâté.

When I was little, my mom took me to a party. She let me dress up for the occasion—I wore a sparkly pink dress with a tutu skirt, even a tiara. I was excited to meet fancy, beautiful people and eat fancy, beautiful food. There was one particularly glamorous and stunning woman named Victoria who I couldn't take my eyes off. She was graceful and willowy; everything on her shone and sparkled, from her glittery toenails to her diamond earrings. She ate with tiny little nibbles, her chewing barely visible. And when she spoke, her voice was like a song that I wanted to sing along to. And she just *loved*, just *adored*, the duck liver pâté.

I wanted some of that duck liver pâté.

I wanted it *bad*.

I had the sense that I wasn't supposed to have any—it was clearly the somber color of grown-up food, and not the brightly packaged and colored foods that are usually given to children—but while everyone engaged in party chitchat, I went up to the little table and scooped some on my plate, along with a cracker, like Victoria had done. Then I snuck under the table and, though it reminded me of Hunter's poops, I smeared some of this special stuff onto the cracker and put it into my mouth, so sure I had to love it, like Victoria did.

But here's the thing. It was awful. So very, very awful. It tasted like—no surprise—the word *liver* itself—mushy and brown and stinky. It tasted so bad I had to spit it out right there on the wood floor under the table. A little pet wiener dog came to my rescue, wolfing down the evidence.

It was weird. I knew that it was something I should appreciate, but I couldn't. I hadn't expected it to taste like birthday cake or mint-chocolate-chip ice cream, but I *had* expected it to be something I could at least manage to swallow. But all I had was a bad taste in my mouth.

Yes, this is a little like that moment. Nick is about to ask me to the Cotillion. He likes me. A lot. He's brought me flowers, made me jewelry, and now he's taking me to an actual dinner! I should feel victorious. *Triumphant. Appreciative.* But somehow this moment feels a lot like duck liver pâté. I've got another bad taste in my mouth.

Sticks + Stones

Mabry is sitting at a table in the food court already, a textbook and a notebook open in front of her. "Hey, Bean Breath," she says when she sees Thad.

"Hey," he says, and adds on, lamely, "Onion Head. Are you doing homework?"

"I got here early."

"Yeah, I can see that," he says. "But *why* are you here so early?"

"Can we not talk about it?"

"Yeah, sure." He feels like it's a strange thing for *her* to say, but he also feels hungry. Very hungry. He slides his skateboard under the table and pulls some money out of his pocket. "Want a taco?"

Mabry gives him a crooked smile and picks up a balled-up wrapper. "Already had one. With two packages of hot sauce. It was that kind of a day."

He grins. "You really *are* learning, my cricket."

"Grasshopper," she says.

He leaves his skateboard under the table, goes to the Macho Nacho stand, and orders a burrito.

"Anything else?" the man behind the counter asks.

Thad looks over his shoulder at Mabry. She's leaning on her elbows, just staring at the table—something's not right. He orders her a side of chips and guac.

He brings the food to the table. "I thought you could use this," he says, setting the guacamole down in front of her.

"Thanks." She looks up at him, surprised.

He feels some heat rise to his face, so he says, "Well, go ahead, eat! It wasn't *free*."

She takes the lid off the guacamole container. "Guess what?"

"Chicken butt," he says, taking a huge bite of burrito. It annoys him when she starts a conversation this way; he always wants to come up with something extraordinarily funny in response, but he usually falls flat.

"Sirina asked this guy Kipper to the Cotillion."

He lets his mouth drop open, despite its fullness. "No way!" He can't help feeling amused. *Jeez*, is he turning into a girl now that Mabry is his only friend?

"Yep," she says. "I had *no* idea. Zip. Zero."

"Seriously?"

"None." She looks down at the table. "That's one of the reasons she won't talk to me anymore."

"Dude, what do you mean she won't she talk to you anymore?"

"Like I said, can we not talk about it?"

"Yeah, no problem." He feels sad for her, and he knows he should say something, but he has no idea what. He can't say Sirina's a *wipe*, like

Nick, because it's just not true. He can't say Sirina will get over it, whatever it is, because he's not sure that's true, either.

He watches her scoop some guacamole onto a chip, but she doesn't put it in her mouth. He puts three dry chips in his own mouth and swallows hard.

He clears his throat and tries to make his voice a little jokey. "So what about Nick? When are you going to—?" He swipes his hand across his throat.

She looks up at him quickly, and back down at the table. She presses her finger against the table grate, mindlessly.

Her silence makes him want to stop eating.

"He asked me to meet him at Schatzi's on Saturday night," she finally says, without looking at Thad. "I think he's going to ask me then."

And you're going to tell him no, right? He wants to ask, but can't bring himself to do it. There's something about the way she's acting that he doesn't like.

She breathes out heavily. "I had no idea how hard this heartbreaking stuff would be."

His stomach churns slightly. He can't help but wonder, *You're still going with me, aren't you?* He studies her, but she's staring into her guacamole. He feels pinpricks under his skin. He takes a sip of his Dr Pepper.

She pushes the guacamole across the table. "Here, you have it. I can't eat."

"Nah, I'm okay," he says.

Her head snaps up. "You're refusing guacamole?"

He just shrugs. "Sorry. I guess I'm sick of it."

"Sick of it? No, don't be sorry," she says, a smile starting. "It gives me hope."

"What do you mean?"

"Hope that maybe we won't end up right back here in the food court on the night of the Cotillion."

Oh. Okay. Everything's okay. He feels suddenly starved of oxygen, and takes in a long breath. His face softens with relief.

"Seriously," she says. "Now I can finally see if you actually exist outside of this mall, or if you'll evaporate once you leave the food court."

"Now *that* would be worth a YoJo," Thad jokes.

She tries to stomp on his foot, but her own foot hits his skateboard, under the table.

"Oh!" she says suddenly. Her eyes widen. "I found your skateboard."

He smirks. "Um, hey, Sherlock, it's not lost, I just *stashed it* under the table."

"Not this one, dummy. Your dad's."

He blinks. *Am I hearing her correctly?*

She continues. "The one you lost."

He feels her words swirl around his head like a random sentence that has to be diagramed. *Dad's. Skateboard. Lost.* "You found—what? *Where?*"

"Yeah, you know, your dad's skateboard. You told us you'd lost it, that first day Sirina and I saw you here." She gives him a confused smile. "Anyway, Officer Dirk has it. I found it under his desk—that's a whole *other* story. Your last name was written on it. I told him it was probably yours, but he was like, *Get out of my office this exact second.*"

Where is it now? he wants to ask, but he's suddenly too exhausted to talk. He feels dizzy. He looks around for something fixed, something not moving, to stare at. But everywhere he looks, he sees motion. Feet walking. Escalators moving. Wheels rolling. Nothing is still.

"Thad? Why are you acting so weird?"

He tries to steady himself by fixing his eyes on the grout line between two tiles on the floor. Something straight, linear. Stable. Simple. The opposite of *everything* right now.

Mabry keeps talking. "I was hoping he would just give it to me and I could try to skate it over. 'Course I'd probably fall flat on my face."

"*Ride*, you mean."

"Huh?"

Annoyance creeps into his voice. "You *ride* a skateboard. You don't skate it."

"Oh, okay then, whatever," she says, like she's getting irritated. "*Ride*. What's up with you?"

"Well, that kinda"—his voice comes out strained and slow; he feels tight with anxiety—"sucks."

"What? I thought you'd be happy."

He shakes his head. He knows he's coming across all wrong, like he's mad at her. He *is* upset, but he realizes now it's not so much about getting caught anymore—it's about letting her down. If they have the skateboard, they picked it up at the crime scene. If they picked it up, they might know he's the one who broke the window. Now they'll never let him enroll in school, much less go to that dance. He'll have to miss it, and worse, she will, too. Unless—

"Collins?"

"What?" She looks at him like he's a human puzzle.

He takes a breath. He practically has to squeeze the words out. "About the dance."

"The Cotillion?" Her voice breaks.

"Uh, yeah," he says. He takes a breath. "I think you *should* go with Nick."

"*Oh. My. God,*" she says. "Are you seriously flaking on me?

"No, I'm not—"

"I can't *believe* this."

"Collins!" he says louder. She's getting the entirely wrong impression. "I need you to listen to me for a second—"

"I should have seen—"

"I mean it," he cuts her off. He listens to her exhale with frustration, and he tries to breathe normally himself. "Okay, first, I *do* want to go with you, but here's the thing. I don't think the school's going to let me."

"*What? Why not?*"

"You know how you found my skateboard?"

"Yeah?"

"And you told Officer Dirk it was mine?"

"Well, *yeah*?"

"Well, he's probably had it since I punched out that window, okay? Like, waiting for me to confess or something."

"You? *You* punched out that window? You're the one?" She seems baffled. "But why would you *do* that?"

So he tells her.

It had seemed like a good idea. The last time he'd set foot in Hubert C. Frost was when he was in elementary school and the class took a bus over to see the middle-school band's holiday performance. It was enough to put an end to his childhood dream of playing the drums.

But that day, weeks ago, facing the nerve-racking expectation that he'd be going to school—regular school—soon, he thought he'd go check it out again. This time, on his own terms. Walk the halls, learn the math wing from the language labs, see where the cafeteria was, where his locker might be. Maybe lurk a little—from a distance—see if there were any recognizable faces. With his navy-blue sweatshirt on, and the hood up over his head, he could pass for any other eighth grader. He could be practically anonymous, nearly invisible. The thought filled him with a sense of freedom. Of relief.

When he'd gone in through one of the back doors, school had been out for about twenty minutes. It was like after a long day of being traipsed through, the building itself was taking a little break from the hectic pace of the school day. Lights were turned off, breezes came through open windows, voices in the hall were lively and at ease.

"Check me out!" He'd overheard a voice from another nearby hall. Then laughter.

He'd peeked around the corner, down the hall. He squinted. Was that Nick Wainwright? And Abe Mahal? He thought so. They were there with another guy he didn't recognize. The guys were all fake fighting, throwing air punches and ducking, basically taking advantage of the empty hallways. It looked kind of fun.

"Watch this!" Nick had spun around, kicking in the air. He fell on his hip, got up and dusted off his jeans, and accepted being laughed at.

"*Nice* moves," Abe had joked.

"Hi-*yah!*" the other guy had called out, and tried the spin-kick himself. But he'd accidentally spun a little too much and kicked a little too much, and got Abe right in the crotch.

Abe had crumpled to the ground, clutching his jeans.

"Wow, sorry, dude," the kid said, while everyone else laughed.

"Hey, Abe, you okay, man?" Nick had asked, his face looking like it was trying to decide between amusement and concern.

From the ground, Abe had groaned, "Nick, man, I don't think I can walk anymore."

Nick had turned to the spin-kicker. "What are you trying to do? Get him enrolled in the Special Olympics?" And then, to Abe, Nick said,

"Hey, don't worry. We're right here next to the handicapped elevators, so I can wheel you in, like some sort of freak."

Thad felt a swell of anger. The guys had all burst out in laughter, which, it turns, out, is harder to hear over the sound of breaking glass.

Now Thad looks across the table at Mabry, who is staring at him with an open mouth, like she needs a little more explanation. So he adds, "Yeah, so they were just being dipsquats, I know, but it just—" He has to stop talking. His vocal cords feel like they've been strung too tight.

"*Oh,*" she says, like she finally understands. "Yeah. Your mom."

After a few moments, he clears his throat. "It's like they were making fun of *her*—not Abe." He traces a scar on his hand. "And that word—*freak*. It just got to me."

"Well," she says. "Just FYI. Abe actually *is* a freak. A walking, running, fully mobile freak."

"Yeah." He gives her a fraction of a smile. "But you're talking to me *now*. Not the me back then, before"—he suddenly stops himself before he can say anything gag-worthy like *before you*—"I just felt like I needed to punch something, you know what I mean?"

"Yeah," she says. "I do."

Her answer surprises him.

"You do?" he asks.

"Well, I haven't punched out any windows, but I do know what that feeling is. It's called *passion*."

He snort-laughs. "Actually, I think it's called a misdemeanor."

"Yeah, resulting from passion," she says. "Because you love your mother so much."

Okay, he thinks, *so for Mother's Day, what should I give her? A felony?* He almost says this out loud, but Mabry's not looking like she wants to joke around.

This all feels too serious. He can't help but add, "Yeah, well, I shouldn't have done it. It's not like you flip out when people use paper shredders or anything."

"Why would I?"

"You know," he tries to joke. It's lame. "Flat Stanley?"

"Oh, right." She doesn't laugh, though—no surprise. "No, but you know what you should have done?"

"What?"

"You should have *told* me. But you didn't. You just used me to get back at Nick." She is looking at him like he's a stranger.

"*Well.*" His neck feels hot. He runs a finger under the edge of his T-shirt collar. "Okay, well, fine. I wanted to tell you. Yes, that was the plan. But that's the thing. Nick's actually the winner, not me. He's taking you to the dance. And *you*—you got what you wanted."

He hopes she'll correct him. She doesn't. She just continues to stare at him, like things are tightening inside of her. Her jaw seems to harden. Her eyes get sharp. A cord flinches in her neck.

"You should have at least stopped me from writing those stupid articles."

"That's one of the reasons I *didn't* tell you," Thad says. "How would I have known back then that you wouldn't have turned me in?"

"Yeah, and guess what? I basically turned you in today. Because I *didn't* know," she says.

"You know what? I'm actually kind of relieved," he tells her. No more wondering. No more worrying. Whatever it's going to be, it will *be* by tomorrow.

She shakes her head. "And now you want me to go to the Cotillion with Nick?"

No, not really, he thinks. But instead he says, "I just want you to be able to *go.*" If nothing else, she should give him credit for that, right?

But instead, she stands up and says, "God, who *are* you?" And then she walks away from the table faster than any of the bored housewives who speed-walk around the mall, and she almost trips on the toe of her own flip-flop. Which would be funny to him if anything felt funny anymore.

Lock + Key

'm sorry, I'm sorry, I'm sorry, Thad thinks, all the way home on his skateboard. *I'm sorry about the window. I'm sorry about the stupid articles. I'm sorry I can't go to the dance. What am I supposed to do about it? Wear a freaking T-shirt with* I'm sorry *printed all over it?* Get the words stamped on his forehead, tattooed on his chest? How does anyone ever make anything right anyway? It's not like you can ever rewind and redo things in life, like you can on TV.

The door's unlocked again, so he goes right in. Aunt Nora's not in the kitchen, which gives him a chance to do this right.

He goes over to the manila folder. Officer Dirk's business card is clipped to the inside cover.

He picks up the phone and dials the number.

"OFFICER DIRK HERE."

"This is Thad Bell."

"THAD."

"You might want to come over," he tells him.

"SO YOU'RE FINALLY READY."

Thad is slightly stunned, but not at all surprised. So Dirk did know. All this time.

"I am."

"HEADING OVER NOW."

Thad hangs up the phone and puts the kettle on.

"You're making tea?" Aunt Nora asks, coming into the kitchen.

"Yep. Sit down," he tells her. "We're about to have company."

"Company?" She seems baffled.

"Your friend. Dirk."

"Dirk? He's coming? Now?" She pats her hair and looks down at herself, as if she's forgotten what she's wearing. "Well, why?"

"Because I know where dad's skateboard is, and you're probably not going to like how it got there."

So she sits.

besar *to kiss*

yo beso

tú besas

ella besa

nosotros besamos

ellos besan

Schatzi's.

We are here. It's Saturday night at the mall, and it's just the two of us, Nick and me. The Mariela-flavored me. I want to be happy—I *should* be happy. Okay, so maybe there's no candlelight, and maybe you can see Macho Nacho and the whole food court from the window overlooking the mall, but all in all, it's pretty darn romantic. We are in a sit-down restaurant. In a booth. Nick is sitting on the same side as me. We have a waiter (named Bart), and we are possibly in love, or something like it. This has to be it. I mean, he's *mi hombre*, right? *Mi amor*, I remind myself.

So I really shouldn't be thinking too much about *mi amigo*.

Bart is not a very good waiter. He hasn't refilled my Coke or brought us silverware. He even made a joke about how far our allowances will go in a place like this (which, as it turns out, is not very). He places our cheese-dip "fundue" in the middle of the table, and drops a basket of bread dippers right next to it.

"Ladies first," Nick says.

I reach for a dipper, and then stop myself. Mariela wouldn't eat with her hands, I remember. "I think I need a plate. And a fork."

"Right," Nick says. And then he raises his hand like he's an honor-roll student in a social studies class.

Bart does notice, thankfully. "'Sup, little buddy?" he asks.

I feel the awkwardness simmering inside of me.

"Um, it's just that we need, um, *plates*? And *utensils*?"

"But's it *fundue*," Bart says. "A traditional finger food."

Nick clears his throat. "It's just that—the *lady*—would like them."

I feel like such an imposter. If Nick could see the usual me—the hanging-out-with-Thad me—would we even be sitting here together tonight?

Bart brings back two napkin-rolled forks and knives and two miniature plates, and follows it up with an unnecessary bow. Nick smiles at me.

I smile back. I try to enjoy myself. I'm the closest I'll be for a while to being on a real date, in a real restaurant, with waiters who wear tuxedos and ferry around bottles of wine. Where there will be candles with real flames. Where items on the menu will require familiarity with a second language. Where the larger waiters aren't giving the smaller ones wedgies in the kitchen.

I use my fork to place the dipper into the fundue and put it on my tiny plate. I take a small bite of mine and try to chew politely.

He gives me an awkward smile, and looks at his dipper, and says, "So, I wanted to ask you something."

What are the chances he'll ask me what my favorite food is? I wonder in a flurry of panic. *Or my middle name?* But I know it's going to happen, and instead of the excitement I had expected, I feel sick inside.

"Mabry." Under the table, he takes my hand in his. He fixes his eyes on mine. "Will you please go to the Cotillion with me?"

This is the moment. I open my mouth. I take a breath. *Yes* is the word I'm supposed to say. I once very much wanted to say *Yes! Yes! Yes! With all my heart, yes!* But here, now, I can't get that simple word out.

Because I don't want to anymore. The *yes* doesn't feel real. Nothing about it feels real. My whole fascination with Nick feels like a stage set.

All I can wish for is that life had sound tracks like *La Vida Rica*— heavy, serious, mood-setting music. It just makes sad things easier. Without it, the words cut through the air like missiles, blowing through the space between us that is yet undefined.

My heartbeat is starting to speed up, sweat is starting to swim around under my skin, making its way to my pores. All my forehead muscles seem to be migrating toward the ceiling.

"Nick?" I pause. If only you could buy time as easily as you can buy some heart-shaped jewelry at the mall kiosk. "I'm sorry. But, I, uh, think I have to break up with you."

It's the first time I've ever uttered that phrase to anyone, and the words seem both heavy and trivial at the same time. They're just words, my head says. Still, even if they can't break bones, words can definitely break hearts, and possibly damage other organs. I mean, when my heart is breaking, try to convince me that my spleen isn't somehow involved.

"Break up?" Nick's face seems to melt a little. His eyebrows drop and his cheeks sink. "Why?"

I shake my head, like if I try hard enough, an acceptable answer will pop up, like a Magic 8 Ball. It doesn't. How do you explain to someone that everything you thought you wanted was all wrong? That you were living someone else's life—a character on TV's! That you feel now like an exhausted actor who just wants to call it a day and go home? That "real" feels like a whole different thing than it did just a month ago?

He stares, as if in a trance, at the fundue bowl. And I realize that this heartbreaking business really sucks big-time.

"I'm sorry, Nick."

He releases my hand under the table. It's clammy and wet, and I have to wipe it dry on the hem of my skirt.

"I thought this is what you wanted," he says without looking at me.

"It was." It all feels so once-upon-a-time.

"I thought we, you know, *liked* each other."

"We did! We *do*, but—"

Through the glass that separates the restaurant from the mall, I see a hand waving manically. I squint. I see that the hand belongs to Thad Bell. When he sees me gawking at him, he gestures for me to come out.

"Hey, Nick?" I say. "I'll be right back."

"Where are you going?" But he still gets up and lets me out of the booth. Or maybe I've sort of nudged him out of the way.

I get through the entrance and am face-to-face with Thad. "What are you doing here?" I ask. My voice comes out annoyed, but really, I'm not sure how I feel. Yes, maybe annoyed, but also excited and scared and curious and thrilled and confused and, well, basically, like a bolt of electricity has just traveled through me but I'm still trying to figure out what happened, and if I can move, if I'm hurt, if I'm okay, or what.

"Hi," he says. He looks nervous. He is holding a cabbage, or at least something that looks like a cabbage. "Am I too late? Did you already say yes?"

"No, I—" It seems too hard to explain what just happened.

"Oh, good." He seems to melt a little with relief. "Because guess what?"

Chicken butt? I'm tempted to say, but I'm not really in a chicken-butt kind of mood. "What?"

"I can go." He looks strangely excited.

It's like my thoughts are trapped in molasses. "Go?" Though I have no idea what's going on, I *am* sure of the fact that my face is practically doing acrobatics, trying to find a proper expression.

"I confessed about the window. I told the school what happened. And apparently, the kids who get into trouble are the ones who *aren't* in school. So, instead of banning me from school property, like I thought they would, they made me re-enroll. You're actually looking at the newest student at Hubert C. Frost." Thad looks relieved, maybe even a little happy. "Officer Dirk knew the whole time. He was just hoping I'd turn myself in. It just took me a while to do it. But it's done."

"Oh, well that's—good." My head feels jammed, like a broken printer.

"Yeah, so, all right, Collins, here goes," Thad says, clasping that cabbage-thing in front of him.

My nerves start to bundle together. My scalp starts to feel hot and sticky. I can't move.

"Will you go to this stupid Cotillion thing with me after all?"

"Thad, I—I mean, I'm still trying to understand this."

"I can go to the Cotillion. The *dance*." He smiles. "That stupid dance."

All I can do is stare at him and manage a couple blinks.

"Okay, Collins, here's something you can probably understand. Maybe I need to speak your language," he says, smirking and turning a little pink. "I, uh, have *feelings*."

"Feelings?"

"Yeah. About you," he says. "I mean, I think you might be right. About those things."

I blink again. I breathe. I wiggle my toes. Amazingly, *he* has feelings, but I seem to be completely out of them. It's like when you stub your toe on something and you have that weird blank space in time where you don't feel anything yet, but you know some sort of pain is about to make itself known.

But Thad is standing there, staring at me with those stupid penny-colored eyes, pushing the cabbage-thing into my hands, and now my feelings start to rush in.

Not the feelings he is probably hoping for.

No.

They are sharp feelings. Red feelings. Boiling feelings. I. Am. Livid. I mean, he can go to the dance, and then he can't, and then he wants me to go with Nick, and *then* he wants to go with me to the dance that he made fun of in the first place—*now* that I'm so over the idea of going anyway? And here he is pulling out this "feelings" thing, like he has *any* *right* to use that on me. Feelings are *my* territory.

"Collins?" Thad says, a look of uncertainty taking over. "I, uh—"

"*You know what, Thad Bell?*" I say, I actually yell. "*This isn't about you anymore. AND IT NEVER WAS!*"

I storm away and thrust myself back into the booth next to Nick, flinging the paper cabbage thing onto the bench next to me.

"You okay?" he asks. "What happened?"

"Nothing." *Except my world just spun off its axis. That's all.* "Sorry."

I take a sip of water and try to calm down.

"Do you want some more food or anything?"

"No, I'm"—*incredibly ready for this night to be over*—"okay."

Now I take a deep breath. "I'm really sorry about the Cotillion."

"That's okay," he says. "I really did want to go with you, but I might ask Ariana."

"Oh," I say. *So I haven't ruined him for all other women, I suppose.*

Even though I won't be going to the Cotillion, and I feel sad and a little lonely, I start to feel something else. Something bigger. I feel free. It's not the kind of freedom that makes you want to spin around in circles and shout joyous things, but the kind of freedom that makes you realize you are no longer shackled, like you've been released into a brand-new, unfamiliar world. Free, yes, but a little scared. Like Graciela when she found her way out of the cave after months of being confined.

He studies me for a moment and leans in close to me, "I guess it's too late to ask you for a kiss."

"Uh—" I say. This isn't the first kiss I've been waiting on. Served up with a breakup? With fundue on my breath? A pity kiss? After a fight with Thad Bell? *Really?*

"Sorry." He shakes his head, looking embarrassed. "I shouldn't have asked."

We pay the check and get up to leave. At the hostess's stand, I turn toward him.

"What did Thad want anyway?" Nick asks.

I shake my head. "He was just—passing by."

"How's he doing?"

"He's—" All sorts of adjectives come to mind. *Annoying, funny, sad, infuriating, cute, awful, awesome, exasperating, fragile, strong, sneaky, sweet, flawed, smart.* "Complicated."

Nick nods. "He's had it rough. I can't believe all the stuff you told me about him."

And then it starts coming together, like the missing pieces of that puzzle have been found and are being put into place. "Wait. Is that why you changed your description all of a sudden?"

He gives me a squinty, guilty look.

"So you *did* see him break the window?"

He nods. "I didn't get a great look, obviously. That was the truth. I wouldn't have realized it was him if I didn't see you guys together at the mall that day."

"So that's why you changed your story."

"Yeah. I didn't want him to get in trouble," Nick says. "He didn't need that. Plus, I realized I was kind of a— I mean, I think he overheard me making some stupid joke about a wheelchair. I didn't mean anything by it, but he might have heard me."

I look at him. I feel a sudden surge of affection. "Nick?"

"Yeah?"

"You know that kiss?" Maybe I can channel Mariela, for one last hurrah. And then I can let her go forever. She's nothing but trouble.

I lean toward him. He leans toward me.

In three. I recite the definition in my head, which I know by heart: to press, purse, and then part the lips. *There is only about an inch between us. I can feel the warmth of his breath; I can smell the salt from his dipper.*

Two. *Maybe a centimeter of space between us now. Or would that be a millimeter? A hectometer? Why am I thinking about metrics right now!?*

One. *My lips purse and pucker forward like a magnet is pulling them toward his. And then our lips touch. His are weirdly, surprisingly muscular, like he works them out—*

It's happening. Our lips are pressing together, and now we must part them slightly. I try, but maybe too hard, because I end up clamping my lips back together, and he pulls back, and when he does, we emit a smacking sound.

I'm really confounded. *That's* a kiss? The world falls to its knees for *that*? I feel like a bonfire that's been soaked with an ice-cold bucket of water. Long-burning flames are now little plumes of smoke. You couldn't roast a marshmallow over this.

And it doesn't help that I'm still thinking about Thad.

Then we hear, "Hey, get a booth." It's Bart. He winks at me. Then he hands me the cabbage bouquet. "You almost left this."

"Thanks," I say.

"What is that anyway?" Nick asks.

And for the first time I look at it. I mean *really* look at it. And I realize it's not just any paper cabbage. It's a true crafting project. It's a handmade king protea.

No, not something you can get with a Ding Dong. At all.

"Just something," I say. A boulder of an understatement. "From Thad."

"Poor guy. But I get it. I guess I'm glad he hit the window and not me," Nick says.

I sigh. "Well, he wouldn't want you to feel sorry for him."

Nick shakes his head. "I mean, I do feel bad for him, but it's not that. I just, you know—when stuff like that happens, I can see why he'd be so angry all the time."

Angry. But tonight that wasn't him; that was me. *He* wasn't angry tonight, not at all. No, the image of Thad's face when I yelled at him is seared into my memory. It is *broken*.

*Heart*broken.

And with a thrust of clarity, I realize something. *Well, congratulations, Mabry Collins. Applaud yourself. You just broke your first heart.*

"Well, bye, Mabry," Nick says.

"Bye."

And it isn't Nick's. Not at all.

quedar *to stay, to remain*

yo quedo
tú quedas
ella queda
nosotros quedamos
ellos quedan

For the next few hours, the scene with Thad replays in my head over and over again. It's torturous. I really wish I *was* on *La Vida Rica*. That some producer could just call *CUT!* and the scenes would end up in some digital trash can, never to be seen again. But instead, it's like an episode set on a loop, ending with me spewing out words very loudly at Thad.

I keep checking my phone. Maybe Thad's texted. Maybe Sirina's called. Maybe everything really is okay. But it's not, and I feel like there are weights pulling me down, dangling off my (uneven) earlobes and my fingers, dragging behind my feet on the floor. I brush my teeth—normally I'd floss, too, but tonight it feels like too much work, like running ten laps around the field.

I so wish I could call Sirina. I need her. Maybe I can send her the most brilliant good-night text ever. One that will make her miss me to the depths of her being. But I can't think of anything clever—it's like a fire inside me has been stomped out. And there's the risk that my message would just sit there, unacknowledged and unanswered, a little piece of myself rotting away somewhere in cyberspace.

And there's Thad. The crushed, bewildered look on his face when I yelled at him. My memory serves up the image with a cracking sound. I feel a stream of sorrow.

I think about running downstairs and crying to my mom, but then I hear her laugh flutter up the stairs. It's something Stephen said, no doubt. And it makes me feel even more alone. I mean, what if what they have *is* true love? What if the true love that I thought existed isn't even real? That it's as made-for-TV as the remote control? That it's no more real than the fake desert that Aurelio is *still* somehow crawling across. *Día cuarenta y tres.*

I stuff my face back into my pillow. It can't be. It just can't.

I roll over and try to get comfortable. It's not hard to still my body—I'm so incredibly tired—but my mind is on a separate course. It won't shut up. It keeps whirling and twirling and spinning out thoughts that poke at me like little pins.

I try to breathe deeply. I mean, I actually succeed in doing that, but instead of feeling calm, I feel more awake.

But I tell myself, all's fair in love and war, after all. That's what they say.

Crack.

But it doesn't feel fair.

Fine. I'll apologize to Thad. Then maybe my HEAD WILL SHUT UP SO I CAN GO TO SLEEP!

I roll back over and grab my phone.

I thumb-type it out. *Sorry about tonite. I'm pooped. We can talk about it tomorrow.*

And I hit Send.

And then I realize I WILL NEVER, EVER SLEEP AGAIN BECAUSE I JUST RUINED MY WHOLE ENTIRE LIFE.

Because what I *thought* I typed is not what I *actually* typed at all. What a difference—a crucial difference—one letter can make.

Because here's what I wrote:

Sorry about tonite. I pooped. We can talk about it tomorrow.

Oh. My. Dear. God. I *pooped* and we can *talk about it* tomorrow!? What in the name of *Dios mío* HAVE I DONE!? AND THAT IS A REAL QUESTION!

I spend the next ten minutes furiously texting him things like: *Don't read that txt! And I meant I'm pooped, like tried.*

Frantic texts lead to more typos. So, great, now I sound constipated.

TIRED! I text.

And I finally start to weep with exhaustion. I power my phone off and put it down on the table next to me. I lay my head on my pillow and cross my arms like an X over my chest, so when I die of humiliation and they find me in the morning, I'll have salvaged a bit of dignity and have left this world gracefully and composed.

Over + Done

T had throws up on the way home. In someone's bushes.

It's sudden. And confusing. He never got his burrito at the mall, so he's pretty sure it's not food poisoning. And, anyway, it's not just his stomach. Is it possible to feel dizzy in your chest? Everything from his throat to his lower belly feels tingly, carbonated, and his head is starting to ache.

He's short of breath, too. It's like he can't take in a full lungful of air, whenever he sees it in his head—Mabry kissing Nick. This is bad. He must be coming down with something awful. Miserable.

He has to walk home. The skating is making him feel worse—dizzier, more panicky. He can't remember when he felt this awful—he hates to pull a Mabry, but it feels quite possible that he could be dying. Is this how his dad felt right before he died? He hopes not. He really hopes not, but love and pain seem to come together like a package deal. A combo meal in the drive-through of life.

He gets to the front door and dry heaves right there on the porch. Aunt Nora opens the door and takes in a breath when she sees him. "Thaddeus? Are you okay?"

He moans. He doesn't even have the energy for a proper reply, and anyway, he's sure from the looks of him, it's not needed.

"Oh, honey." Her voice is warm. Concerned. Good old Aunt Nora.

He stumbles inside. She places her hand on his forehead. "No temperature, so that's good. Probably a bad cold," she says. "Why don't you go on up to your room and I'll bring you some soup."

He's never had a cold like this.

He manages to ask how his mom is.

"She's doing better than you, I think." Aunt Nora gives him a smile, but it's a weak and worried one. "You look pretty bad. You need some rest."

Even though he doesn't feel like he *can* rest, he goes up to his room and lies down on the bed without even taking off his shoes. He curls over on his side and listens to his own breath. His throat is tight, he realizes. That's why it hurts.

Aunt Nora brings him some herbal tea. "It might help. It's that lemon ginger."

He'll try anything. He takes a sip. "Thank you," he says. He's not sure the tea will make him feel better, but there's something about her trying that does.

"Are you hungry?"

"No." And that's the weird truth. He couldn't eat a single nacho, not even if it was put in front of him, not even if it was covered in extra cheese.

"When did you start feeling sick?" she asks.

"I don't know," he says. And it hits him. It's only been about thirty-five minutes. Since Mabry Collins yelled at him and then kissed Nick Wainwright right on the lips.

Oh. No. *Oh no no no no.*

Could this be—?

He doesn't even want to let the word pop into his head. But it doesn't seem to need his permission.

Lovesickness?

He heaves again. Aunt Nora scurries out and comes back with a bucket, just in time. He throws up the ginger tea, which still tastes gingery and pleasant, even as it comes out.

But this can't be *that*. There's no way. Just because he has feelings, it doesn't mean *that*. Because that kind of love doesn't actually exist. It doesn't. It doesn't. It does *not*.

In Mabry's silly little world, love is hearts and flowers and candlelight and that kind of crap. But what does she know? If love is hearts, it is hearts that will never beat again. And sure, maybe love means flowers—mums dying in the windowsill of a hospital room. And maybe it means candlelight—of birthdays never had.

Death. Now *that* is the ultimate breakup.

Mabry knows nothing about love. *Not. A. Thing.*

If he's sick of anything, it's Mabry. Mabrysickness. Now *that's* real.

Later, when his phone buzzes, he picks it up. He can't sleep anyway. It's a text. From her. Of course. It would be.

Sorry about tonite. I pooped. We can talk about it tomorrow.

She pooped? *And* she wants to talk about it tomorrow? Then her other texts come in. She's trying desperately to cover for her mortifying typo. He feels the ghost of a laugh inside of him. Oh, *duuuuude*. He would have so much fun with this if he wasn't done with her.

But he's *so* done with her.

THE VINDICATOR

The Official News Blog of Hubert C. Frost Middle School

Girl's Entire Life Ruined, Over

While other girls are busy buying dresses and shoes for the famed Cotillion, eighth grader Mabry Collins is slowly dying in her small upstairs bedroom. A recent turn of events, including losing her best friend, has turned her heart into a shriveled black pump—one that isn't expected to last much longer.

There have been no crowds of well-wishers or get-well-soon cards flowing in through the mail, but Collins says she doesn't hold that against anyone. "I've a had a full life [click for more]

IN OTHER NEWS . . .

There Really Is No Other News When You're Dying

Mabry, see me.

289

pensar *to think*

yo pienso

tú piensas

ella piensa

nosotros pensamos

ellos piensan

It's Sunday night. At dinner, Stephen blathers on about something and my mom responds to all his blather. Then things get quiet suddenly and she says, "Mabry, aren't you listening?"

It's not even worth lying about. "Sorry. I was just thinking."

"Thinking?" Stephen says, getting his joke face on. "What's *that*? There's got to be an app for that."

My mom just gives him a tight little smile. To me, she says, "I was thinking we could go dress shopping tomorrow. For the Cotillion."

"Oh."

"*Oh?*" My mom's eyebrows pull together in confusion.

"I'm not going," I say.

Even though I'm staring into my Brussels sprouts, I feel all their curious looks darting across the table. My mom puts her hand to my forehead. "You okay?"

But I'm *not* okay. I'm *not*, I'm *not*, even though The Former Man of My Dreams asked me to go the Cotillion with him. Even though I got what I thought I wanted.

"She looks tired," Stephen says, like I'm not at the table.

"She looks ugly," A-Bag adds.

My mom doesn't even start berating him. I glance up. She looks too concerned about me. So I just say, "Your imaginary girlfriend is ugly," to him, and he tells me how lame I am, and then my mom tells us both to be quiet and stop picking on each other, and everything goes back to normal, at least on the surface.

I check my phone. No Thad. No Sirina.

A little part of me is hoping that maybe Thad's just having a Funyun moment. I mean, it's possible, right?

Okay, probably not.

Well, Thad can go skate off the edge of the world, for all I care. He can laugh at all my poop typos and THEN go skate off the edge of a cliff. He can laugh at all my typos, IGNORE THEM, and then go skate off of Mount Kilimanjaro. For all I care.

And Sirina. I'm as lonely and miserable as I was when she went away to her epilepsy camp last summer and left me to fend for myself for four full weeks. No, wait. This is worse. There are no miles to blame for our separation. The thought makes me even more lonely and miserable.

Doesn't she miss me at all? I hold the phone in my hand and stare at it. I will it to ring. Nothing happens, so I intensify my stare and start sending telepathic messages to Sirina. *Call me. Call me. Call me.* And then, for good measure, I throw in a *Call me, please, my tufted-head paper cutter.*

The only thing that happens is that I get confirmation that my telepathy skills suck.

No, under the surface, nothing is right in this world.

Later that night, when I'm curled into a ball on my floor, A-Bag passes by my room. He sees me and pauses at my doorway. "Sick again? What is it this time? Cholera? Consumption?"

"Shut up!" I say without thinking. Now I have to soften my words because I'm thirsty. "Sorry. Can you get me a glass of water?"

"What do I look like, *Mom?*" he says.

He's just being his usual mean self, but right now I feel so awful that I just start crying. He walks in and flops to the floor next to me. "What's *wrong* with you?" he asks, stretching his legs out and using my curled-up body as a footrest.

"I'm sure *you* could write up a pretty good list," I mumble.

He gives me an evil laugh. Then he says, "Yeah, but I'd have to be pretty bored to do it. So just tell me."

"Why do you care all of a sudden?"

He shrugs. "I don't know, it's just crazy that you're not going to that dance. *You* of all people. Even *I* went to that stupid Cotillion."

Which is true. And normally it would really get to me, but now, I just don't care about it. It just all seems so ridiculous.

"Is Sirina going?" he asks.

"Yeah."

"And you're *not*?"

"No."

He lets out a big sigh. "Oh, man," he groans. "This is serious, then."

"Uh." I give him a look like he's crazy. "This is not your problem."

He raises his eyebrows and looks at me. "Well, it kind of is. I'm your big brother."

"And?"

"I *mean*"—he puts the soles of his feet on my back and rocks me back and forth—"if you want to go, I'll take you."

"What?" I laugh. I actually laugh.

"Oh, is that funny?"

"Yeah, sort of."

He thumps my back with the balls of his feet, so that my laughter breaks into staccato.

"But you're off the hook. I'm not going. I don't even *want* to go anymore," I say, still being bounced around.

Finally, he stands up. "Fine, my work here is done. Glad I could cheer you up. And even gladder you don't need me to go to that *Cartellion* with you."

I crack a smile for him. "Thanks, though," I call to him as he leaves my room. A few minutes later, he comes back with a full glass of water.

I can hardly believe it. Maybe Earth got a little heavier. Maybe the cosmos is shifting in some way. Maybe some of the stars are being written out of the universal script.

He puts it down on the table next to my bed. And then he pinches my cheek. Hard. "Aw, my little loser sister. She's so *cute*! Such a little cockroach!"

Which would normally annoy the crap out of me. But today, it's just nice to know that in this new, different world, *not everything* has changed.

saber *to know*

yo sé
tú sabes
ella sabe
nosotros sabemos
ellos saben

It's the night of the Cotillion. And my feet are moving. But not in the way I ever expected, no. Not at all.

Outrageous. This is *outrageous.*

My feet are doing things without the permission of my brain. They are playing this game where they trade off stepping in front of the other, almost like it's some sort of race. I keep telling them to stop, but that only seems to make them go faster.

I try bargaining with them—*just let me figure out what to say!*—but they don't listen. I don't really know what's in it for them. For the first time in my life, I hope they trip on something. An unexpected rise in the sidewalk, a rogue tree root, my own heel, *something*! I ask them very nicely to slow down; they rudely do not. I remind them that they're in flip-flops, not running shoes, but it's almost like they're asking for blisters.

They don't care. They just don't care. I argue with them the whole way there. They finally come to a sudden stop in front of Thad's town house.

"Now what?" I ask them. They offer nothing. In fact, it's like they're suddenly struck dumb. It's like they've been set in cement.

"Seriously?" I look down at them, the stubborn things. The skin at the base of my left big toe has been worn through, sacrificed, I realize with annoyance.

"Move!" I tell them. They do not. "Come on!" I cry out. They just sit there like stubborn mules. I wonder if I can—

"Collins?"

It's Thad's voice that makes me freeze in place. I'm bent over with my hands on my right shin, trying to get the thing to budge.

"Uh, hi."

"Are you lost or something?" He has stepped out onto his front stoop, and doesn't sound all that happy to see me.

"*No,*" I say, still crouched.

"I know that, *duh,*" he says, shaking his head. "What are you doing down there?"

I stand up slowly. Very slowly. And self-consciously face him. "Nothing," I say.

He starts to crack a smile, but it's like his face wrestles it away. "It looked like your foot was caught in an invisible raccoon trap."

"Well, it *wasn't,*" I say.

A laugh crackles up through his throat. And even though it hits me how incredibly stupid my response was, I don't laugh. Well, I try not to, but my chest and throat quiver a little, and my nostrils start to spasm. I try to breathe the laugh away, but it doesn't work. It erupts from me. But it's one of those laughs that feels inappropriate—a laugh that comes at the wrong time, embarrassing you and everyone around you, like when someone falls down but actually gets hurt. We both turn bright red.

"So, uh." His laugh quiets, pretty abruptly. He steps off the stoop and onto the sidewalk where I am. "So why exactly are you here?"

"I thought you were coming back to school. You said you were."

"I've been sick," he says.

It doesn't feel like he's telling the truth exactly, but it doesn't feel like a lie.

"Like, how sick?"

"I don't know, just sick."

"Like, on-medicine sick?"

"I don't think there's, like, an approved drug—" There's a hint of a smirk, but it disappears quickly. "You still haven't told me why you're here."

"Sorry I yelled at you that night," I say. "If I was a jerk or anything. I don't want to be a jerk anymore."

"So just don't," he says. So Thad-like.

There's a word for how I feel right now. I don't know why the poor sheep got saddled with this kind of word, but it did. *Sheepish*. "You don't give lessons on how to get your best friends back, do you?"

"Best friends?"

"You and Sirina," I say. "Like, how to unbreak hearts?" I make myself laugh at my own joke, even though it's not really a joke at all.

He stares at me. "You should be able to figure that out on your own by now."

And maybe I should. "Okay, I'm sorry I asked. I'll figure it out."

He's still looking at me as if he's waiting for me to start trying. Right now. So I exhale and say, "Okay, I guess I'm here because I've been thinking a lot."

"*Have you,*" he says. "Well, good for you."

But I continue. "You know how you wanted me to find those flaws in Nick?"

"Barely," he says. He crosses his arms over his chest.

I remind myself that Thad's been hurt. Really hurt, not just by me. Heartbroken by life, in a way that I haven't. "Well, I finally came up with one—the only one that matters."

He glances away. "Yeah, well, Mabry, he's almost perfect, then. But I don't really care about that anymore."

"It's that—"

He shuts his eyes. "Doesn't matter."

"The one major flaw—"

His jaw clenches. "Don't care."

"—is that he's not *you*."

He quickly turns to face me. "*Well*. Lucky him."

This isn't at all what I envisioned. Where's his thankful embrace? Where's his long-yearning kiss? I shift my weight from foot to foot. Inside the house, a woman passes by a window in a wheelchair.

I clear my throat. "Is that your mom?"

His turns toward his house and sees her. "Yep."

"How is she?"

He takes a breath. "She's, you know, a little better."

Our eyes meet, and when they do, it's like there's some magical force keeping them connected. I can practically feel my pupils grow. Though we're not touching, the nerves in my body start to magnetize, as if they're all pulling forward, reaching for him.

A car drives by and Thad's eyes snap away from mine, breaking the spell. His mother crosses back across the kitchen in her chair. "I guess you better go," I say, and wait for him to argue. Or hope for him to argue. Whatever. I *esperar*. In Spanish, that one word means both of those things, which makes perfect sense right now. Waiting and hoping. Hoping and waiting. It is its own state of existence.

But he just says, "Aren't you supposed to be at the dance tonight?"

"Nope."

"Why not?"

"I told Nick no. I didn't want to go with him."

He squints at me. "You *kissed* him. I saw you."

He saw me? Is that why he's acting so weird? I shake my head. "Yeah, well, I did it for you."

"Oh, wow," he says, flatly. "Well, thanks. You're so *thoughtful*."

"He's not such a smear, Thad. He changed his description of the guy who broke the window when he realized *you* were the one who did it."

He takes a deep breath and looks away. "Okay, well, dude, please don't do me any more of those kinds of favors, because that made me retch."

"Fine," I say. "Deal." Then I dare myself to ask my next question. "Thad, did you—?" I look up at him. He is staring at me curiously. "Did you mean what you said?"

"You mean about the invisible raccoon trap? *Collins*." He rolls his eyes and acts exasperated. "You should *know* that there are no such things as invisible raccoon traps." Then he laughs a little. It's not his normal feral cry, but it'll do. For now.

Ha-ha. Hardy har har. I glare at him. "You know what I'm talking about. What you said that night. Your *feelings*."

Please say yes. Please say yes. Please say yes.

But he lets his head drop sideways, and his smile goes all crooked, winding up almost apologetically on his right cheek.

"Never mind," I exhale. I feel jellylike, exhausted. "Okay, I guess I'll go."

I turn to walk away.

He grabs my hand.

I whirl around.

"I also meant what I said about your earlobes."

"My earlobes! *Great*."

"More like, it's easier not to crush on someone when you can focus on something stupid like that."

My arms wrap around him just as quickly as his wrap around me. He pulls me tighter to him, and my cheek presses into his neck. A Cottonelle commercial blares from someone's television through an open window. A car alarm goes off in the distance. And even though he *does* smell a little like jalapeños, I am certain that nothing in the history of the world has ever felt this good. I need all my senses to describe what I feel—orange and crackling and melodic and hot and safe and sweet. Like a new emotion has just been invented for us.

I feel that glorious beating. This time, I'm not sure whether it's in my chest or his. Mine. No his. Wait, mine. His. *Jeez*. I'm glad I have only one heart, not five. Love just must be so confusing for the worm! I snort into his neck, practically giving him a hickey with my nose. So gross.

"Are you *laughing*?" He pulls away just enough to see my face.

"Sorry. I was just thinking." I wipe his neck.

"Should I ask?"

"Maybe not."

"Tell me anyway."

"I was just thinking about worms," I say.

"Dude, *seriously*?"

"Did you know they have five hearts?"

He laughs. *His* laugh.

I smile. I've missed that safari sound.

Then he says, "What other crazy things go on in that head?"

"Well, lots of things," I say.

"No doubt."

"But not everything's so crazy."

"No?" He moves my hair back from my shoulders.

"No," I say. "I've been thinking about what you said. About writing about things that really matter."

"Like what?" he asks.

"Like can I meet your mom?"

Tú + Yo

unt Nora helps Thad's mom put on a new red sweat suit while he and Mabry share a Little Naked Debbie and thumb-wrestle in the kitchen.

"You can come in now," Aunt Nora says.

His mom's sitting up in her chair, her feet bare. She smiles at them when they walk in the room.

"Mom, this is Mabry. But you can call her Collins if you want."

Mabry gives him a quick *ha, ha, ha* look and turns to his mom and smiles. He's warned her not to try the handshake thing, that sometimes she's too tired for even a handshake at this time in the evening, so he's glad to see Mabry clasp her hands in front of her. "I've been wanting to meet you," Mabry says.

He knows his mom can't actually say the same. She hasn't exactly known Mabry existed until about forty-two minutes ago. He bites his bottom lip and feels the tremor in his ankle. He *is* a little nervous.

"It's so nice to meet you," his mom says. She smiles. And she *does* lift her elbow from the armrest. She *does* slowly reach her hand toward Mabry. Mabry smiles, takes her hand, and gives it a gentle pump.

Aunt Nora beams at Thad from across the room.

"Mom?" he says. "We'll be out in the kitchen—"

"Thad, just wait. I want to show you something."

Mabry looks hesitant. "Should I—?" She points toward the kitchen.

Thad feels a little shy about it, but his mom answers. "You can stay here." Then she sits up a little straighter in her chair. "Okay, let me give this a try. Watch my right leg."

He does, they all do, but nothing happens. He takes a quick glance at his mom's face—the effort shows in her tightening forehead and her stiff smile. He fights the urge to help her, and instead, smiles patiently even when his eyebrows want to pull together with concern. She stares down at her foot, concentrating. And then, slowly, her right leg lifts off the leg rest, just an inch or so. It hovers—just a second feels like a tiny eternity to him—and then she releases it with a gust of a laugh.

Mabry is beaming, even though she doesn't really understand how amazing it is.

Thad wants to jump up and down, but feels that shyness again. "That's awesome," he says, just about four decibels below where he really wants to.

"Hang on," his mom says. And then, still as slowly, her left leg lifts a fraction of an inch. Two-tenths. Okay, maybe a tenth.

He feels the tear prickle. Oh no. Not here. Not now. No way. The only way to combat the tears is to do something else with these crazy, overwhelming feelings. So he does. "Well, is that it?" He smiles. "I mean, we actually have an audience today."

She laughs. Aunt Nora laughs. And Mabry laughs. Okay, she snorts.

His mom looks at Mabry. "You must think we're all nuts."

"Not all of you," Mabry says, eyeing Thad. "Just one of you."

And then he laughs, too. And feels a ripple of something.

A ripple of something.

A ripple of *feelings*. Lots of *feelings*.

Okay, fine, *love*.

Love.

He can't think of the word without also thinking of Mabry. So, even if she is ridiculous, which she *is*, maybe she was right. Just a little bit right. Maybe it exists in ways that he never knew.

First it's a flutter. And then there's a surge of it, like a tsunami. And for the first time since the accident, love feels a little bit okay.

empezar *to begin*

yo empiezo

tú empiezas

ella empieza

nosotros empezamos

ellos empiezan

"**W**hat if she won't come to the door?"

"No way, dude. I'm not letting you chicken out now," Thad says. He grabs my free hand, and it takes me a little bubble-bursting second to realize he's just trying to keep me from bolting down the street. "Come on." He pulls me down the walkway toward her front door.

"But wait. What's my first line again?" I ask.

"There are no lines." He looks at me and smirks. "I can't believe I'm going to say this, I really can't, but just speak from your heart. *There.* Gah!" He makes a coughy-gaggy sound.

I look at him. "You *really* just said that."

"I know. *I know.* It's just sometimes I have to speak to you in your own language. As much as it kills me a little inside."

He's still holding my hand. Or maybe I'm holding his. Very tight. I look at him. He nods and squeezes my hand. "You can do this."

"What if she hates it?"

"She's not going to hate it, Mabry."

Mabry. He's called me Mabry. For the first time ever, not Collins. It makes me blush.

He steps onto the porch, my hand still in his, so I go along with him. Then he releases my hand and pulls the draft of the article I've been working on out of his pocket. He unfolds the paper, smooths it out, and hands it to me.

"Okay, you're all set," he says, and presses the doorbell.

Even the three-tone chime makes me miss her. Ringing it always meant the next few hours would be spent with my best friend. Ringing it always was practically the theme song for friendship.

I see people moving around inside through the window along the side of the door. Then it opens and Sirina says, "Oh. It's you."

Her face is blank. Her words are matter-of-fact. I had hoped for at least an exclamation mark, if not a heartfelt hug. I mean, it's been weeks since we've spoken.

"Yeah," I say. So brilliant.

She and Thad say hi to each other, and then she looks at me, her face still blank. I decide she should be a professional poker player. I just can't seem to read her.

"So." I take a breath and look down at the paper. "I wrote something for you. Well, I mean, not for you, but kind of, like, thinking about you. I mean, I know how much the YoJo meant to you, but I was thinking, how can I make it all better—"

Thad is pressing his sneaker against mine. *"Just read it,"* he says quietly, his coppery-brown eyes pleading.

"Right," I say. I look at Sirina. She looks back at me, her mouth slightly open. She looks like she's almost *something*—appalled, amused, baffled—but I can't tell what.

I clear my throat and read. "Last year, Ashley Walker, now fourteen, went on the dream vacation of a lifetime: a ski trip to Colorado. But she had a horrible accident while atop that mountain. Not only did her pelvis get crushed, but also her *dreams*."

I look back up at Sirina. Finally, an expression! Even if it is *aghast*.

"Go on," Thad says.

"But it's not the physical devastation that causes Ashley the most pain. Since she's been out of school, struggling to keep up online, her friends have moved on without her."

I glance up at Sirina again. Now she is sort of wincing.

"Jessica Sawyer, age fifteen, has the same dreams of any other girl her age. She longs to go to school dances, she dreams of walking on the beach, she yearns to dance tango. But her disability keeps her like a prisoner in her own home, a girl trying to live a life where wheels aren't always welcome. Her only social outlet, she reports, is 'liking things on Facebook.'"

"Is this *real*?" Sirina asks.

I look up from the page. Despite the fact that I'm starting to shrink a little inside, I say, "It turns out there are lots of kids in the county who have disabilities and can't get to school. I wanted to share their stories."

"But 'crushed dreams and pelvises,' Mabry? A little sensitivity maybe?" Her eyebrows lift. "And for the record, not every fifteen-year-old girl 'yearns to dance tango.'"

"Well, so, I need a good editor," I say, a little apologetically. Then in a quieter voice, I say, "I need *you*."

Her face softens. "Well, how did you—? I mean, where did you get all this?"

"Thad and his family helped me. His mom's in a wheelchair. She talked to her doctors and therapists, and they got me in touch with a lot of people. There's more. A guy with cerebral palsy who has to rely on a bad satellite Internet connection. A blind girl whose guide dog died. There's a bunch of kids who have trouble going to school. And I know you know some, too. What about all those kids you met at that camp last summer?"

I don't add *when you abandoned me for four weeks*.

"Camp Amberbrook," she says.

"Right," I say. "You told me one of the girls was having ten seizures a day. That's got to get in the way of school."

"Wow," she finally says. At least, her words say it. Her face, not so much.

I finally break down. "Oh, Sirina! Let's take another shot at the YoJo. Or being best friends again. Or both!"

She finally smiles at me, but it's a tight smile that looks almost painful on her face.

"Can you at least think about it?" I plead.

"Okay."

Thad tells us he'll wait down by the sidewalk. Sirina leans on the doorjamb. "Well, this is—"

"Weird, I know."

"I was going to say *a surprise*, but you're right. It's a little weird. But it's *you*. You keep things—interesting."

"Not boring?" I ask.

"Not at all. You never were."

Say it, I tell myself. *Just* say it. So I do.

"Sirina, I miss you." And then I just say more words, which make me feel *even more* exposed. "I *love* you."

She lifts her eyebrows.

"Not in a *La Vida Rica* way, of course," I add. And it's true. *La Vida*

Rica doesn't do friendship well. It's always people in love or people fighting. People in lies and people betrayed.

"I miss you too, Mabry," she says, but her words are quiet and she's not really looking at me. She opens her mouth to say something else, but closes it again.

Her pocket buzzes. She takes her phone out and looks at it. "Hey, Mabry? I kind of want to take this," she says. And then, in a quieter voice, she says, "It's Kipper."

"Oh. Okay."

"Hey, I'll call you right back," she says into the phone. She slips it back into her pocket, and says to me, "Well, thanks for coming."

Thanks for coming? What is this? A *business* memo?

I start to walk away, but she says my name. I turn around. "Just so we're clear." She smiles. "I never, ever want to kiss you on the mouth. Ever. But I love you, too."

So I just do it—I fling myself around and just hug her. She smells like Sour Patch Kids, and right now, it smells better than any flower ever could. She hugs me back, and a piece of my hair gets caught in her watch, but I don't care. Even with a little pain in my scalp, this is the best I've felt in a long time.

It's getting late. It's getting dark. And technically, Thad *has* to hold my hand on the way back to my house, which I'm trying to be very cool about. So I give Sirina's hand one last little squeeze and say, "Go talk to Kipper."

"Wait," she says. She pulls back just enough to see me. "We're going to need photos, interviews, everything. And of course, some *major* editing. It's a whole different category—Education in Our World? Wait, no, maybe Modern Life. And we could enter it as a feature, I think, instead of a series. But it's a good story. And a good start."

I smile.

She smiles.

"And if we're going to win the YoJo, we've only got a few weeks. We better get started *ASAP*. Like, tomorrow morning—here, okay?"

"Okay," I say. I feel giddy.

In my head, I see it. Sirina and I growing up together. Sirina and I being each other's bridesmaids. *Wait*—our husbands will be best friends; it will be a double wedding! There will be king proteas involved. And gazebos. Sirina and I will pass our children off as cousins, and we'll spend holidays together for the rest of our lives. I can practically see the photo montage. Our kids dressed as Skittle-faced monkey wrenches or peanut-headed sock puppets for Halloween. Summer vacations at the beach. I see us growing old together. Waving from a ship. Flying over Europe. Riding in a rickshaw in Asia. In a carriage in Central Park.

Maybe friendship is actually the best kind of romance there is.

We hug again, just a quick good-bye with promises to see each other in the morning, and Thad and I start back to my house. I stand on the skateboard and he walks, pulling me by the hand, just so I can get the hang of it. I've told him it's strictly for research. He tells me he believes me.

But a block away he stops, kind of suddenly. I wobble on the board, and he grabs both my hands.

"Why are we stopping?"

"Just look," he says.

I do. There, stuck in the middle of the sidewalk, is a lone worm.

"Five hearts, right?"

"Right," I say.

"From this day on, whenever I see a worm on the sidewalk, I'll think of you," he tells me.

"You mean it?"

"With all my hearts."

I know the smile on my own face is probably a pretty goofy one, possibly smile number ninety-three, but I don't even care. The one on his face can't be much better.

My phone buzzes in my back pocket. He puts his thumbs through my belt loops while I get my phone out. "Just to help steady you," he explains.

I tell him I believe him.

The text is from Her. My Sirina, *Mi Mejor Amiga*.

Good night, my razor-backed ostrich feather, her message reads.

And it is a good night. A great night. The *bueno*-est of *noches* indeed.

I smile and type back, *Good night, my shea-butter blowfish.*

And Thad kneels down to move the worm carefully to the grass.

The Unbreaking

At first, just existing feels like betrayal. Not just a betrayal of your own heart, but of your lost love. Loneliness threatens to swallow you up, but you still have to brush your hair. Floss your teeth. Put things into your mouth and chew and swallow them. You still have to put one foot in front of the other and move along. Life just doesn't wait. The world has no patience for a broken heart. Hair mats and tangles. Stomachs growl. Clothes wear out. Teeth rot.

And then—something catches you off guard. You laugh at something, maybe by accident. It's just a reflex. But still, you start to remember what it feels like not to ache so much. It's like cracking through an invisible surface, and not knowing how to climb back under.

If, that is, you want to climb back under. Because up here, out here, you can breathe a little deeper. It's a little warmer here. And brighter, too—you can see colors again. And your heart—it still somehow beats. You can feel the stubborn pulse on the inside of your wrist. You can feel the blood, how it sometimes rushes around inside you like it has a mind of its own, in and out through your cobbled-together heart. Sometimes very fast.

It's a different world, a strange one. But maybe it's not so bad. There are pretty things here. Nice things. Soft things. Shiny things. Things you could like. People you could like. People you could love.

And maybe even some you already do.

—El Fin—

agradecer *to thank*

yo agradezco

I'd first like to thank my mom, Delores Bucknam, for her constant love and encouragement, for her sense of humor, for her odd little quirks, and for her stubborn belief in me. For years ago bringing me the palm-size copy of *El Libro Semanal*, with the shirtless man and a bare-shouldered beauty on the cover, and for reminding me that you never know where you'll find your next idea. I thought I knew everything about heartbreak until I lost you.

Warm embraces to my friends and family who helped me through her loss and the writing of this book, which went hand in hand: Michele Nesmith, The Best Friend One Could Ever Hope For. Seriously, she should run workshops. To Kylie Stewart, who never met a 'chong she didn't like. Unless it has gluten. To Joe McGrath for reading, and reading, and reading again, and for expanding my heart in all the good ways. To Dad and Anna, Lois, Uschi, Deanna, and Andrea. Big, fat "fundue" pots of love to all of you.

Extra hearts to Ashley Rock, who is the nimble-footed walrus cheek behind many of the good-night texts. And to Casper, the little blond thing that makes sure I'm up every morning to write. All right, fine, he's more concerned about his kibble than my writing, but the point is that he pants and paces and nudges and sneezes until I'm up.

A dole of doves to my agent, Holly Root, who deserves more thanks than I can give her here. There are mountains that should be shouted from; choirs of praise that should be sung. Oceans of gratitude that should be swum in order to fully express my appreciation for the many things she's done and continues to do for me.

Passionate thanks to all the editorial staff I've worked with at Disney Hyperion, including Julie Moody, Abby Ranger, Lisa Yoskowitz, and Laura Schreiber. Julie, a bonus heart-shaped box of chocolates to you for all the hard work and insight that brought this book into its own. Admiring glances of gratitude to Stephanie Lurie for her support; Dina Sherman, who is simply awesome in all her work with libraries and educators; Emma Trithart, for her cover illustrations; and Maria Elias for her cover design.

Bouquets of fragrant flowers to authors Alison Cherry and Nancy Cavanaugh for helping me write, rinse, and repeat. And Alison, an origami swan to you for sharing your secret Facebook inbox messages with me when needed. And, yes, sometimes they are needed.

Muchas gracias to both Don Stewart and Donna Schillinger for help with my *español*. Let it be known, however, that any errors are all *mío*.

Moons and stars of thanks to the Brush Creek Foundation for the Arts in Saratoga, Wyoming, and Playa in Summer Lake, Oregon, for providing me (and many other writers and artists) with the gift of time, space, and inspiration. You are national treasures.

Many *x*'s and *o*'s to fans of *Fetching* and to my new readers for reaching these very last lines. If a squirm of a hundred earthworms equals five hundred hearts, I wish them all to you.